THE CRY
OF THE
HANGKAKA

THE CRY
OF THE
HANGKAKA

Anne Woodborne

Published in 2016 by Modjaji Books
PO Box 385, Athlone, 7760, Cape Town, South Africa
www.modjajibooks.co.za

Edited by Karen Jennings
Cover artwork by Judy Woodborne (www.judywoodborne.co.za)
Cover text by Danielle Clough
Book layout by Andy Thesen

Printed and bound by Megadigital, Cape Town
ISBN: 978-1-920590-60-4
ebook: 978-1-928215-38-7

The dead come to me in dreams with wet eyes, as if they have swum the waters of those mythical rivers of the underworld, the Acheron and Cocytus, rivers of woe and lamentation. They crowd around me, their pallid faces slick with an underwater sheen; they watch and wait. As I sink into a deep sleep they seduce me with their surreal images.

I wake from such a dream one night and, in my drowsiness, sense the presence of my mother hovering over me, leaning on a stick, trying to peer into my dream. I turn on my pillow to escape her; I've shut the memory of Irene away between the heavy covers of a photo album and in a box containing a twig of dried heather, pearl drop-earrings and suede gloves carrying a lingering scent of lily-of-the-valley. The old yearning, like a heart wringing itself, has not tempted me to open these mementoes.

Yet, as I slip back into my dream, I find myself in my childhood bed, iron-framed, shrouded in a mosquito net. I hear the skeletal fingers of the locust bean tree scratching on the tin roof. The snakes slither from tree branch to roof, rustling through the leaves then thudding onto the corrugated tin. The drums begin their thrumming from the surrounding villages, an obbligato beat to underscore the soft crooning of the Hausa servants around the fire in the compound. Jack's drainpipe snores rip the air from the bedroom he shares with Irene. The doll from Madeira sits, glassy brown eyes snap open and stare into space. Her concertina lungs wheeze a cry of 'Mama-Mama' through her painted lips. From the night sky drifts the jarring two-note cry of the hangkaka. The mechanical clanking of the dredger down on the riverbed pushes me back into the time of my childhood. I shrink into my nine-year-old body. The night noises of Dorowa lull me into a dream about my mother.

Part One

SHE'S MY shadow. Whenever I turn, wherever I look, she's there. I see her first thing in the morning when her face is new, before she remembers what's happened. I feel her warm body close to mine like a hot-water bottle at night before I sleep. If the black dog nightmare wakes me, I see her walking like a ghost up and down at the end of the bed in the dark room.

Mom smells like sunshine and lilies. Her sweet lily smell comes from a small blue bottle called 'Lily of the Valley'. Mom dabs the neck of the bottle on the inside of my wrist – I breathe in the scent and imagine Mom and I in a place where lilies grow. 'Fields of lilies were crushed to make this exquisite perfume,' Mom says.

Her black hair hangs like a silk curtain when she bends to turn the key of the jewellery box. She opens the lid and the tiny ballerina, painted gold and pink, pops up and turns on her toes. She holds her arms above her head in a circle. Mom shows me her reflections dancing in the small mirrors behind her. The music tinkles like a fairy dance.

'The Blue Danube,' Mom says. 'Your father held me in his arms when we danced to this waltz, many, many times ... to think I was once so happy.'

Mom's tears shine like the pearl earrings she puts in the red velvet drawer in the box. They roll down her cheeks.

When Mom's almost happy, her voice sounds like milkshake with bubbles on top. When she's sad or angry, her voice sounds like burnt onions.

Mom's lonely. 'You're my only companion, Karin,' she says. 'Our world has shrunk to these four walls and the beach – just the two of us.' Sometimes she hugs me so I can't breathe; her arms and hands are so strong. Sometimes her eyes look as if they can't see me even when I'm right next to her.

I love watching Mom's hands. They're busy-bee hands. Her fingers are long and strong. They push sewing needles into material and wind wool around silver knitting needles. They cut vegetables and meat to cook. They make sheets smooth with a hot iron. Mom irons everything we wear so we can be neat and clean. When she dresses me she sings under her breath, 'Little Karin is so sweet, always clean, always neat.'

The sun splashes a block of gold through the window onto the floor so Mom and I can be warm like marshmallows melting in front of a fire. Mom shows me how to cut pictures out of a magazine. Her scissors are small with sharp cutters like a bird's beak. She's turning the page in her hand to snip round a bunch of flowers. She looks up when she hears a swish and sees a blue envelope slide under the front door. 'What's this?' Mom says. She puts down the scissors and walks to the letter. Her eyebrows wave into worry lines. 'Please God, not another lawyer's letter?'

She picks up the letter and reads – *Sender: John Robert Carmichael, Kincardine, Invergowrie Street, Perth, Scotland.*

She rips open the thin blue paper folds. Mom sucks in her breath. Her eyes move from side to side. She reads the words running like crab legs wet with black ink sideways across the page. 'Oh my – aah – unhh.' She moans, 'Oh, Jack, Jack.'

She holds in her breath for a long time then aaghs. Her eyes shine blue sparkles, a tear falls down her cheek. Her eyebrows undo their worry lines and jump into thin black moons. Her eyes are so sharp they look as if they could pin me down on the floor.

Mom presses the letter to her heart and puffs air out again. Her legs walk tchik-tchik. I snip paper with her scissors. She bends down, 'Feel my heart, Karin.'

I put my hand on her apron top. I can feel Mom's heart. It's jumping up and down under her clothes. She's excited. I run to my parting present, a painted rocking pony from my father. He gave me this when he divorced Mom and me. Rocky has a red saddle, brown eyes and brown spots on her white body. Her little black hooves look as if they can run to the ends of the earth. I jump onto the saddle and rock to the beating of Mom's heart. Thump-thump. I feel everything Mom feels.

Her mouth stretches wide in a happy smile. She looks surprised. 'Jack wants to marry me.'

Who's Jack? The only Jack I know is my jack-in-the-box. But clown Jack can't write letters.

Mom walks up and down with quick steps. She's talking to herself, sounding out her thoughts. 'Do you know what this means, Irene? It's your passport out, a chance for a new life, a new beginning.'

She stares through the window, her hand on her mouth. 'Oh, but I must think ... what if ... Scotland will be so very different.' She shakes her head, pushes back her black curls. 'No, I should go ... I'll take Karin. I deserve a second chance after what that basta–' she looks at me to see if I'm listening, '... did to me.'

Mom doesn't notice when I don't eat my meat at supper tonight. I only like food that slides down my throat without chewing. I'm too worried to chew. I worry about Mom all the time. But when I don't eat, Mom's nose twitches, her eyes get big and she tries to push the fork into my mouth. I zip my lips up tight. 'This is war, Karin,' Mom's face turns red and her voice sounds like burnt onions. Then she fills a big spoon with castor oil and brings it right close to my mouth. When

I smell the oily, sick-making stuff, I begin to cry, then I eat.

'Met lang tande,' Mom says.

Mom spoke Afrikaans when she was with my father although she is English-speaking. Mom told me they got divorced because my father drank and chased women. I have a picture in my head of my father running down the road drinking out of a bottle, chasing women away.

But tonight Mom is happy, I've never seen her so happy. She listens to a programme on the radio. There's the sound of a fish horn blowing then a voice says, 'Snoektown calling – the craziest station south of the line with Cecil Wightman.' Mom laughs at his jokes. I don't think I have ever heard Mom laugh out loud before. This is better than Christmas. Christmas in this tiny flat above the Main Road is lonely. Mom is sad and cries for all the things she's lost.

I climb onto the bench on the balcony high above the cars in the street. I can see half a moon and the stars blink at me. I wonder if I will see these same stars in Scotland. Mom says she's taking me there. I turn to ask Mom but she's rubbing cream onto her face and pulling her eyebrow hairs out with a little tweezer. Plucking, she calls it.

When it's dark, I climb into bed with Mom. I snuggle-wriggle into her back. 'You're like a tick,' she says.

The wind rocks the night. I hear the whooshing of the wind from the sea up the Main Road, round the roof tops, through the trees. The windows rattle, the floors creak. I hear the clickety-clack of the train next to the beach.

'We're leaving soon, Karin, we're going to have a new life,' Mom says in a sleepy voice. I play with Mom's curls. I take pictures of our life out of my memorybook. I see Mom bending over the roses in the garden of the house where we used to live, she gives me one to smell, I see her baking cakes in the kitchen, I see her sitting on the stairs crying when the divorce papers come, I see Mom lying in this bed, staring at the wall and saying, 'Divorce is worse than death. It's like being buried alive.' Then I fall asleep and dream of Rocky's little black hooves running to the ends of the earth.

When Aunt Rose smiles two big holes show in her cheeks. Mom calls them dimples. She says Aunt Rose is a saucy minx, but Aunt Rose is not smiling now. She's sucking smoke from a cigarette into her mouth and blowing it out through her nose. She listens to Mom with her eyes popping out of her head. She shakes her brown hair tied up in sausages on top of her head.

'I'm going to marry Jack and that's that,' Mom says. She waves the blue letter in Aunt Rose's face. 'This is my passport to a new, better life.' She holds up her left hand, 'Look, no rings, Rose. I'm free to do what I want. I threw Good-for-nothing's rings into the sea.'

Aunt Rose sucks hard at her cigarette and pushes the smoke through her mouth as she speaks. 'Pops would turn in his grave if he knew. What did he always say? "Marry in haste, repent at leisure." You only saw Jack for three weeks before he went back to Scotland, Irene. You don't know him at all.'

Mom leans close to Aunt Rose, 'I saw enough at the holiday farm. Jack is a perfect gentleman.'

'Why has Jack never married? He's over forty.' Auntie Rose stares at Mom with her brown button eyes.

'I don't know. I don't care. I have to go, Rose, and the Northern Hemisphere sounds just fine to me.'

Aunt Rose snorts and pushes her cigarette into the sand. 'You don't need a man in your life, Irene, you can be happy without one.'

'Perhaps you can. You're not tied down by a five-year-old. I'm lonely.'

Aunt Rose shooshes her, puts a finger on her lips. She watches me playing in the sand.

'She's almost six. She'll grow up.'

'Rose, I want to put distance between myself and that … man. I don't want any reminders of my old life.'

Mom's forgotten. She has me.

'Irene.'

Mom doesn't stop wrapping her blue and white plates in newspaper. She puts them in a wooden box. Uncle Dan coughs. He turns his hat around in his hands. He has a long nose like Mom but his head is almost bald. Mom has got bunches of black hair that curl past her shoulders.

'What about all the mines left floating in the Atlantic since the war? Your ship could easily set one off. Doesn't this worry you?'

'No.'

Mom picks up a glass duck, the head comes off like a cork. 'Hmm,' she says, 'this is crystal. I'll keep it. And these flying ducks – I can put them on a wall in Scotland.'

Uncle Dan puts his hat on his head and hammers nails into the lid of the box. 'What about food for this child?' Bang-bang. 'Have you thought about that, Irene?' He looks at Mom through his bushy eyebrows. Bang. 'They still have food rationing and coupons in Scotland. Powdered eggs and Spam. Not good for the child.'

Mom's lips squeeze together. 'She hardly eats anyway.'

'You're breaking Ma's heart, Irene, I hope you realise she isn't strong.'

'I can't worry about broken hearts, including my own, Dan. It's been three years since the divorce. I've got to get out of this rut, mines or no mines, food rations or not, broken hearts are last on my list.'

Mom is taking me to say goodbye to my Ouma, my Daddy's mother, before we sail on the big boat. Mom has tied a bow in my hair and put me in a dress with tucks and pleats and embroidery on the Peter Pan collar. She sewed the dress herself. I watched her push and pull the needle and cotton through the material for days.

I walk through the door and arms reach out and hold me tight, hands push my face into soft bosoms covered with frilly bits. I can't breathe; I'm squeezed tight by these arms that shake me up and down. A strange voice cries in my ear, 'Foeitog, Irene, wat 'n oulike kind.'

The arms let me go. Pheew. I suck in air.

'Karin, say hello to your Aunt Nerie,' Mom says.

Aunt Nerie holds me away from her, looks at me as if I am a prize she has just won, then pulls me close to her bosoms again. 'Darr-ling child.'

Her voice purrs like a kitten, her eyes, yellow-green, stare at me, her mouth painted pink stretches wide, showing her wet shiny teeth. Her short yellow hair looks like the halo of the angel in Mom's Bible. She turns me this way and that, whispering under her breath, as if she has only just discovered me, her brother's child.

'Kyk na haar mooi gesiggie,' she touches the bow in my hair, touches my hands and knees. She presses her lips to my face in lots of quick kisses. Mwah-mwah.

Mom sits on the couch and watches, she sits stiff as a stick, her nose twitches as if there's a bad smell nearby. My Ouma crouches like a black-widow spider on an upright chair. Her grey hair is scraped back from her forehead into a doughnut shape on top. Her eyes have no colour; they look at Mom as if she's an insect she would like to bite. Her fingers curl like spider-legs over the top of her walking stick; the skin of her face is like the dough Mom push-pulls into bread. She has little furry black moles on her face. I can't stop looking at them.

Aunt Nerie whispers in my ear, 'Jou ouma is so lelik soos die nag, nie waar nie?'

I turn away from Ouma's dough face and doughnut hair to my exciting auntie who fusses over me like a mother hen. She cuts a piece of cake thick with butter icing from a plate on the table and pops it into my mouth. She feeds me with small pieces as if I am her baby bird in her nest.

Mom and Ouma stare at each other across the room. They wait for the other to speak. Mom hunches her shoulders under her green dress, her pearl earrings shine under her black hair, but her eyebrows rush together in angry squiggles. Ouma mumbles under her breath and stamps her stick on the floor. She puffs up her chest under the black dress she always wears. 'Because she's mourning her dead children,' Mom once told me.

'So, Irene, you're going take this arme kind away from her family to a strange country because you're going to marry a rooinek.' Stamp goes her stick. Thud. 'What's that you say? A Scotsman? Maak nie saak nie, hulle is almal dieselfde. Murdering Engelse. Alfred, Laawd Kitchener, spawn of Satan.'

Two red spots jump onto Mom's cheeks. Aunt Nerie looks at her mother, 'Ag, Moeder, hou nou op. Bly tog stil. Irene has come to say goodbye. Don't start again about the concentration camps and the dead children. We know you suffered. It's enough. It happened almost fifty years ago.'

Ouma holds her breath until I think she is going to burst, her nose holes open wide to suck in air, her chest sticks out; our eyes watch while she holds her breath then whoosh, lets it all out. She scrapes her teeth together scritch-scritch. She pulls her spiderweb crochet blanket over her knees and stares at Mom with her colourless eyes, 'Ek sal nooit vergeet nie. Nooit.' She lifts her stick, waves it at Aunt Nerie, then bangs it down hard.

Aunt Nerie lifts me off her lap, puts me down. 'Verskoon my asseblief.' She disappears down the passage, into a side room.

I follow her, my shoes trotting on the wooden floor. I look into the room where Auntie Nerie stands; it's a bathroom. She is staring at her face in the mirror; she strokes the skin on her cheeks, wipes the crumbs from her mouth. She bends to the laundry basket, lifts the lid, scratches in the dirty clothes. Pulls out a bottle full of orangey-brown water. Opens the lid and puts the bottle to her mouth. Throws back her head and drinks loudly. Glug-glug. Her throat swallows, her eyes close. She licks her lips. Then back to the bottle. Long swallows. Now I know she's really my father's sister. She puffs air out of her cheeks, closes the bottle, then hides it in the basket. She turns and sees me in the doorway, my eyes open wide. She walks to me, drops on one knee, puts one finger on her lips squeezed together like a kiss, then she winks. I know what she means. It's a secret.

'Nothing like brandy to calm the nerves,' she says.

We walk back to the sitting room, hand in hand.

Mom and I are walking along the catwalk next to the sea. 'Is this a walk for cats?' I ask. 'Is it too narrow for people?' But people walk along here every day, below the railway line and above the rocks and the sea.

Mom doesn't answer. She's looking at the far away mountains across the bay. The wind lifts her hair and makes it wave like a flag behind her.

'False Bay,' she says, the wind grabbing her words from her mouth before they sound. 'False as men's hearts.'

We climb down steps onto a little shell beach and sit on rocks warm as toast next to a tidal pool. 'When it's high tide the pool disappears,' Mom says.

My legs are bare and my brown hair blows across my face. The sun has taken the colour out of my thin cotton dress. Mom bends down into the pool, her hand dips into the water. I bend next to her, and pull hair out of her eyes. I put my hands on either side of her face and kiss her nose. Her eyes are deep blue like the sea, her mouth is the same shape as a bow. We have been alone together my whole life from the first moment I knew I was me.

Mom shows me the sea creatures hiding in the cracks of rocks – blue-black mussels and orange-brown limpets. 'Here's a Venus ear,' she gives me a red-brown shell shaped like an ear. The inside shines like Mom's pearl earrings. Green sea-urchins, round like balls, creamy-green starfish. Seaweed like moss sticking to rocks. Seaweed like flat black snakes bobbing up and down on the water. Mom points to a flower under the water. 'Look, Karin, this isn't a flower, it's really a sea creature. See its waving tentacles.'

I watch the tiny pink-orange arms waving, they're waving goodbye.

'Remember everything you see, Karin, we may never come back here,' Mom says.

I look at the sea heaving, at the train crawling like a caterpillar round the mountain across the bay, at the fishing boats, the white sand, the soft blue sky. The sea shooshes me into a daydream. Mom and I will be shut in this daydream in my memorybook forever.

Tomorrow we will catch the train to the harbour where the Carnarvon Castle ship waits for us at the docks.

The trunk sits in the middle of the room. Mom has almost finished packing. Mom's green travel suit and my red jacket and leggings lie on the chair for us to wear when we leave.

Mom and I are cosy in bed together. I know Mom's tired; her eyelids almost close over her blue eyes. Her eyelashes want to sweep her cheeks, but she's telling me a story.

'Something you should know before we go,' she says. 'You were not an accident, Karin. Your father and I wanted to have a baby to save our marriage. He promised he would stop drinking and chasing women. He wanted a son. I will never forget the look on his face when he came to the hospital. The nurse was going to put you in his arms but when she said you were a girl, he turned away.' Her shoulders shake, a tear crawls out of one eye, then the other. 'And that, as they say, was that. Finito. The end.'

I listen to Mom but I'm also looking through the pictures in my memorybook and I can't find one of my father. I can't remember seeing him; I have no picture of him in my head.

Leaving is a big worry. Mom's face is white; she holds my hand tightly as we stand at the rails. We're waving little squares of handkerchiefs to Uncle Dan and Aunt Rose down below on the docks. They wave handkerchiefs back. Crowds of people have come to say goodbye to people sailing on the Carnarvon Castle. It doesn't really look like a castle. It's pointy in the front, has two big funnels and a wooden deck running all the way round the top of the ship.

Mom sings in a shaky voice, 'Wish me luck as you wave me goodbye, Cheerio, here we go on our way.' She says they used to sing this song to all the soldiers going to war.

The tug boat pushes the end of the ship away from the wharf, sailors drop thick ropes into the dark-green, greasy sea in the harbour. The ship moves slowly to the opening in the harbour wall. Uncle Dan and Aunt Rose are just two dots. The tug hoots, the ship's funnel shouts a deep goodbye and we're out in the open sea. Mom and I move to the back of the ship where the ship leaves a carpet of white foam. We watch Table Mountain get smaller until it slips into the sea.

'Well,' says Mom. 'I've burnt my boats now.'

We walk down all the stairs, through the passages until we find our cabin deep in the bottom of the boat. I don't like the smell of hot painted metal. It's dark in the cabin. Bunk beds sit on top of one another. The ship starts to roll up and down and side to side. 'We're sailing through the Cape Rollers,' Mom says. 'Giant waves.'

At first I think its fun, but soon I feel sick and dizzy. Mom finds a bucket and leaves it next to my bunk. I have to lie down all the time. The minute I lift my head, I get sick. The pillow is hard with stripy material and the grey blanket is heavy and scratchy. Mom's bought me red leggings, a jacket and bonnet. They have tens and tens of buttons. When I need to pee, Mom can't undo the buttons fast enough and I wet myself. Mom gets cross with me and slaps my bare legs. Her nose twitches and her eyes shoot blue sparks.

Sometimes she just sits at the end of my bunk and stares at the wall. Bulkhead, she calls it. I'm too sick to worry about her, but she doesn't look happy, her face is white and cross. Sometimes she won't answer me. I don't like it when Mom won't speak to me, when she's locked herself away in her thoughts.

It seems as if I have been on this bunk at the bottom of the ship forever. If I'm hungry, Mom brings me soup or toast. When I'm bored, she reads the story of Pinocchio. When we come to the part where Pinocchio and Geppetto find themselves in the belly of the whale, I say to Mom, 'Just like us, we're having the same adventure.'

But she pulls her eyebrows together and stares away from me.

One morning when it's still dark, Mom wakes me up. She starts to dress me in a padded vest with tiny buttons, a blue jersey, the red leggings and jacket. Her face and hands are cold. They shake.

I touch her cheek. 'Mom, what's wrong?'

'We're here,' she says. 'In Liverpool. We docked in the night.'

Then I feel that the ship is standing still. 'Is it Scotland?'

'Not yet.'

We go on deck to look. The sky is a dark grey blanket shutting out the sun, the air is cold like inside a fridge. Mom and I shiver. The buildings are old and grey, or dirty red. So many metal ships and cranes. The harbour water is oily black. Mom and I hold hands tightly as we walk down the gangplank. It takes so long to find our trunk and suitcases. Mom has to find a man to carry them on a trolley. Porter, she calls him. There's a train at the other end of the docks. Mom says it's an express that will take us all the way to Scotland.

We wait for people to fill the train. A whistle blows, the wheels screech, the train moves clickety-click slowly from the harbour through the town. The sky is still a grey blanket, the smell of smoke burns my nose. Mom keeps a hankie over her nose and mouth. The train goes faster and faster when we leave Liverpool behind and there are fields, telephone poles and little houses and farms. Then we go so fast – everything whizzes past.

I'm tired and thirsty. Mom brings me cocoa and sandwiches with stinky pink meat on them. The flying fields and trees make me dizzy; I slip onto the seat and sleep.

I wake when it's night. The train is going so fast, it rocks from side to side. I'm thirsty, I need to pee, I cry, 'Mom, Mom', then wet myself.

Mom looks at me, then covers her face with her hands. 'Not now, Karin,' she says. 'Try and sleep.'

But I can't. I smell and my wet leggings scratch.

Mom stares at her ghost face in the window. The black rushes past. Clickety-clack don't look back, the wheels say, but I do look back. I don't like this speedy train; I'm tired of moving in rocking ships and trains over tens and tens of miles. We're moving into the long black night like a tunnel. Mom is stuck to the sight of her white ghost face in the window. I sob into my hands. I can't see a moon or stars. I want to go home to the warm yellow sun, the sand and the sea. I'm tired of moving ... I want my pony ... I want ... home.

I'm painting a blue sky with a flat brush on a big piece of paper. I wash my brush in the jar, dip it in the yellow and paint a round sun in the corner with lines coming out of it. I paint a green sea with red fishing boats. I put stick figures on the sand – that's Mom and me watching the sea although we are really tens and tens of miles away in Scotland. Mom brings me to this nursery school every morning.

Mom and Jack are married now. Mom shows me a photograph of herself and Jack on their wedding day standing in front of arches and pillars. 'Not real,' Mom says. 'This photograph was taken in a studio.'

I look at them dressed up in wedding clothes. Mom's smile doesn't look real either, it looks as if somebody stuck it on her face. Her eyes look shiny-worried. Her black hair waves at the side of her face under a black hat with a veil and black dots like insects on it. She wears a flower on her fur coat. Jack wears a flower on his suit and a hankie sticking out of his pocket in a triangle. He combs his hair back from his forehead and keeps it in place with thick gooey stuff he calls Brylcreem.

He doesn't smile, he has little hoods on his eyes and his nose is like a bird's beak. My teacher gives me a gold star for this painting. 'Lots of detail,' she says.

The bell rings. My stomach gives a little shake. Mom isn't coming to fetch me today because she has errands to run. 'You're a big girl now, Karin,' she says. 'You can find your way home. There's a red letter box on the corner of Mellville Street where we live. You'll see the signpost. Mellville starts with M like Mom.'

My feet in their black shoes tap along the pavement. I feel very small like a mouse scurrying next to tall, stone buildings. My heart pumps worry through my body; I'm scared I will get lost in these streets of Perth because they all look the same. Little cobblestones and grey block buildings. Mom has promised me she will be home by the time I get there. I see a red letterbox in the distance and run towards it. This must be the road – I see an M on the signpost. Rows of houses that are really flats. I run down the road in a panic now. Rows of windows with curtains and doors. I stop at one. Yes, I know this door. I run inside and hop up the stairs to the first floor. Here is our door, our green mat. I throw myself at it, turning the knob at the same time, but it is locked. It won't open. 'Mo-om, Mo-om.' My thin voice trembles up the stairwell. Silence. There's nobody at home.

I sink onto the cement step at the top of the stairs with a sob. Sick panic rushes into my stomach. What if Mom never comes home again? What if something happens to her? I will be left alone in a strange city full of people who speak funny English. Scots brogue, Mom calls it.

I begin to cry with a wailing sound, spit rolls down my chin onto my blue jersey. The cement step is cold under my red kilt. Suddenly I hear footsteps below me and my wailing stops. My heart thumps. Surely this must be Mom? But it is Jack who climbs onto the landing, his face under his felt hat pops up like a jack-in-the-box towards the sound of my crying. His eyebrows lift at the sight of my shaking body, wet jersey, crying face. He pretends to be surprised, but his eyes look happy-cruel.

'Wha's this?' He stands over me, his mouth twists. 'A snivellin' bairn on the doorstep?'

I look into his cold grey winter eyes and see he's a hawk looking for something to eat. A sour smell comes from him. I make nn-nnhing noises in my throat. His eyebrows pull together in a black bristly line over his bird beak nose. He is so close I can sniff two smells on his breath; cigarette smoke and something like Auntie Nerie's brandy. I can see yellow spots in his grey eyes and the black dots of beard showing on his skin.

'Is the babbie cryin' because her mither's no here? Eh? Och, wha' a shame. Precious little lambkin's too scared to stay by herself for one second? Pathetic wee rabbit. What are ye goin' tae do when we leave, yer mither an' I. Hey?' He pauses to wag a finger in my face. 'An' we're no' takin' ye with us, mind. Oh, no. I'm no' takin' any crybaby wi' me. Who will ye cry to then?'

What does he mean, leave behind?

I hear Mom's voice on the landing. 'Jack?' Mom's walking up the stairs. She looks beautiful to me in her blue coat and red scarf. My heart wants to jump out of my throat. Her smile goes away, her eyes see my tears, Jack's wagging finger. 'What's going on here?'

Jack turns to her and pushes out his chin; his voice is thunder banging in the sky. 'It's aboot time ye disciplined this child, Irene. She'll have to stop this bawlin' and greetin' every time ye're oot o' her sight.'

He takes a box of Woodbines out of his jacket pocket, lights a cigarette and blows the smoke in Mom's face. 'Wha's goin' to happen when we leave? Have ye told her yet? No.'

Mom looks guilty and worried. She unlocks the door. She and Jack step inside and argue as they take off their scarves, hats and coats.

'When were ye goin' to tell her?'

'Waiting for the right moment.'

'Cathy and Lizzie won't put up wi' her nonsense ... I can tell ye that.'

'She's only a child.'

'Well, she'll have to learn. Ye knew from the beginning, Irene, I wouldna take a child to the tropics. She's better off here at school.'

'We've never been apart.'

'I dinna care ...'

I cry, 'Mommy. Mommy.'

Quick as a flash, Jack turns his beak nose down to me. 'Shoosh wi' yer "Mommy" malarkey. Ye're no a babbie anymore. Grow up. Say Mither ...'

'Jack. You have no right ...'

'I do now, Irene. She does wha' I tell her tae do.'

They throw words at each other. My eyes move from face to face. Jack's eyes come out on stalks, his mouth shoots out the words, Mom's eyes look sad. I learn the truth behind their words. They will sail for Nigeria on the Balmoral Castle in a few weeks, leaving me behind with Cathy and Lizzie, Jack's sisters, in the house they call Kincardine.

I don't sleep with Mom anymore. I lie in my dark room on my own. I listen to the sound of their voices, sometimes soft, sometimes fast and loud. I think about what's happened and I put this picture in my memorybook. I can say whatever I want in my head. Jack won't hear me. *Mom, Mumsey, Momma.*

They're rushing up and down the flat. Jack and Mom. They're leaving today. When Mom's not packing and sorting, she tells me what I must do while she is away. 'Brush your teeth, Karin, eat all your food, brush your hair. Don't forget to put on clean underwear every morning.' She's packed my clothes in a small brown suitcase.

Mom dresses in her green suit, she pulls her black curls into a ball on her neck, clips pearl earrings on her ears. She rubs cream into her skin so it looks extra smooth, paints her lips with a red stick, makes her eyelashes black with a tiny brush. Her eyes shine double blue. She pats lily-of-the-valley perfume behind her ears, in the dip in her throat. The strong, sweet smell makes my nose twitch.

'Always look your best, Karin.' Mom brushes my hair. 'People judge you by your appearance.'

The taxi takes us to a brick house at the end of a long street. There are no trees, no grass, only a street of red-brown brick houses with chimneys. The front door opens and I smell what's inside the Kincardine house. Boiled cabbage, mothballs, something stronger than cigarettes, and something rotten.

Four people stand in the hallway. Cathy, Jack's sister has the same hoody eyes, she's short and plump with a flower apron that wraps around her body over a skirt and jersey, her short hair stands in a fuzz around her head. Her husband, Alan McCracken, looks over the top of his glasses. He wears a jacket and tie. He's got a smoke pipe in his hand. Mom bends down and whispers their names in my ear. 'This is Mavis,' she says. 'She will take you to school and look after you.' Mavis looks at me with black eyes and sticks out her tongue. 'Then – Lizzie,' Mom puts her arm around my shoulders and smiles at Jack's family. Lizzie smiles back, her lips stretch open over big plastic teeth. Jack also has false teeth. He puts them in a glass of water next to his bed every night. I don't like Jack's family, they don't look happy to see me at all.

When Mom bends to kiss me goodbye, she whispers, 'Be a good girl, Karin.'

I hang on to her sleeve. 'Don't go, Mom. Please.' I look up at Jack. His hoods come down over his eyes and his black bristle brows join in the middle of his nose. But Mom just whispers, 'Be a big girl, Karin, don't cry. Time will go quickly.'

Mom's eyes have a happy sparkle as if she is going on a big adventure, and she is. She has a new husband and they are going on a long ship voyage to a country called Nigeria. She showed me a map of the world while she was packing. She pointed to a band around the middle. 'These are the Tropics,' she said. 'The Tropic of Capricorn and the Tropic of Cancer. The equator is in the middle. You were born under the sign of Cancer, and I, under the sign of Capricorn. You're a crab running sideways under my mountain goat hooves.'

She and Jack will live near a tin mine where he works.

I watch the taxi until it turns the corner at the end of the street. I want to run after it, but I swallow my tears until my throat aches. I cry myself to sleep in the bedroom I share with Mavis who won't talk to me. Before I sleep I look at all the pictures in my memorybook – Mom knitting with clicking silver needles and jerseys growing from her busy fingers; Mom cooking and cleaning, everything in its place; the smell of Mom's perfume; playing at the beach with Mom. It's cold and grey here, I feel so lost, so lonely. I feel like a puppy that's been left alone on the side of a long empty road.

'Karin.'

Cathy coughs out my name through the slimy goo in her throat; yellow-green globs she's always spitting into her hankie. She's got pouches and wrinkles round her mouth and chin. She looks like a droopy cartoon dog. A cigarette sticks to her bottom lip and hangs down with a red tip over the bread she's cutting. When she speaks the cigarette wobbles and shakes ash onto the slices of bread. She half-shuts the hoods on her eyes so the smoke won't go into them.

'Karin? Make yersel' useful noo an' fetch the wee pan an' brush frae under the sink and sweep oot the grate so we can get a fire goin' in here.'

She grips the cigarette with her lips. More grey flakes fall. She opens her hoods and looks through the window at the black patch of sky above the roof of the coal shed. 'It's gettin' awfu' cold in here.'

I open the curtains under the sink, they're stiff with crusts of dried dirt. I smell something sour and rotten but I find the brush and pan and begin to sweep the ash from yesterday's fire. A rail hangs from the mantelpiece, it holds dish cloths, socks and underwear – baggy flannel bloomers, Cathy calls them.

Cathy stops cutting the bread. She piles some coal and sticks of wood into the grate, crumples newspaper and lights the pile. She takes the cigarette from her wet lips and flicks it with her thumb and first finger into the grate. She smiles at me. Like Lizzie and Jack, her teeth are big and false, they click together when she speaks. Sometimes they pop out of her gums.

'Put the ash in newspaper, lovey, an' roll it up – there ye are, there's newspaper behind the coal scuttle. Aye, there's a lass.'

I make a parcel of the ash and give it to Cathy. She walks across the kitchen. The backs of her slippers are trodden down. They make a slap-slap noise on the linoleum floor.

Later we sit at the round table. A light bulb hangs down from the ceiling shining a circle of bright light on us. The rest of the room is shadowy. The sky's as black as soot. There are brown stains on the tablecloth. Alan stoops into his chair and flicks the newspaper open and reads. Lizzie rubs her hands together, the tip of her nose is pink, her eyes watery. 'Och, wha' a day. As cold as a witch's breath ootside ...'

Mavis drops her school case on the floor and slides into a chair opposite me. Her eyes stare at me; they say, 'Don't move, don't speak.'

'Says here there's twenty-three feet o' snow in the Highlands,' Alan says.

'Awa' wi' ye! An' there's going to be a shortage o' coal, they said on the news.'

Cathy brings a pan from the stove and plops grey blobs of something on our plates.

'Powdered eggs again?' says Lizzie.

'Och, aye, wha' else?'

Slap-slap across the floor. Cathy drops the pan in the sink. She puts a slice of bread on my plate. 'Here ye go, Karin, eat up.'

I reach for the butter and jam. Mavis' hand shoots across the table and puts them out of my reach. She watches me. She's the cat. I'm the mouse. I try again. Mavis puts her arm around both bowls of butter and jam.

Cathy has hawk eyes like Jack, they see everything; her little hoods flick from Mavis to me. 'Och weel, ye see Karin, we're still bound tae wartime rations, ye ken, a half poond o' butter a week. Our Mavis is a big, braw girrl an' needs her sustenance. Here, ye can put this on yer bread.' She pushes a plate with a knob of white fat on it close to me. 'Lard,' she says.

There's a lump in my throat, tears prickle my eyes. I think of Mom sailing away across the sea with Jack. I remember the teas with Mom in the flat on Mellville Street in front of the fire. A white tablecloth, yellow omelette with grated cheese on top or a sausage, on pretty plates. Warm toast, curls of butter, red berry jam.

Alan makes a noise behind his newspaper.

'Ahemm. Cathy? I thought ye had an agreement wi' Jack's new wife? She was goin' tae pay ye board and lodging fer the bairn? Doesna that buy her some butter an' jam? Eh?'

'Haud yer tongue, McCracken. The money Irene gives me doesna go verra far. There's expenses ye ken nought aboot. There's bus fare, school fees.' Her teeth clack together. Her jaws close tight.

'Weel, I thought I would just ask – seems a little bit o' jam and butter wouldna harm anyone.'

Alan folds his newspaper and sets it down. The McCrackens bend to their plates of food. Their sets of teeth clack like the castanets of the dancers in Madeira when Mom and I leaned over the rail to watch. I take tiny bites of dry bread and grey eggs. Mavis watches me. Once when I couldn't eat Cathy's boiled cabbage and fatty meat, Mavis cried out, 'Look, Ma, our food's nae guid enough fer her,' and she'd grabbed my plate away from under my nose and gobbled the food. Mavis talks about me as if I'm not sitting there.

A few days after I came to live at the house called Kincardine, Mavis came into the kitchen where I was sitting with Cathy in front of the fire.

She stamped one foot, put a hand on her hip and pointed at me. 'I'm no sleepin' wi' her in my room fer anither night, Ma, do ye hear? She cries in her pillow. She thinks I canna hear, but it keeps me awake. I canna stand her blubbin', I tell ye.'

'Och, weel, dinna fash yersel', my pet,' Cathy's rough, coughy voice stopped Mavis. 'We'll think o' somethin'.'

They moved my mattress into Lizzie's bedroom, on the floor next to her bed. Every night Lizzie takes her teeth out and puts them in a glass of water with a pink pill that turns the water into pink foam. Her teeth smile in the glass but not in her mouth. Lizzie's face shrinks without her teeth, her hair is a brown frizz she gets from a tube she calls Toni Perm. Her empty mouth makes a tiny circle when she snores.

The bedroom smells of mothballs and air that's stuck in the room forever. They never open the curtain or a window. Lizzie's clothes pile up over the furniture and carpet. Nobody makes the beds. I think of Mom's white teeth that don't come out at night, of Aunt Rose's dimple smile, of Aunt Nerie's wet tooth pink lip smile.

I can read. Miss McConachie has taught me to read everything. I read all the advertisements on shop windows, on boards, on the sides of red buses on the ride to and from school every day. I read the McCracken newspapers and all the books I can find. I read faster and better because reading takes away the loneliness, fills the empty hole Mom's left in my chest. I want to surprise her when she gets back.

> Kitchen soap skin isn't kissable but a velvety skin is an aid to romance.
> Make your skin adorably soft with Eve toilet soap 2 ½ d.

> Oh what a lovely pudding!
> What joy in a pudding that turns out
> perfectly. Atora, the good beef suet.

> My doctor recommends
> Camel cigarettes for smoking pleasure.

On the first day of school at the Perth Academy, Mavis tells me to sit in front of the bus. She sits at the back with her friends. 'Remember,' she says. 'I dinna ken ye. Ye dinna live wi' us.'

Children push and shove past me when the bus stops. They run up the steep hill to the red brick school building. I follow them. A bell rings. A grown-up's hand pulls me along, takes me to a classroom. 'Miss McConachie' says the sign on the door. Confused and excited, I hang my coat, my beret and my scarf on a hook. I sit next to a small girl with gold-brown pigtails. Her face has a pointy chin and sharp round eyes, her ears stick up like a pixie's.

Miss McConachie walks into the room, she carries a small stick in her hand. She speaks in a loud voice, her lips are scarlet-red, she wears a red jersey, a brown skirt. Her brown eyes look everywhere at once, they see everything. Her brown hair lies flat and neat like a nut helmet. 'You, you and you.' She points the stick at me, the pixie girl beside me and a boy behind us. 'Tae the front. Bring yer books. Look sharp noo.'

There's a book on my desk with a picture of a small girl and boy on the cover. We stand in front of the class and try to read the words with Miss McConachie saying them out loud. Then she just points the stick. Soon we remember all the words. All the children stand in front, three by three, in turns. We follow the words in the book when they read.

Miss McConachie teaches us spelling, the times tables, we learn to recite the tables aloud every morning, then Miss McConachie tests us. She teaches us to write the alphabet, then to write words, then sentences. She says long sentences out loud and we have to listen and write the words in our books. She calls this dictation.

Miss McConachie looks at her wristwatch a lot. We jump from reading to writing, to reciting the times tables, to spelling tests, to mental arithmetic, to dictation. We never stop working and learning. When I ride home on the bus, my head spins from all the work my brain has had to do. Miss McConachie is very strict; she keeps us on our toes with her wristwatch and her short stick and her loud voice.

The pixie girl becomes my friend. Her name is Yvonne. We sit together in class and on the low wall in the playground at break time. She shows me her collection. Coloured transfers of flowers, fairies, angels, woods and animals.

'Ye look through my book at all the transfers. If ye like one, you push it up like a bookmark, then mebbe we can swap. Where's yer collection?'

I tell Yvonne I don't have one.

'Here ye are then, ye can start yer collection wi' these.' She hands me some of her pictures. Yvonne reminds me of Mom. She's also like a busy-bee, she has a busy-bee mind, she's always thinking and talking, always doing something.

At home I find the Peter Pan book Mom gave me when she left. I put the transfers, one on each page, in this book. I show Cathy. 'Can you buy me some more transfers with the money Mom gives you?' I ask.

Cathy puffs for a second on her cigarettes, screws up her eyes then says, 'I tell ye what, Karin, if ye sweep oot the grates in the kitchen an' the parlour every Saturday mornin' an' help me wi' the dishes, I'll buy ye transfers every week.'

Yvonne and I are in a bubble of friendship. At school we sit together the whole day. We go through our collections at break time, swapping, comparing our treasures. Dragons, knights in armour, castles, forests, angels, fairies, children, animals especially horses. The best ones are the glossy-shiny, embossed pictures. She doesn't ask me questions like the other children do. 'Why do ye talk sae funny?' 'Where do ye come frae?' 'Are yer parents no' Scots?' She accepts me. She's quick and clever in class. I learn to think quickly like Yvonne.

Cathy discovers me reading a newspaper one Saturday morning. Her eyes behind the hoods and swirls of cigarette smoke look at me with interest. She asks me questions about my schoolwork. Then every night after supper, we sit in front of the fire in the parlour and she tests me on my spelling, my reading and my times tables. She waves her red-tipped cigarette around, like Miss McConachie waves her short stick. Her eyes shine in the firelight. She's lazy about doing housework but not about doing schoolwork with me. She barks out questions one after the other. Her plastic teeth shine in the firelight when I get them right.

'Guid girl, Karin. I'll make a scholar oot o' ye yet. Ye'll be top o' yer class or my name's no Cathy McCracken.'

But I have a worry. When I go to bed at night on the floor next to Frizzie-Lizzie, I have trouble remembering Mom. I can't remember her smell or her voice. Frizzie-

Lizzie smells like mothballs and her snores whistle through the little empty hole of her mouth at night. Mom's memory is blurry. Lizzie, Cathy and the rest of the McCrackens, Yvonne and Miss McConachie are more real to me.

I try to remember when she left. Mom's been gone forever. She doesn't write letters. She doesn't know I can read and write. She left at the start of a new year when it was still winter. There have been two springs, two summers, an autumn and a winter. I don't know how long Mom has been gone. It feels like years. I've had a birthday, soon I will have another. With a shock I realise Mom has been gone for tens and tens of days, so many I can't count. 'Only eighteen months, Karin,' Mom said when she left. 'Time will go quickly.'

'Karin.'

I'm clearing out the grate. It's Saturday morning and a patch of blue sky shows over the roof of the coal shed, but still we had a fire last night.

Cathy stops swishing the breakfast dishes in grey, sudsy water to cough into her hankie. She wipes her mouth. 'Yer mother will be back one o' these days.'

I turn to look at her. 'How do you know?'

'Jack wrote an' told us. Said they'll be back by the end o' June an' that's no verra far off – a week or two.' She stacks the plates then looks at me. 'Ye'll hae to gie yersel' a guid scrub before they gang here. Ye dinna look verra clean tae me.'

I look down at my brown kilt. It has wrinkles and stains. My orange jersey has blobs of porridge down the front. Sometimes I forget to brush my teeth and hair. Cathy doesn't mind.

Another Saturday morning. I've forgotten Mom is supposed to be arriving back in Scotland. Cathy and I are listening to music on the BBC station. The orchestra makes the sound of wind whipping up a storm of waves around the cliffs and rocks – they rise higher and higher.

Cathy says, 'It's the Glasgow Philharmonic – they're playing music called *The Hebrides.*'

The Hebrides. They're islands in the stormy North Sea at the top of Scotland, Miss McConachie told us. Cathy stops washing dishes to listen. I lean on the broom I'm using to sweep the floor.

Lizzie bursts into the kitchen like the rushing wind. 'They're here!' Her eyes pop out at Cathy.

'Eh?' Cathy turns, the sudden movement loosens a long stick of ash from the tip of her cigarette. 'Who's here?'

'Them. Jack an' her mither.'

They turn to look at me. I see worry and shock in their eyes. It's as if they are really seeing me for the first time. I look down at my clothes. I'm wearing the same dirty kilt and jersey. My hair is an unbrushed bush.

Cathy stubs out her cigarette in a saucer. 'Will ye look at the child? Surely Jack gave us the wrong dates then? Lizzie, do somethin' wi' the bairn. Wash her face. Brush her hair fer Godssake. Hurry.'

My heart jumps. Is Mom really here? I feel as if I'm waking up from a dream. My mouth is dry. I try to say 'Mom' but it comes out in a croak. I turn to the door and there she is. But she's a stranger. She's walking across the room to me, her arms outstretched but I don't know her anymore. I'm shy, I hang my head. She kneels down and I remember the sweet smell of lily-of-the-valley.

'Karin? It's me.'

I try to smile but my lips are stiff. I look at Cathy. She nods as if to say, 'It's alright – it really is yer mither.'

Mom, the stranger, pulls out a chair, sits on it then pulls me on her lap. She begins to look like Mom but she's older; I can see lines in the corners of her eyes, her hair's pulled back tightly. On top of her head is a little green hat with a feather.

Jack stands in the doorway. He doesn't look at me, he's watching Mom, waiting to hear what she says.

Mom moves her eyes over me. 'How you've grown, Karin.'

Cathy opens her mouth. 'Och, Jack, Irene. I wasna expectin' ye today but come in, sit down, Jack. Welcome hame.'

Her wrinkles and pouches shake around her chin. Her head seems to shrink into her pinafore. I see how tired and old she looks, how her eyes look at Mom who does not fit into this kitchen, into this house. Mom who looks as if she's just stepped out of a shop in a smart red suit with a black belt and black high-heeled shoes.

Mom stares at me closely; her mouth drops open, the thin lines of her eyebrows lift, then rush together. 'Karin? Didn't you brush your teeth this morning? Why are you so dirty?' She bends her nose to sniff me. 'You smell.'

Mom looks around at the grimy kitchen, at Cathy and Lizzie. 'But I don't understand. Why is everything so ... so ...?'

Her voice stops. She feels my arms and legs, pulls my mouth open, gasps. She pulls at my kilt and jersey.

'What's been going on here? Cathy? I paid board and lodging for Karin. Why is she so thin? So dirty?' Mom's voice rings in my ears. I feel dizzy.

Cathy curls her lip as she stares at Mom. 'I dinna ken wha' ye're on aboot. There's nothin' wrong wi' yer precious bairn.'

'She ate wha' we ate.' Lizzie rubs her hands.

I can see Mom doesn't believe them. 'But she's so thin.' Her voice gets louder. 'It doesn't look as if she's been fed properly.'

Mom stares around her – at the dirty linoleum, the stained green curtains sagging at the window. Her eyes begin to pop. Two red spots show on her cheeks, the tip of her nose twitches. I feel the heat of her body.

Jack's voice behind Mom breaks the silence. 'Not now, Irene,' he says. 'Leave it fer now. Ye can hae a word wi' them later.' He bends and whispers in her ear. 'Ye're tired. Get the bairn's belongings and let's go. The taxi's still outside.'

But Mom's on her feet. 'Not later, Jack. Now.'

Her eyes rush around the room and down to me as if to make sure she's right about what she sees.

'Why is it, Cathy, that although I paid board and lodging for Karin, it's obvious she hasn't been fed properly and hasn't been taken care of?'

Cathy takes her cigarette from her lips, waves it at Mom and sneers, 'How dare ye? Who are ye tae question me? A divorced woman who latched onto, or should I say, entrapped my brother wi' yer feminine wiles.' She runs out of breath and huffs deeply.

Lizzie's watery eyes move from Mom to Cathy and she nods every time Cathy speaks.

Cathy pushes her quivery chin forward. 'Why did ye no take care o' yer own child? Eh?'

Mom moves closer to Cathy, begins to raise her hand. Cathy shrinks backward, her eyes defiant. She spits and her teeth come loose from her gums. She lifts her hand to push them back into place.

'Who do ye think ye are? Eh, Irene? Ye colonial upstart, ye hussy wi' yer airs and graces.'

Mom turns to Jack. 'Right, we're leaving now. Where are her things?'

She marches down the passage to Mavis' room but Mavis blocks her by standing in the doorway with her arms folded. Her black eyes challenge Mom.

'Irene,' Jack shouts, following her. 'Leave it fer noo. We'll come back tae fetch her things.'

'No,' Mom shouts back. 'I'm never coming back to this ... this pigsty.' She says to Mavis, 'Get out of my way.'

Mavis jerks her chin towards Lizzie's bedroom door. 'She doesna sleep here – she shares Lizzie's bedroom.'

Mom pushes open the door to Lizzie's room. She stands in the doorway and looks at a mountain of clothes, high as Ben Nevis. There's a moment of silence as we all wait. I stand close to Mom and look at what she is seeing and smelling for the first time. Jack, Lizzie and Cathy crowd behind us.

Clutter piled on clutter, heaps of Lizzie's clothes, coats, dresses, skirts, underwear, stockings, shoes. None of them clean. Stained, dirt-encrusted, rotting crumpled clothes. Closed curtains and window. Lizzie's belongings in a stinky tomb. Unmade bed and unmade mattress on the floor. I have made a little nest out of pillow, sheet and blanket that I step into every night. The glass that holds Lizzie's teeth while she sleeps has layers of dried pink foam stains.

'Dear ... God!' Mom whispers. 'Never ... never ... my whole life. God. Never ... stinking mess. Grown women ... like pigs.'

She stoops to pick up the sheet on my mattress. It's grey and wrinkled. She turns to Cathy. 'This is where my daughter slept? For eighteen months?' She rips the sheet into strips. 'This isn't fit to sleep on.'

'Irene!' Jack roars, his grey eyes shoot sparks. 'Enough. Let's go.'

Mom grabs my hand and marches to the front door. Mavis sends me one last look of hatred. Mom places her black high-heels down the steps as if shaking the dust off them, her face is almost as red as her suit, she clutches her handbag in one hand and my arm in the other. Jack breathes heavily at our heels. Outside he reaches for a cigarette in his pocket and lights it. His skin looks sallow in the sudden blaze.

I turn my head and try to wave goodbye to Cathy and Lizzie but Mom jerks me forward. They stand in the front doorway, huddled together. Cathy's faded eyes, the whites made yellow by her drifting cigarette smoke, glare at Mom's back. She folds her arms, her eyes blink with concentration. I can see she's thinking of one last thing to say. 'Dinna ever darken my doorstep agin, do ye hear, Irene, ye ungratefu' hussy?'

Mom shouts, 'I wouldn't set foot in this house even if you paid me.'

The taxi driver turns a surprised face in our direction. Jack climbs into the front with him. Mom and I, into the back. I kneel on the seat and look through the back window. Cathy and Lizzie stare after us with resentful eyes. They shrink along with the house, then disappear as we turn the corner. I feel sorry for them. My heart twists in my chest. Another goodbye.

Jack is angry with Mom, he puffs non-stop at his cigarette. His face turns sideways to stare at her; I see the look in one of his hoody eyes, his nose a beak, ready to snap.

'Irene ...'

'Don't say a word, Jack.' Her eyes swivel to look at him, she leans forward and hisses, 'I don't care what you say. I will not leave her behind with those women again. She WILL go back to Dorowa with us.'

It's the middle of the day when we arrive at the flat in Mellville Street. Yet the first thing Mom does is run a bath of hot water. She soaks and scrubs me and washes my hair. She brushes my teeth until my gums bleed. She combs the tangles from my hair in front of the fire. I feel drowsy and clean. But I can see the angry way Mom and Jack look at each other. The air snaps and crackles between them just like the fire.

'Are ye satisfied noo, Irene?' Jack says at last. 'Ye coulda curbed yer tongue. Ye've offended my sisters wi' yer insults an' no a word o' thanks.'

'Do I look as if I care, Jack? I refuse to discuss your sisters with you now.' Mom lowers her eyes to examine my scalp.

'They did their best.'

'Not good enough,' Mom snaps.

The next morning Mom goes shopping for new clothes. She didn't bring any of my old clothes back from the Kincardine house. Jack and I are left alone. I sit on my bed in Mom's dressing gown, too scared to leave the room. Jack strides up and down the passage, smoke flaring from his mouth and nostrils. He smokes one Woodbine after another, lighting a new cigarette from the butt of the old. I watch the tip gleam red as he sucks on the filter end. He jingles his money in his pocket. When he passes the door, his eyes under their hoods slide sideways at me. I sit on the bed and pretend not to see him. I have my Peter Pan book of transfers on my lap and I read the story and look at my collection, hoping Mom will come home soon.

She arrives with bags of clothes, and dresses me immediately in a corduroy green dress, a beige jersey with embroidered flowers and long socks. I still wear my old brown school shoes.

When we left Kincardine, I read every advertisement to Mom in the taxi on the way back to Mellville Street. 'I'm flabbergasted,' Mom says, looking at me with pride. 'You can read like an adult, Karin.' But now she hands me two children's comics to read – the *Dandy* and the *Beano*.

Mom and Jack have been home a week and it seems as if they have never been away. Jack is there all the time and I don't like it; I don't like sharing Mom. And she gives him so much attention I know she puts him first. When we lived in the flat in our old life, I couldn't always reach Mom, she was often somewhere else in her thoughts. But now her attention is always on Jack, as if she has to keep him happy. I feel sick and angry when I see them kissing each other as if they're limpets sticking together.

She talks to him in her bubbly, milkshake voice.

'Would you like a cup of tea, Jack?' 'What would you like to eat for breakfast, lunch, supper?' 'Are you hungry? Are you cold? Should I light a fire?'

They argue about me going back to Nigeria with them. Mom won't back down and Jack won't give in. Then Jack gets news from Amalgamated Tin Mines of Nigeria that they will open a boarding school for the children of their workers.

'Och, weel, that changes things, Irene, she won't be around tha' much.' He turns his nose and hard eyes on me. 'Verra weel. Ye can come but wi' these conditions. Children should be seen an' no heard. Ye do as ye're told at all times.' He holds up a warning finger. 'An' no greetin'. I canna stand a bairn that's always blubbin'. If ye dinna behave, ye'll come straight back to Scotland to boarding school.'

I never talk to Jack. I can see that he doesn't like little girls. He is the same as my father. I leave them alone and sit in my room reading or doing my next favourite thing, drawing and painting.

Mom and Jack sit in front of the fire in the sitting room. Mom knits and Jack smokes and listens to the radio. Jack listens every day to a man singing; his name is Harry Lauder. Jack tells Mom over and over again, 'He's my idol, there's none like him – Harry Lauder.'

Harry Lauder's voice sounds old and shaky; he makes jokes and laughs at them in a crazy high giggle like an old woman. He sings Scottish songs. '*I luv a lassie, a bonnie, bonnie lassie, she's as pui-ir* (when he hangs onto "puir" I think of a dog howling) *as the lilies in the dell, she's as sweet as the heather, the bonnie purple heather, Lily my Scots bluebell.*' And '*Roamin' in the gloamin', wi' a lassie by my side, roamin' in the gloamin' by the bonnie banks of Clyde.*'

Jack looks at Mom when Harry Lauder sings these words. 'Irene, we'll catch a bus to Scone' – (he says Scoon) – 'an' go fer walks in the countryside there.' He smiles and pushes his cheeks into flat cushions. 'I want tae show ye the Scottish countryside before we go back tae Dorowa – it's almost autumn an' it's especially beautiful. I spent a lot o' time in the Scone countryside when I was a boy.'

So we catch a bus to Scone and go 'roamin' in the gloamin'' although it's the middle of the day. I trail behind Mom and Jack, kicking my shoes through a carpet of gold and orange and rotting brown leaves. The autumn leaves on the trees shine like precious metals.

We have tea and scones in the corner café when we've crossed the old stone bridge over the river Tay. The bell jingles on top of the café door as we step out onto the street.

A faint noise comes up from the river. 'What's that?' Mom says. We stand at the side of the road and turn our heads. A long black roofless car comes crawling towards us. People gather around it, smiling, cheering and waving. Mom catches Jack's arm and says in a breathless voice. 'Is that ...?'

'Aye, I think so.'

The car is almost upon us. A lady in a bright blue dress and gloves and hat, made of dyed blue feathers, sits on the back seat. She looks at the crowd gathering around the car and smiles with happy surprise and waves, first one hand then the other in their blue gloves. Mom waves back and shouts, 'Love from South Africa.' She picks me up so I can see the blue lady. 'Wave, Karin, that's the Queen – Queen Elizabeth.'

The lady turns her head when she hears Mom and looks directly at her. She nods her head, her smile grows wider. I can feel Mom's heart thumping next to mine.

A queen? But she doesn't look like a queen. Her face is round as a pancake, and her body as stout as a plump pigeon.

'Will ye wheesht, Irene,' Jack scowls, his eyebrows join in the middle. 'Dinna carry on so – she's nought but anither Scotswoman.'

I'm sick, my chest is on fire. I can't talk, walk or eat without coughing my lungs out. My eyes stream tears from the fits of coughing that choke me. 'It's whooping cough,' Dr McLeod tells Mom after he examines me. 'Bed rest, plenty of fluids. I'll write a prescription for something to ease her cough.'

I'm in bed for six weeks. I whoop, I wheeze, I cough. My eyes water.

One evening after supper, I lie back on my pillows, struggling to breathe and I hear Jack say, 'I'm off tae the pub.'

Mom says nothing but later, when Jack returns, I hear them argue.

'You've had too much to drink, Jack.'

'I had a few drams – thassall.'

'More than that – you reek of whiskey.'

'Irene, haud yer tongue. I'm used tae havin' a dram in the pub every so often.'

'Why don't you drink at home?'

'Irene, if ye must look after yer sick child, I need to find some male company an' drink a wee dram wi' them. I'm no used tae havin' children around.'

Their voices drone on and on, hypnotising me – up, down, soft, loud. I fall into a feverish sleep.

One morning, when the whooping cough has left me weak, I see Jack lifting heavy suitcases from the top of the wardrobe. Mom dusts and polishes them, puts tissue paper at the bottom. Then she packs Jack's clothes, all freshly dry-cleaned and laundered. Jack sits at his desk, writing his name and forwarding address in his black crab writing onto little tickets.

John Carmichael
C/o The Amalgamated Tin Mines of Nigeria
Dorowa Mining Camp via Jos
Nigeria

'When's he going?' I whisper in Mom's ear.

'Who's "he"?' Mom tightens her lips, she shoots me a hard look as she rolls Jack's socks. 'Jack's going ahead to see that an extra room is built on our bungalow for you. Children have always come home to Scotland to boarding school before, but this has changed. You'll be going to a boarding school in Jos.'

She puts a pile of ironed handkerchiefs on top of Jack's shirts. 'Try and show some gratitude, Karin, try and call him Uncle Jack.'

Never, never, a voice whispers in my head. *You don't have a father and Jack's not your uncle.*

My voice talks in my head because Jack will never let me speak. It's my badgirl voice. But I say nothing to Mom. A big burst of sunshine is exploding in my chest because Mom and I will be alone for Christmas and her birthday. We will be alone in Perth for weeks, then together on the sea voyage without Jack. My heart is doing a dance of joy. I am full of sunshine bliss.

The needle burns in my arm, but when I yelp, Dr Mcleod says, 'Better this than black water fever.' He turns to Mom who pulls her arm out of her sweater and camel hair coat. 'A bigger dose for you, my dear, let me know if there are any unpleasant side effects like dizziness and fainting.'

Last week we had injections for yellow fever and we swallow yellow quinine tablets every day to prevent malaria.

We're walking home, Mom and I, my hand is on her arm. I'm happy although my arm is stinging. I have her all to myself. I don't feel jealous of Jack because he's far away. I'm thinking happy thoughts; I look up and see a poster on a wall, a blown-up photograph of Mom's face stares down at me.

'Mom,' I say, 'it's you.' The same long nose, the thin eyebrows, the mouth shaped like a bow, wide-apart eyes. I look again. But the hair isn't black like Mom's, it's lighter.

Mom turns her eyes to the poster. 'It's Greta Garbo, Karin, she's starring in a film called *Two-faced Woman*.'

We pass a second-hand book shop, as wide as two doorways, almost hidden between a tobacconist and a draper's shop. Just inside the door there's a small table with piles of books on top; a small green book catches my eye. I pull Mom into the shop and pick it up. It's very old; it has gold embossed lettering and flower patterns on the cover. The gold letters spell *Siward Silk-hair, the Viking*. Siward Silk-hair. I sound the name in my head. What a strange name. The front cover shows a long boat with a dragon neck and head in the front. A boy with long strands of yellow hair stands ready to jump onto the beach, his shield in one hand, his sword in the other. A grey wolf stands at his side. I open the cover. It says Pocket Edition. It fits perfectly in my hands.

'Mom? Please?'

She pushes her lips out, shakes her head as she looks at the small print. 'Karin, you won't be able to read this, it's too difficult.'

'Ple-ease. I need more books to read when we're at the mining camp before school starts.'

I think of the Spanish doll Mom brought back from Las Palmas. The box says 'Walkie-Talkie Doll.' The stupid doll squeaks 'Mama-Mama'. She totters on stiff legs then falls over. She has a red frilly dress and bonnet. She is the most boring present Mom has ever given me. I open my mouth to tell Mom I don't like dolls but she's seen the price on the book. One shilling, six pence. She changes her mind. 'All right, make sure you read it. I'd better buy a dictionary as well.'

The fire crackles out fireflies. Mom hums in the kitchen as she opens packets of greasy, salty fish and chips. My stomach growls. I open the book and sniff the pages. I think I can smell the special smell of books – cut wood, gum, ink, leather. I turn my head and smell the salty oiliness. I hear Mom's hum become a moan. I run to the kitchen and see Mom slide down the front of the stove. I kneel at her side, touching her face – cold, sweaty, white as the stove.

'Mom?'

'Bring me water.' She croaks.

I fill a glass and trickle drops into her mouth.

'Help me up.'

I pull on her arms, she gets to her knees, then pulls herself bent-over onto the counter. We stagger like a three-legged race to the lounge. Mom sinks onto the sofa.

'Must rest.' She whispers.

I watch firelight flicker yellow-orange patterns onto her face. She settles deep into the cushions and sleeps.

I eat fish and chips standing up at the table in the kitchen. I pour tomato sauce on the plate and dip the chips. On the table there's a big envelope with a stamp 'Elder-Dempster Lines'. I pull out a little book with a picture of a ship on choppy seas under large red and gold letters. 'South Africa in Seventeen Days'. The name of the ship is 'ACCRA'. Inside is a passenger list. I find Mom's name – Mrs I. Carmichael and child. The labels Mom must tie on our suitcases have red flags and gold crowns. Soon we'll be on swaying trains and rocking boats again. Train, boat, train. Liverpool, Lagos, Jos.

The tugboat pushes the *Accra* away from the docks at Liverpool. Mom and I stand at the rails in the icy wind. She's wearing her red suit, a warm cap, and her fox fur cape round her shoulders, and gloves. Her cheeks are pink, her eyes water from the wind. I'm wearing a thick blue woollen coat and beret and red gloves that Mom knitted for me. There's nobody to wave us goodbye on the docks. The tug pushes us past the pier head and blasts three toots from its funnel. The *Accra* answers with a long deep hoot from one thick red funnel. We're on our way. We're out on the choppy green waves of the Irish Sea, looking back at the coast. Dark grey clouds chase each other across a sulky sky. The air is cold in my nostrils and smells of briny sea and oily-metal, a mix that used to make me feel sick.

Down below in our cabin on C deck, Mom unpacks our few clothes. I stand on a chair and look out of the porthole. Half the circle is sea, half is sky. Sometimes it's all sea or all sky, depending on how the ship is riding the waves. I'm excited by the humming of the huge engines, the hot clamminess of windowless passages and painted bulkheads. I have to learn the geography of the *Accra* while we're here. Layers of decks and passages (gangways), stairs (companionways) doors (hatches). Dining-room, library, lounge, dancing- room, the bow and the stern, port and starboard.

We sail through a storm when we pass the Bay of Biscay; black banks of clouds pour icy rain from a sky the colour of metal. The howling wind whips the sea into mountain peaks and the ship creaks and heaves up the sides and down into valleys of heavy water. When we pass Portugal, the storm blows over and a pale sun comes out of hiding. People stroll round and round the promenade deck, play games. They throw rubber rings onto painted circles. Hit feathered cocks over a high net with tiny rackets. Dance, watch films at night. Play cards, drink at the bar and eat big meals three times a day. Beef tea made from Oxo cubes at eleven in the morning.

Mom has made friends – her shipboard friends, she says. Two old missionaries, Alice and Edward, sit on deck chairs with Mom every day. 'We're going back to our mission church at Takaradi,' they tell her. 'We are dying to return to our work there, ministering to our children in Christ.'

Alice and Mom knit and Edward, his glasses sitting on the end of his nose, reads the paper or stares out to sea. 'Oh, we can't wait,' they say. 'England isn't home to us anymore.'

Henry joins them when he finishes ten fast laps round the deck. Henry is alone. He is a little man who looks like a cricket, a man with dark-grey curls and springy legs. Henry's dark eyes looks at everybody with interest, he knows a lot. He asks Mom questions about her life in Cape Town because he is going there. I think Henry may be interested in Mom, his eyes watch her closely, he smiles at her and talks as if he's interested in her life. But Mom won't tell him much about our old life in Cape Town, about her failure in marriage.

One morning Henry says. 'Have you noticed who is on board with us?'

'Who?' ask Mom and Alice.

Henry points his chin to a young woman sitting under a companionway on her own. She wears a scarf and sunglasses, reads a book. I wonder if she's a spy. Alice puts down her knitting, her eyes peer over the rims of her glasses, waiting for Henry's answer.

'Don't you know?' Henry pretends to be surprised. 'My dear ladies, that's Ruth Khama. Haven't you heard about her?'

'Aah,' says Alice, looking at the lady with interest.

But Mom carries on – one plain, one purl – knitting with fast fingers and flashing needles. My mother has never heard of Ruth Khama. 'Who is she?'

Edward leans towards her, his white hair wispy in the breeze, his eyes are serious in their wrinkled pouches.

'My dear Irene, she married Seretse Khama last year in a registry office in Kensington ...'

'But who is Seretse Khama?'

'He's the chief of the Bamangwato tribe ...' Edward says.

'In Bechuanaland. A British Protectorate,' says Henry.

Alice turns in her seat, her eyes flick to Ruth Khama from time to time. 'It's caused a diplomatic storm,' she whispers. 'The Government of South Africa – your country, my dear.' Mom counts her stitches. 'Well, your government says he is not fit to rule his tribe since he married Ruth Khama.'

'The South African Government has also made it illegal for mixed marriages to take place,' Edward says.

Alice clucks her tongue. 'Poor woman – she's persona non grata in her own country, in Bechuanaland and South Africa, although I'm sure she'll never go there.'

'All these stupid laws,' says Henry, 'putting barriers between people. But ... she's not alone on the ship. Members of her husband's tribe are accompanying her on this sea voyage.'

I'm tired of listening to grown up talk. I'm bored, bored, bored. I run past Ruth Khama but she doesn't look up from her book. I jump over deck quoits, skip under badminton nets, run past windows of the common rooms, until I see one with shelves of books. I find the nearest hatch and see the room is a library and writing room.

The books are locked behind glass doors. I look at them with longing. There's writing paper with 'Elder-Dempster Line' and the drawing of an ocean liner at the top. My pencils and crayons are on C deck in our cabin. I turn to leave the library to fetch them when I see a pile of magazines in a box. A sign says 'Do not remove.'

I look at the top magazine. *LIFE* is written in red letters on top. *June 1945*. There's a photograph of soldiers going through barbed wire fences. Hanging onto the fences or lying next to them are scarecrows in rags, walking skeletons. Joints sticking out, eyes sunk deep into their skulls, slow-moving, dying spider-people. There are piles of dead bodies, people like bald rag dolls, legs and arms all mixed up. I open the pages.

'American Soldiers liberate Nazi Death Camps. General Eisenhower insists his soldiers see what they are fighting against.'

A photograph of small children in striped clothes sitting like rabbits next to the barbed wire fence. 'Children's Block 66 at Buchenwald.' Then 'BUCHENWALD, AUSCHWITZ, DACHAU, BERGEN-BELSEN, MAUTHAUSEN, RAVENSBRUCK.'

Only witches can grind and spit out these hell names with their yellow rotting fangs. Gghh – zzz – tzz. This isn't Hansel and Gretel, it's not a fairy tale, it's real life and they do throw children to burn in ovens.

I turn and run back onto the deck, run to where Mom sits on her chair, knitting, talking. I pull her arm, 'MOM. Come.'

She drops her knitting. Her face is white, her eyes wide. 'Karin, what's wrong?'

I pull her to the reading room, pull her through the door, show her the *LIFE* magazine. I can't speak. I point to the pictures, the headlines.

Mom eyes run over the pages. 'God, Karin, trust you to find this.'

'I don't understand.'

Mom sighs, 'It was the war. The Nazis blamed the Jews for all their troubles ...'

'Are all these people Jews?'

'Not all of them, but most of them ...'

'But what's wrong with being a Jew?'

'It's complicated ... the leader of the Nazis ...' She says words like 'genocide' and 'holocaust'.

'It could have been us,' I say.

'We're not Jews.'

'But we could have been.'

The night is soft and warm. I sit on a bench on the deck, in the dark, watching people dance round the room inside in the bright light. Like watching a film. Mom thinks I'm below sleeping in my bunk, but I'm not able to sleep because of all the pictures I've seen today. The breeze from the sea cools my hot forehead, the waves slap against the sides of the ship. I don't want to let Mom out of my sight because of the hell names and photographs.

Mom sits at a table, talking to Henry and Alice and Edward. She's wearing a royal blue dress with a tight belt. The skirt falls down long past her knees. 'It's the New Look,' she says.

Men play their instruments sitting on a small stage higher than the dance floor. The man with the saxophone says into the microphone, 'Good evening, ladies and gentlemen, welcome to the sound of the Dick Loxton Quartet. Tonight we bring you music from the big band of Guy Lombardo.' People clap.

The man bows. 'We start our selection by playing *Stormy Weather*, *I'm Confessin' That I Love You*, and *Have You Ever Seen a Dream Walkin'?*'

Ruth Khama is on the other side of the room. Her face is white as paper, her hair shines pale gold. She sits with three black men; her entourage, Mom calls them. She wears a plain silver-green dress; she dances with each of the black men, one by one. Two of the men wear dark suits but the third wears an African shirt of bright colours over khaki trousers.

One of Ruth Khama's men, one in a suit, strolls over to Mom, bends his head and offers her his arm. Mom turns her head, refusing to dance. I can't hear what she says, but Henry, Alice and Edward look at her in shock. The man bows again and returns to his table. Mom sits with her head bent as Alice whispers in her ear.

Nothing is the way I thought it would be on this trip. I thought with Jack out of the way, everything would be perfect, but it's not.

Inside the cabin, the bulkheads shine white, the dark sea slops against the porthole. When it falls away, I see pinpricks of stars in the night sky. I take my clothes off, put on my pyjamas and jump onto the top bunk. I pick up my little green book, *Siward Silk-hair, the Viking*. I touch the bumps of the gold embossed pattern of chains crossing each other. The pages whisper open. Siward was the younger son of King Sveinn of Norway. An eighteen-year-old boy with a beautiful face, hair like thin ropes of yellow silk and eyes the colour of summer skies. He had blue tattoos round his wrists and throat, wore gold rings round his neck and wrists. He carried a dagger and a sword. He had a big grey wolf called Pall as a pet. He lived in the ninth century. So long ago, tens and tens of years ago. I can't imagine it.

> Some of the old men saw signs in the sea and the sky. Orm the Necromancer, with his rheumy old eyes, saw dragons flying in the sky above the Borg of Horstadt. Only once before had he seen such an omen: at the time of the Great Famine when the crops and the animals and many of the townsfolk perished in the long night of the dread winter.
> Now old King Sveinn lay dead on the pyre of his boat, the long black flat-bottomed boat, his oar- steed. He was laid on a pyre of dried wood, covered in bear furs, wearing his golden crown, his shield on his chest. At the last minute, Siward had put the sword in his dead father's hand although he had died from a creeping sickness in bed and not on the battlefield. Would it fool the gods of Asgard into opening the portals of Valhalla?
> The wind picked up and bore the funeral boat down the long Vik to the sea. Jarls of Horstadt beat skin drums, blew on rams' horns. Karls lit torches, sent burning arrows to land on the oar-steed. Flames grew hungry and licked the wood, the furs, sending plumes of orange fire into the sky, casting orange reflections onto the water.

I've been in the reading room, sitting at a writing desk with my book and my dictionary. I look up all the words I don't know. If I can't be at school, I will learn new words.

I haven't seen Mom since breakfast. Now I can't find her. I run around the promenade deck looking in all the windows. A bubble of panic is in my chest, choking my throat. Then I see a bent-over body at a table in the corner of the lounge; I run towards her. Mom's wearing a scarf over her head, sunglasses on her nose. There she is alone in a corner. She's looking out to sea. She's very still.

Henry appears, walks around the tables and chairs. 'Do you mind if I join you, Irene?' He looks at her.

Mom takes off her sunglasses, waves her hand to a seat.

Henry says, 'Irene, why aren't you sitting outside? It's such a lovely morning.' He watches her, but Mom lowers her eyelids. 'Are you avoiding us?'

Mom shakes her head.

'Is it because of what happened last night?'

Mom's eyelids shoot up. 'You know it is.'

'But, Irene, what did you expect? How could you make such a racist comment –"I don't dance with black men"? Yes, you were rude and ungracious.'

Mom's eyes flash. 'Alice and Ted scolded me as if I were a delinquent two-year-old.'

I'm shrinking into my shoes. Oh, this is red hot shame.

Bad girl whispers, *It's Jack's fault.*

'Irene, you could have just said you were sitting the dance out, you were tired – anything but your racist slap-in-the-face.'

'Oh, stop, Henry,' Mom twists her mouth. 'This is how I grew up – with segregation. I just said it, I wasn't thinking.'

Henry looks at Mom. I can see he's disappointed in her.

'You don't dance with black men. I suppose you don't dance with Jewish men either?'

Mom tightens her lips; there are two spots of red on her cheeks.

'Let me introduce myself properly. My name is Henry Grossman. I'm Jewish, Irene.' Henry's voice gets loud. He slaps his chest. 'Yes, that's right. I'm Jewish and we danced last night. How do you feel about that?'

Mom can't speak. She stutters. 'But ... but ...'

'I didn't tell you? Why would I after you mentioned your husband is anti-semitic?'

Mom shakes her head.

Henry stands over her, leans down to look in her eyes. 'A word of advice, Irene, think for yourself – don't just take on the attitudes of your husband or your country.' He turns away. 'You don't know what to say or think, do you, Irene? I won't embarrass you with my company anymore. You're disembarking at Lagos the day after tomorrow and I carry on to Cape Town.'

He bows to Mom, smiles at me and walks away.

Lagos is like the scab on my knee. A rough crust on top and stinky pus underneath. The light is clear and everything – the sea, the trees, the harbour – looks as if it has been drawn with the sharpest points of pencil crayons.

The night before, the coast of Nigeria was a thin blue line on the horizon. Now the *Accra* waits for the tug boat to push her in to the Apapa Quay. I can see bits of rusty tin roofs, narrow streets. 'Lagos is built on swamps taken back from the sea and four islands,' Mom says. 'Long bridges join everything.'

We stand on the deck, breathing in the strange smells of Lagos – sour, rotting smells from the lagoon mix with the salty tang of the sea. The sea is light green close to the shore. I can almost see to the bottom. Little canoes leave the harbour, wooden dug-outs, racing across this ice-cream-coloured sea towards the ship. Two brown men sit in each canoe, paddling their home-made oars with short, quick strokes. They are bare except for little nappies between their legs. They shout as they paddle. When they reach the ship, they rest their oars, turn their faces up to the passengers standing at the railings, peering down on them. Their teeth flash white in wide smiles. 'Dash,' they call. 'Dash.' The word floats up as the men stand in rocking canoes, their arms and fingers stretched up-up to the watching passengers.

'Mom, what does dash mean, what do they want?'

But Mom's face is dreamy; she's lost in a trance as she stares down at the shimmering water. Her skin takes on a greeny colour from the water and her eyes mirror the lapping waves. I see passengers throw money down to them. Silver crowns and shillings float down to the water like confetti. Brown bodies dive into the sea, following the glint of coins as they spiral down into the clear depths. The men swim like brown eels, bodies wriggling after the sparkles, breath held until they catch them in their fingers. Woolly heads bob to the surface, hands wave their little silver coins.

Mom and I walk down the gangplank. How strange it is to stand on land and not rolling sea. We walk to the customs shed and join the queue under C's. The customs man opens our trunk and suitcases, gives Mom a form to fill in.

'Anyt'ing to declaa? What be purpose to come to Nigeria? I see. Husband work on de tin mines at Jos? Oh, yess.'

The customs man wears a red fez and khaki jacket. His spectacles sit on the edge of his nose as he searches through Mom's layers of ironed, starched linen, her clothes so carefully wrapped in tissue paper. He opens Mom's blue satin hat box, scrabbles through her hats, her gloves, the lace hankies and boxes of jewellery she keeps in the corner pockets.

He's satisfied. He stamps labels with a 'cleared' sign and draws a tick on each suitcase with yellow chalk. 'Next.' He turns to the passenger behind us.

Mom struggles to close the lids, nothing lies flat anymore. She re-opens the hat box and takes out straw hats. A porter loads our bags onto a trolley. We leave the hot shed.

Outside sunlight hits us like the blast from an oven. We stagger and blink our eyes; the strong Nigerian sun blinds us. Its greedy rays suck beads of sweat from our skin. We push our straw hats onto our heads and Mom fishes sunglasses from her handbag. Our slippery hands clutch each other. So much noise comes from an open air market. Loud voices – shouting, calling, laughing, talking – join to make a babbling noise. Large women sit or stand everywhere surrounded by their baskets of fruit and vegetables – green plantains, mangos and paw-paws. They sell eggs, beadwork, tin mugs, live chickens squawk in small coops.

Mom says, 'These are Yoruban women – they live in the south.'

They waddle around each other, talking in loud voices, the bows of their scarves are like bright flower petals. Their dresses have colours I've seen on parrots – orange, red, purple, green.

I see a figure crouching on the ground and walk closer to look. It is an ancient woman, thin and bony, her eyes full of red threads, her top lip stretched over teeth that stick out over her bottom lip. There's a strange smell coming from the basket at her feet. At first I think her baskets hold dried plants. But I see with a shiver of terror that beside the bunches of leaves, pods and feathers, are skulls of dead dogs, birds and monkeys. A little black monkey like a furry mummy stares up at me with dead black eyes. Paper-thin bird skulls, snake skins, bat wings, dogs' paws, deer's antlers. She's a witch, I'm sure. She stares with empty eyes into the distance, her skinny arms clinging to her knees, her dry lips sticking to her over-sized yellow teeth. I step back, my eyes fixed on her and her dead things.

Mom calls. Our luggage is being loaded into the boot of a taxi. 'Karin, hurry up. I have a dreadful headache already from this noise ... and the smell.' She wipes the sweat on her face, smearing her lipstick and her mascara. 'Damn heat. I don't know why I bother with make-up. I forgot how the sun melts everything.'

We climb into the taxi, the driver starts the engine.

'Mom,' I'm stuck with the picture of the old woman and her baskets. 'Why is she selling dead animals and skulls and feathers?'

Before she can answer, the driver, in a striped shirt and a beaded purple cap turns his head. 'Dose tings, dey be for juju. You mix de ash of de burnt feather, scrape de monkeys' bones, mix dem to a powda, den mix wid watta of boiled leaves, den you drink. Maybe, if you be lucky, you t'row up de sickness.' He smiles. 'But sometime, de people don't get betta, dey get sicka an' dey die.'

He turns to face the traffic, then honks his horn with his fist as a silver-painted truck, loaded with squawking chickens for the market, heads for us. As it swerves, I see words painted in bright red capitals above the eyeglass-shaped windows: TO THEE OUR GOD WE FLY.

'Heh-heh,' the Yoruban driver rumbles, his chest shakes. 'Dey be goin' to fly to God for sure, if dey be drivin' like dat.'

We drive down streets lined with palm trees, their fronds shivering in the breeze from the sea. Every second palm tree has empty bottles tied to their trunks.

'Look,' Mom says, fanning herself with her hat. 'They tie bottles to the tree to collect sap. When the sap ferments, it becomes frothy. Then people drink it. They call it palm wine.'

We cross a bridge. The water lies still and flat with a grey-purple shine on the smooth top.

'Aagh,' gasps Mom as she rolls up the window. 'What a stench. Watch out for the mosquitoes, Karin, get rid of them before they bite.' She slaps at her leg.

At the Queen Victoria Hotel pink paint peels off the walls. Ferns spring out of red pots next to the front door. We're sweaty and sticky; Mom has wet triangles under her arms. She pays the driver and the hotel porter carries our suitcase. The trunk and other cases wait for us on the train. It's dusk – it seems time is standing still or just hanging in the sky like the flat red sun over the turquoise sea. Outside, people dressed in long white gowns kneel and pray to the sinking sun, their heads pressed to the sand, their bottoms sticking up in the air. I can hear bits of hymn songs. We watch as the sun slips into the sea.

'Why…?'

'No more questions,' Mom says. 'To bed. We have a long, tiring journey ahead of us tomorrow.'

Mom unties the folds of mosquito nets and tucks the ends under the mattress.

I fall asleep, listening to the whirr of the fan, the murmur of Mom's voice, the tiny buzzing of mosquitoes at the net.

I dream of mountains of dead bodies and skeletons, animal and human. I dream of witches dancing with glee as more and more bodies pile up. They hang up their hell names made from twisted wire that they take from barbed wire fences and keep fires burning in their ovens. I see Mom dressed as a witch, her black hair sticking out like electric shocks. She screeches at Jack, 'I danced with a Jew, Jack, I danced with a Jew'. The witches scream, 'Genocide of the Jews. Jews. Genocide.'

The train puffs slowly along the tracks through thick forests. The leaves and branches are all tangled together. 'Mangrove forests.' Mom knows as much as a guide book. Mom says it's all uphill to the Jos Plateau where our journey ends. We pass villages where ground has been cleared, villages with round mud huts. Roofs made of palm tree branches or reeds and streams of running bare children, with round bellies too big for their stick legs and arms. They cry, 'Dash, dash.' Catching up with the train, crying up into the windows. 'Daa-ash.'

Mom and I sit in silence on green leather seats. Stare at the slow-moving countryside. Mom is white, tired, she has shadows under her eyes. Her grey dress is creased; she has wet patches under her arms again. She scratches her leg where a mosquito bit her in the taxi. This is going to be a long slow journey, two days puffing up to the Plateau, then on the third day when we reach a town called Zaria, we change trains and go in another direction to Jos.

I sit opposite Mom. I have a chocolate box on my lap with paper and pens and pencil crayons in it and my Siward the Viking book. Mom puts a fold-down table between us.

I unpack my Elder-Dempster writing pages. I write on top of a page 'My African Journey'. Then, a list of names of villages and towns we pass through. Abeokuto, Ibadan, Ilorin, Jebba, Mokwa. I have never heard names that sound like these before.

The train stops for an hour at Ibadan. The carriages steam on the hot track, the metal wheels creak. The sun beats down on the town and the nearby market-place. Mom won't get off the train to stretch our legs. She says it's too hot. She buys a bunch of bananas from a Nigerian woman through the open window. She almost buys a round silver tin with a lid, patterns beaten onto the silver, but she changes her mind. She seems too tired to think.

The rocking train makes me drowsy. I lie down on the leather seat and drift in and out of sleep. Mom wakes me. We walk down the corridor, stepping over a swaying open metal plate to get to another carriage. We sit next to the window, a table with a white cloth between us. The waiter brings us soup plates filled with rice and something yellow. 'Chicken curry,' Mom says. A new taste. I eat it with slices of mango, tomato and bananas.

We sleep in the afternoon, Mom and I, our elbows propped up on the armrest at the window. We leave the forests, the train rocks across fields of yellow grass and short trees. Humps of dry soil. 'Termites,' Mom says. I forget she's been here before. We slow down as we pass by villages and small towns but do not stop. Every village has crowds of running children. Their cries follow the track of the train. 'Dash. Dash.'

I sleep easily, rocked by the rhythm of the train. I wake from time to time to see Mom staring at her ghost face in the window, as she did when we were racing through the black night in Scotland. But here in the night sky there's a bright moon and showers of stars.

The next morning we do not go to the dining-car for breakfast. Mom sends for tea. 'I'm not hungry,' she says. I have dry toast with my tea. I'm not hungry either. Mom's face is yellow and sweaty. Her hair sticks to her forehead. She sways in front of a round mirror above the basin. Her eyes are wide and staring. There are half-circles of blue shadows like bruises under them.

In the afternoon, I wake from a hot sleep to see Mom bending over the basin, vomiting. She wipes her mouth and moans. 'I don't feel well, Karin.' We swallow our bitter quinine pills. Did we remember to take them last night?

I wake on the third day, tasting the bitterness of quinine in my mouth; I have a headache. My body feels as if it has been roasting in an oven in the night.

Mom looks at me. 'You're yellow.' We stare at each other, two yellow faces bobbing on the swaying train. My head feels light as if it's full of air, like a balloon. 'We'll soon be there,' Mom says. 'Zaria by eleven this morning – change trains, another few hours, then Jos.'

The station at Zaria is bright with flowers. Heat throbs in waves as we stand on the platform. Mom's pointing to the white wax flowers of frangipani, the red hibiscus frills when pain hits me behind the eyes. I drop my box. I'm so tired; my fingers take too long to pick up my papers, my pencils and my Siward book. 'Mom – Momma,' my voice is a croak, but Mom moves in slow motion, she's sweating, struggling to speak to the porter who lifts our luggage onto the Jos train.

Brown hands lift me, lay me down on the cold hard seat of the train. I'm shivering now. The train wheels scrii-inch themselves out on the metal rails. We're moving again, across fields of yellow grass dotted with termite mounds and herds of white cattle with humps on their backs.

I'm half asleep. Leaning against the armrest, I look at the sky and see how the blue is turning into clouds of brown sand. The sticky grains surround the train, blotting out everything from view.

'Mom,' I point to swirling dust outside the window.

Mom opens her eyes, pushes herself up against the back of the seat. 'The Harmattan is blowing,' she says. 'This wind begins in the Sahara desert, it sucks up sand into enormous clouds ... covers everything in its path.' She pushes her hair out of her eye, licks her lips. She waves her hand. 'And ... Jack told me sailors at the turn of the century called the Harmattan "the sea of darkness". It can lift tons of dust into the air and drop it as far away as Devon and Cornwell ... once ... a rain of red dust fell out of the sky above Scotland.' Her eyes droop, her head falls onto her chest.

Mom can't talk now and I'm falling, falling like clouds of dust into a sea of flames.

Part Two

I AM born into a new life out of the fire of malaria. I'm in a different country, on another continent, cast away from other children, with no school to go to.

When I open my eyelids one morning, I'm in a world lit with brilliant yellow sunshine. The room I find myself in glows with this golden light. Through the net screens on the windows, I see green, waving shapes of trees. I can smell wood smoke and cooking food. I lift the layers of mosquito nets, slip my bare feet onto the red cement floor and walk on shaky legs, a baby again, to the bathroom. I feel light as air, as if I'm not in my body. I stand on tiptoes, stretch my neck to peer into the mirror with brown spots like freckles. My face is yellow, thin, my eyes huge, my lips dry and cracked. I shiver and shake as I sit on the toilet but my pee isn't burning hot anymore.

Mom is lying in her bed in her room next to the bathroom. Her eyes are closed, her skin shiny with sweat, her hair sticky and long like rats' tails. Her hands lie still on the bedspread. Mom's hands are never still.

'Mom,' I whisper in her ear. She smells of medicine and sick.

She opens her eyes. She can't see me at first, then she tries to smile, she lifts one corner of her mouth. She whispers back but I can't hear the words. I climb on the bed and lie next to her. I feel so weak after walking to the bathroom and Mom's bedroom. We look at each other, then drift in and out of sleep.

A hand shakes me. I hear Jack's voice, 'Awa' wi' ye, back tae yer ane bed.'

I roll off the bed and stumble to my room, my eyes half shut. Before I climb under the mosquito net, I see the pale curve of a moon above the trees. I lie on my bed, smelling the smoke, listening to voices outside. Then hammering on drums far away. And I think of Siward Silk-Hair. I wish I could read.

My first bath at Dorowa. The bath is half a dragon, the bottom half. It stands on claw feet. We fill its belly with water from the taps, the water sploshes, then trickles into the rust-stained dragon belly. It doesn't look like water, it's brown as if it has mixed with soil first. The hot water cylinder above the bath gurgles and creaks as it empties itself.

I imagine Mom and I have been released from the Bergen-Belsen death camp and have to wash the dirt from our bodies. I feel as weak as somebody who has been starved. Mom can't put one of her legs into water; she has a horrible sore where the mosquito bite went septic. She sits in the dragon belly, her back to me, her septic leg sticking up over the edge of the bath. She splashes water over herself.

Mom never bathes with me, she keeps her bosoms a secret, she hides them in satin bras and petticoats. I only see her arms and shoulders when she puffs powder on them. She sits with her back to me now so I can't really see her body. I see her spine bones sticking up through her skin like small ridges on a mountain. We have to bath together quickly so she can collapse on her bed. I dry myself and pull my nightie on.

The next day, after our bath, we creep into the lounge and fall onto ugly, wooden armchairs. I look around. The windows have heavy clumps of creepers around them outside, creepers with hundreds of tiny red flowers. 'Bougainvillea,' Mom says when I ask her. The sun shines through the thin petals and turns the room a rosy colour. Jack's stuff is in one corner – his chair, his books, his tray with bottles of whiskey, yellow tins of Woodbine cigarettes and an ashtray on a table, his radio and gramophone. 'Jack's sanctuary,' Mom says.

She looks at me. 'We should try to eat – get our strength back.' Then she hears the sound of car wheels on the gravel outside. 'That's Jack. Quickly, let's go back to bed.'

Mom and I sit at the dining-room table. I wear a clean nightie, Mom is in her dressing-gown, the green silk one with pink flowers. Her blue eyes have sunk into their sockets; they look like midnight pools against her white skin. She sits with her head on her hands. She has to hold her head up.

I hear feet rushing towards the inside kitchen, bare feet scraping on cement. I hear a whistle coming through someone's teeth.

A brown man rushes through the door; he carries two plates of food, one in each hand. He wears a khaki shirt and shorts, has a red skullcap on his crinkly hair. He smells of smoke. He puts a plate down in front of me and smiles. His teeth don't match each other and they have brown stains. His gums show pink. He puts Mom's plate down. He stands next to her and waits, his feet shuffle a little dance.

'Thank you, Amos, it looks ... good.'

He nods and leaves. We hear the clanging of pots and pans outside. It makes my headache come back. I look at Mom.

'Amos. He's washing pots in the cookhouse outside.'

I look down. It's chicken stew. Chewing is hard work. My jaws are tired after a few mouthfuls. Mom eats a forkful. We swallow our quinine tablets with water. Oh, the horrible bitterness. I try another piece of chicken to make the taste go away.

Mom rings the small brass bell.

My head spins when Amos whirls into the room, like a tornado. He sees the plates are not empty and his brown eyes narrow, his bottom lip sticks out. 'Medem, why you no eat?' He bends over the table to Mom.

'Sorry, Amos,' Mom says. 'My stomach is smaller, I can't eat a lot. I've been too sick.'

'Why you no say? Why you no tell for Amos? I stan' in dat hot place all de mawnin' and cook dis food. For what?' He answers his own question. 'For nuttin'. Aaah.'

He grumbles in his own language, snatches the plates away and rushes outside. We can hear his voice in the cookhouse as he throws pots and pans around.

After our bath the following day, Mom tells Amos to make toast and slice fruit. He puts down our plates on the table, then folds his arms and waits. We empty the plates. Amos spreads his lips in a happy smile. He goes to the door and shouts something to the houseboy outside. 'It's Hausa,' Mom says. 'Amos belongs to the Hausa tribe.'

We rest until afternoon. In the lounge I find a little red book with 'ATMN' – Amalgamated Tin Mines of Nigeria – on the cover. *Hausa for Daily Use.* There are short sentences inside and how to say them in Hausa. Good Day. Good Morning. *Ina kwana.* How is your health? Sweep the floor. Polish the furniture. Wash the dishes.

I turn to the books on Jack's bookshelves. He has books written by Rider Haggard, John Buchan, Walter Scott, poetry by Robert Burns, magazines – *Ellery Queen*, *Men Only*, *Drumbeat* – and old newspapers. On another table a gramophone and a pile of Harry Lauder records sit next to each other. A radio stands alone on the top shelf of the bookcase.

I choose a John Buchan book – *The Thirty-Nine Steps* – and sit on a red leather pouffe. Mom lies back in the wooden slatted chair, her head resting on a cushion. 'Leave Jack's things,' she says. 'He doesn't like you reading his books.'

'Don't tell him.' I'm halfway down the first page.

Mom sighs. She closes her eyes, her hands lie on the folds of her skirt. Her leg hurts. She limps and has a big bandage over the sore.

Wheels crunch outside on the gravel. A car door slams. Mom opens her eyes and lifts her head. I close the book and put it back on the shelf.

Jack strides through the front door into the entrance, a room as big as the one we're sitting in. He throws his strange helmet, stiff and white, onto a chair. He comes into the lounge and stares at me, then Mom. His forehead shines with Brylcreem and sweat, the hard hat leaves a red ridge near his plastered hair. He looks different. He looks hot and bothered. He wears short sleeves and his bare arms are hairy. He wears shorts almost to his knees. His legs are also hairy. He does not look happy to see me.

'Ye're up,' he says.

'Jack,' Mom smiles. 'Aren't you glad we're out of our sick beds?'

He sighs and frowns as if he's been reminded of something unpleasant. 'I'll be glad o' a wee dram, Irene, and not tae be bothered wi' yer questions.'

He pours whiskey into a glass, sits, lights a cigarette and blows choking smoke into the room. He sighs. 'Och, aye.' He swallows whiskey, he's very thirsty. Puff, swallow.

Mom stops smiling.

'So. Aboot time ye were up. I think we'll go fer a wee stroll before the sun goes down. Wha' do ye say? Ye need tae get yer strength back, Irene.'

He sucks on his cigarette until the tip shines red. He coughs. Yetch-yetch. Looks at Mom from under his hoods.

'Jack, I'm still fighting an infection. I can't walk far.'

'Course ye can. Mind over matter.'

Mom sighs, she fiddles with the folds of her skirt. 'Mmm, I'm not sure.'

'Ye ken, Irene, my mither wasna sick a day in her life. Nivver spent a day in bed. Nothin' wrong wi' her until the day she keeled over an' died.'

I see shock in Mom's eyes. 'Jack.'

Jack turns on me, his jack-in-the-box face jumps into place. 'As fer ye, wha' are ye doin' here? Countin' our teeth? Waggin' yer ears? Go an' play ootside while I talk tae yer mither.'

'No, Jack,' says Mom. 'It's too hot. She's been sick ...'

'Nonsense. Put on yer hat an' scoot. Go on – vamoose.'

I'm glad to get away from Jack and his clouds of smoke. I put on my straw hat and wander into the compound. I blink against the glare. I see Amos working in front of the wood stove in the cookhouse. I feel weak; my legs feel like heavy jelly. I walk past oleander and hibiscus bushes, past mango trees, their fruit rotting on the ground. At the back of the compound four mud huts stand in a row. Behind them, the compound drops into a big ditch. Banana trees grow there.

I turn and see a woman sitting on a three-legged stool in front of one of the huts. I walk closer. She pokes a small fire with a stick. Sparks and flames shoot higher. She puts an old tin kettle on stones above the fire. When the water begins to boil, she takes an enamel bowl, fills it with water from a round jug, adds boiling water, then tries the water with her fingers.

I hear a mewing-cat sound behind her. She bends and lifts a brown kicking baby onto her lap, clucks her tongue, then gently lowers the baby into the water. The baby stops kicking, is silent. The woman splashes water onto her belly. The little mouth gurgles and squeaks, the mother's face opens into a cushiony smile and she sings a simple tune over and over. 'Nhey-ne-ne-ne-nee.' Again and again. The baby listens, lying against her mother's arm.

I crouch nearby and watch. The woman turns to me and smiles again.

I'm hypnotised by the warm sun on my back and by the mother's song coming from the back of her throat. I'm hypnotised like the baby. I watch the slow, careful movements, the mother takes her time. No hurry. Not like Mom. The woman holds the baby on one arm and rubs soap over the baby's body with her free hand, splashes water over her with long fingers. The baby is in a trance, it's so peaceful. Warm water, gentle rubbing hands. 'Nhey-ne-ne-ne-nee.'

The mother lifts her baby out of the bowl and puts her on her lap on a raggedy towel. She pats her dry, opens a bottle of Vaseline, scoops jelly onto her fingers and smears it over the brown skin. Scoop, smear, rub. 'Nhey-ne-ne.'

She unwraps her dress, lifts her bosom, big as a melon, to the baby's sucking mouth. She is not shy. As she sucks, the baby closes her eyes, her little hands squeeze into fists then open. Squeeze, open.

Suddenly, I need Mom. I want her. I want her to hug me, rock me. I want her to sing to me. Inside the kitchen door I call 'Mom?' No answer. I call into her bedroom. 'Mom?' No answer. The lounge is empty, it smells of whiskey and cigarette fumes. No sign of Mom and Jack. 'Mo-om,' I call. I feel panic, the same sinking in my stomach when Mom left in the taxi, left me alone in Perth.

I run through the front door onto the gravel driveway. Nobody. I run into the road. I hear only my breath rasp in my chest and throat. Silence. Down the road on the opposite side is a tennis court – it's empty, the net hangs in a heap, the red sand is marked with lots of skidding footprints. At the side of the court there's a big ladder with a chair on top. I run to it, climb the steps and see for the first time the whole of Dorowa mining camp. Four houses, three on this dirt road that slopes up a hill. The fourth house is closer to the mud riverbed where the dredger clunks, day in, day out. It's much bigger than the house we live in. A road lined with trees leads to it. A stoep wraps itself around two sides of the house, and green grass hugs the house like a scarf.

The houses in this road are square with tin roofs, windows with net covers, like blind eyes. Low hills lie where the land meets the sky that rises over everything like an empty blue dome. So blue, so empty, and beyond the blue, black space that never ends. I cannot see anybody even though I turn around in a circle. Only the dredger, clanking like a mechanical praying mantis with a long arm scooping up buckets of mud from the riverbed. Heaps of mud bigger than anthills line the sides of the riverbed.

Then I see them, two small figures walking on the roadside next to the riverbed. Mom hangs onto Jack's arm. I stare. I want to shout but the sound won't reach them. I wish he would walk into the hills and never come back.

Back in my room I sit on the edge of my bed. The Spanish doll from Madeira sits on the chair next to my bed and looks at me with painted brown glassy eyes. How useless is this china creature with her painted face, her nylon ringlets? I pick her up and throw her onto the bed. Her squeeze-box 'maa-maaa' rings out. I throw her against the wall, drag her up by her neck, shake her, bash her face against the iron bed rails. 'Stupid, stupid doll.' I stretch her curls but they spring back into place. I throw her in the corner on the floor. I hate dolls. I don't want to play at being a mother.

I sit at the table and open my Siward book and read …

> Lindisfarne loomed out of the misty grey dawn like the humpbacked shell of a turtle. Olaf gave a shout, 'Land!' and plied the steering board towards the island. Siward climbed out from under the wet sail where he and his men had been crouching for the last two days and nights, swamped by pelting rain and huge icy waves. He felt a shiver of anticipation as the ruins of a monastery shone in a weak sun glinting through the mist.
>
> Siward's men clambered out of the boat, stretching their cramped legs, looking around, taking their bearings.
>
> 'We're not alone, lads,' Gunnar said. Siward saw a group of monks making their way down a hilly slope, wearing brown cassocks emblazoned with golden crosses. 'Welcome if you come in peace.' The leader, an elderly man with a tonsured skull, spoke with authority. 'I'm Brother Cuthbert of the monastery of Lindisfarne. We are the custodians of this seat of learning. Our solitary outpost is a haven for the faithful. Show us your goodwill by leaving your weapons on board.'
>
> Siward looked into Brother Cuthbert's sharp black eyes and said. 'I am Siward, son of the great King Sveinn Estridsson. These are my landsmenn, given to me by my father on his deathbed. We are travelling the seas on our ship, the *Skidbladnir*, to seek our fortune. All we ask is a roof over our heads to rest.'
>
> We're JomsVikings, thought Siward, we're here to train as mercenaries but Brother Cuthbert need not know that now.

Mom looks sick all over again. She slumps in the chair, her face chalk-white, her skin sweaty. She closes her eyes. Jack sips his whiskey, puffs. His face looks like a proud hawk who's won his prey. He smiles, his lips are loose. He turns on the radio and listens to the news. I sulk and stare at them from under my eyelids, hoping Mom will see my pouty lip. She doesn't. She's having trouble keeping her head up and lifting the fork to her mouth as we sit at the dining-room table in silence.

Amos has brought us something that looks like gravel from the road mixed with water and warmed up. Groundnut stew. Yuugh. I'd rather drink beef tea made from oxo cubes. I swallow a few mouthfuls then put my fork down.

'Mom? Will you come and tuck me in?

Jack isn't eating. He drinks his whiskey. 'Off tae bed, are ye? Weel, tha's guid. Oot o' harm's way. Off ye go then.'

'I'll come soon,' Mom says. Her eyelashes stick out like spider legs; they cover her eyes as she sits at the table, resting her head on her hand. Her mouth sags. The dark tails of her hair are pulled into a bun on the back of her neck. She looks like the picture of the Madonna in her Bible. My heart swoops out in resentful love towards her. Why does she have to spend all her time with Jack? I rest my head against her shoulder. She pats me and says, 'Off you go.'

I wait for Mom to come and tuck me in and switch off the light. But she doesn't come. I lie on my stomach under the mosquito net and read again how Siward found a herd of wild horses on Lindisfarne, how he and his men tamed them. I sink into the pillow, close my eyes and make a picture of Siward in my mind. I see him riding the white stallion, king among the mares. He's cantering across the causeway joining the island to the coast. Pall runs next to the horse. His men follow behind riding the remaining horses. I see him coming towards me, his black cloak flies out behind him, his grey wolf cape covers his shoulders. He comes out of the mist, the stallion breathes smoky puffs into the air, he leans down and picks me up in his arms, strong and comforting. I sit in front of him on the saddle, I fit into the curve of his chest. The stallion moves on the causeway, his hooves clip-clopping.

'I am Siward Silk-Hair, the leofman, the beloved of grey wolves, Siward the sea-pirate and land-pirate,' he whispers in my ear. His hair falls around me like a light gold cloak.

Every afternoon when Jack is at work on the dredger, Mom and I walk up the hill behind the Dorowa houses. We reach a place where there's a deep gully and we stop. 'Dere be leopards in dose hills,' Amos warns us.

We rest on a big flat rock, looking down the hill to the backs of the houses. Mom's eyes look back far into our old life. Mom couldn't wait to leave our old life behind. Now she can't stop talking about it.

'You were christened when you were six weeks old,' she says. 'I made a christening robe from white lawn material, with pin tucks and smocking, a bonnet to match. I wrapped you in a shawl knitted from wool so fine that you could pull it through a ring.'

I was christened in the Dutch Reformed Church on Wynberg Hill where my parents were married. 'How happy I was then,' Mom says. 'Blind and stupid but happy.'

After the church service, my father sent us home to Melkboschstrand with his driver. 'I should have known,' Mom says. My father didn't come home. 'It was dusk.' Mom's eyes get dark with sadness. 'I waited at the window, watching the sun go down.'

I see the scene through Mom's eyes – the flat top of the mountain with its cloth of clouds, guarded by a lion's head and a devil's peak. I picture the orange ball of the sun slipping into the sea, the gulls crying their sad screechy cries, waves slapping onto wet sand.

'Then I saw a string of double lights coming closer along the coast road,' Mom's eyes show her anxious waiting. 'Ten or more cars driving to our house on the beach. He brought caterers, a small band, friends – his friends – for an all-night party.'

The smell of blood. Amos holds down a chicken on a stone and slices off the head in one flash of the knife. The head falls, the body runs, with fountains of blood whooshing out of the neck until the headless chicken falls. I feel sick. Amos cleans the knife in a bucket of water, sits the chicken between his knees, plucks out the feathers.

When Amos puts plates of cooked chicken in front of me, I gag. Chicken curry, chicken stew, roast chicken. Fried chicken. I have to force the chicken down my throat. Mom threatens to give me castor oil again. Jack-in-the-box says he will send me back to Scotland on my own for good.

Bola cooks yams and groundnut stew. She rolls the yams into sticky balls with her long fingers and soaks them in the groundnut gravy and sucks and swallows them as if they were the yummiest thing to eat.

Smoke and chicken blood, rotting mangoes. Inside the house, the smell of lavender floor polish, Vim scouring powder, the smell of Brylcreem, of Woodbines, of whiskey fumes, of Jack's sweat and pee. He never pulls the toilet chain. Mom complains. Jack looks at her as if she's crazy. 'We have tae save water, Irene.'

Hot, noisy nights, the beating of drums, chugging of the dredger, slithering of snakes in the trees, the chirping, clicking insects. And the old songs of Harry Lauder. They all sound the same as if the needle is stuck in a time-worn groove. Slow, lonely days. I have no friends. 'There are no children within a radius of fifty miles,' says Mom.

I wake early this morning. I run outside into the cool, crisp air, sit in the gazebo where I can watch everything. The sky turns the colour of a pale peach then a pale lemon, then an egg yolk breaks, spills its yellow into the lemon. The hills shine gold, the gullies are crossed with purple shadows. Gold light comes into the compound, touches the banana leaves, the reed roofs. The sun bursts into heat as it climbs above the hills. The chickens strut between the huts, their feathers creamy-white and brown, their orange claws lifting high like dancers as red beaks peck in the gravel.

Amos' baby mews like a kitten. He ducks out of the door of his hut, already dressed in his khaki shorts and shirt. He drinks from the bucket outside his door, splashes his face, scratches his woolly head, takes a stick to clean his teeth.

Mom stands in the doorway of the bathroom. 'Come,' she hisses. 'Hurry up.' I drag my feet past the beds of zinnias, cannas and dahlias, bursting with colour like orange, yellow and purple bombs. Mom pulls me into the bathroom. 'Quickly, get washed and dressed before Jack wakes up.' Mom's hair curls round her face, her eyes are sleepy.

I open the tin of Gibbs toothpaste, rub my toothbrush in the pink paste and brush my new teeth, too big for my thin face. 'Ye look like a rabbit,' Jack says. I'm glad Jack's toothbrush doesn't touch the Gibbs pink paste; I would hate to share toothpaste from his toothbrush. No. Jack soaks his teeth in the same pink foam his sister, Lizzie, uses. The foam cleans his teeth while he sleeps.

I look at my face in the mirror as I brush my teeth. Jack may be right. I do look a bit like a rabbit, except for my ears. My face is still yellow. My eyes like blue saucers. I'm disappointed I don't have black hair like Mom. I look at her silky black curls and sigh. I brush my straight brown hair. It doesn't shine like Mom's.

Jack and I play cat and mouse in the bathroom. I keep my bedroom door shut unless Jack is at work, so he can use the toilet without me seeing him. I live in dread of surprising him sitting on the toilet, or peeing into the toilet bowl. Sometimes at night I hear him make a long noisy pee, as long and as noisy as a horse's. I hear him sigh and burp, 'Och, aye.'

I'm dressed and clean and quiet. Jack has nothing to complain about. His bristles are shaved, he's dressed for work, his pith helmet sits at the end of the table. His hawk beak nose sticks out, his eyes ignore me.

Amos carries in our breakfast plates, puts them on the table. Breakfast is always the same. Fried eggs, two for Jack, and fried chips. Toast, butter and jam.

We eat in silence. Amos fetches our empty plates. I hear his feet shuffle along the cement walkway, then return quickly. He carries a basket on his arm. His eyes hold a secret, his nostril open wide, his lips shake. He stands next to Jack.

'Masta Jack. Medem. Dis chile' – he points a finger at me – 'dis chile, she be only one chile, no chillen to play wid her. In my village, dere be many chillen, dey play wid sticks and stones, make much play. Amos bring for dis chile somet'ing to play.' He reaches into the basket and lifts out a tiny cushion-kitten of tabby fur; the little face has emerald green eyes and a triangle of a mouth with baby whiskers.

My eyes pop, my hands reach out. 'A kitten, look, Momma, a kitten.'

'Wha' did I tell ye?' Jack says. 'Nivver use tha' Momma baby talk agin.'

I ignore him, saying, 'Oh, thank you, thank you, Amos.' I jump from my chair and clasp the kitten to my chest. Its fur is soft against my cheek.

Jack's black eyebrows rush together. 'Ye might have asked me furst, Amos. In future ye dinna bring anything into this compound without furst askin' me. Do ye hear?'

'Yassa.' Amos flashes his brown-stained teeth. 'Amos chews betel nuts,' Mom says with disapproval. She likes teeth to be shiny-white.

Mom looks at Jack, she waits for him to say something. Then she turns to me. Mom's not happy about the kitten either. She worries about germs. 'Now don't put your mouth on the cat, Karin,' she says. 'You'll swallow a hair and get TB. And you must keep it in your room. I don't want the furniture scratched. And you feed it outside the bathroom door.'

'Just keep the blasted thing oot o' my way,' Jack says, his voice growls, his eyes send hate-rays from under his hoods. He puts his pith helmet on his stiff greasy hair.

'Irene, can ye make sure Obafemi brings my chop-box tae the dredger afore lunch? I'm off – the driver will be here any minute noo.'

I carry the kitten to my bedroom. I hear Jack in the background telling Mom she spoils me and she will regret it, he never had a pet in his life, why must I have one? His voice drones on and on like an angry bee but I don't care. I make a bed for her on the spare blanket. I fetch milk from the pantry, let her drink from a saucer.

I don't want to walk with Mom in the hills this afternoon. I want to stay with my kitten. I have to think of a name for her.

Mom says I have to exercise every day. We leave the house wearing our straw hats. While we walk, Mom worries aloud. We sit on the rock, sharing it with a fat sleeping lizard. I scuffle my shoes in the gravel. Mom stares in front of her without seeing anything.

'You see, Karin, it's a problem when your father loves you too much, you expect the same kind of devotion from all men ... He didn't want me to work, just sit at home and wait for the right man to arrive.'

I picture Mom dressed in her finery, her Greta Garbo face waiting and watching for her Prince Charming.

'... and look what happened, a wolf came in the guise of a charming man who ensnared me ... what a disaster.'

I listen. Mom doesn't expect me to answer.

'Dan was right. He said I'm the sort of woman who needs a man. I like to be admired,' she tosses her hair, strokes her neck. 'What's wrong with that?'

I don't know what Mom's talking about.

I have my own memories. The warm sun on my back reminds me of being on the beach with Mom, of splashing in the small waves, of being wrapped in a towel, of being hot in the sun yet shivery at the same time, of Mom's strong hands drying me, pulling on my clothes, a feeling of being washed out by the sea, bleached out by the sun, walking home in the oven-blast of the sun, then falling onto the sagging bed, into a long afternoon sleep with Mom, my mouth dribbling into her hair.

The battle to defend King Beofric's castle had been long and bloody. The air had rung with the clash of steel and the thunck of arrows. But Siward and his men had been subdued by the brute force of Halkell the Dane's chain-mailed, helmeted warriors. In the aftermath, Siward and his eighty remaining men had been bound round the neck and wrists by a long rope in a line of defeated JomsVikings.

They watched their comrades die one by one at the block, a stone with a shallow groove. Siward watched his men kneel and bare their necks. His heart swelled with sorrow each time the sword rose and fell and the heads rolled, eyes wide and staring, hair bloodied. Erik

Bloodaxe, Magnus Bareleg, Egil the Tall – he had known these men all his life.

Siward knelt, hesitated, then pointed to a burly warrior at Halkell's side. 'Let him hold my hair from my neck, lest it be bloodied when I enter Valhalla,' he said.

Halkell and his men laughed at such vanity, but thought to humour a boy's last wish. The warrior pulled back the silky strands of Siward's hair, gripping them in his bare hands like the reins of a horse.

Siward saw the flash of steel out of the corner of his eye. He braced his body on the stone, then, at the last moment, pulled his head up and back with all his strength, catching the warrior off balance. The sword fell, slicing the warrior's arms through at the elbow.

Siward stood, defiant. Halkell and his men saw with disbelief their warrior's arm stumps gushing blood, saw how he fell senseless to the ground. They stared at Siward, realising how he had tricked them. 'Whippersnapper golden boy outwitted Halkell. For that I will spare your life,' said Halkell.

'And the lives of my men,' demanded Siward.

Dazed by the sudden reversal of fortune, Siward's men staggered from the battlefield, made their way to the *Skidbladnir* and set sail for Lindisfarne.

The Dodge van bumps and bounces along the dirt road like a wild horse. We are peas in a pod, crammed together on a single seat, knocking into each other as the van jumps and sways. Mom, myself, Jack and Ernest, the driver.

I bob up and down on Mom's lap – there's nowhere else to sit. I hang onto the dashboard with my fingers. I'm wet with sweat. Mom holds a hankie on her cheeks and under her eyes, trying to stop her make-up from running down her face. We jog together until Mom is tired of my weight on her legs. She pushes me without warning onto Jack's leg.

I hate the touch of his hairy, clammy skin. I know he doesn't want me bouncing on his leg, like a rodeo rider. I lean forward onto the dashboard, staring at every rock, cactus, termite hill, every village, every donkey to forget I'm sitting on Jack's knee. My eyes burn from sweat, I can hardly breathe.

Ernest the driver leans forward, hugging the steering wheel. He chews on a stick and drives fast to leap over the potholes and the ridges in the road. The drive is so awful I forget where we're going. Oh, yes, we're driving to the Yelwa Club for Sunday lunch. It's the first time Mom and I have left Dorowa since we've been sick.

A wooden truck moves ahead of us, we catch up after a bend in the road. As we get close, I see a bright blue elephant with angry black eyes painted on its back. Next to the eyes is a pair of extra large flapping ears. Under the elephant are two yellow circles with red letters HAL painted in the middle, then I see a bent T at the top of the letters. HALT. Underneath is a sign: HORN BEFORE OVERTAKING!!!

Above the angry elephant white letters say: BLESSED CITY OF UGA.

Ernest pushes his hand on the hooter in a long blast. He swerves past the slow truck, swinging the wheel wildly. I see the other driver turn his head to look at us, I see the whites of his eyes, he swings the other way, heading for the ditch. Boxes, bags and white buckets dance a wild jig in the back of the horn-before-overtaking truck. Ernest's sudden leap bangs me up against Jack's arm and the steering wheel.

Jack's voice says in my ear. 'Did ye see those flappin' ears on yon elephant? They're almost as big as yers.'

My ears burn with shame. I can't see their faces, but I know Mom and Jack are irritated and sweaty because I must be heavy, bouncing on their knees.

'Off wi' ye – back tae yer mither,' Jack's voice in my ear.

I settle on Mom's lap, it's more comfortable, turn my back on Jack and look out of the side window. Mom sighs and wipes her face with her handkerchief. We rock past more huts, Hausa women walking, carrying heavy baskets on their heads, flocks of donkeys and goats. Far ahead, a white building hides among thick clumps of trees.

'Thank God fer the club,' Jack says. 'Thank God fer a few drams an' a wee bit o' chit-chat.'

Ernest crunches onto the gravel driveway, drives round a bed of cannas, then parks in the green shade of a tree. I fall out of the Dodge cabin, Mom and Jack follow. They pull their clothes straight, Jack pats his greasy hair back. He changes the look on his face; he tries on a glad-to-be-here smile and offers Mom his arm. They walk up the steps, arm-in-arm.

Mom hurries to the cloakroom. Jack calls a waiter and orders drinks. Momma returns to where we stand in the entrance waiting for her. Somehow she looks fresh as if she hasn't been sitting in the hot cabin of the Dodge for over an hour. Her yellow seersucker dress has white edges on the collar and sleeves and makes her black hair look even darker.

Jack takes a long swallow of the glass of whiskey the waiter puts in front of him. Mom sips her drink. My Oros has blocks of ice in the glass.

'Jack! Irene!' a deep voice calls.

A tall man comes towards us, his hands stretched in front of him. His eyes are the colour of sultanas, they look everywhere and miss nothing, they sweep over Mom and me. The top of his head is bald but he has curls round his ears and in his neck. Behind him, a small, neat woman. She has quick, brown eyes. She smiles at me and nods her head.

She bends down. 'Feelin' better, are ye, lovey?'

Jack stands and shakes the man's hand. 'Rob! Helen! Guid tae see ye.'

'We missed you at the New Year dance, Jack. Irene?' Rob smiles.

Helen says, 'Och, we had a wonderful evenin'.' She holds Rob's arm and nods. 'Two waiters had tae carry in the haggis – it was tha' heavy. An' we had a piper.'

'Is tha' so?' Jack's hoods lift; he's missed a treat.

'Yes, a piper. Where there's a Scotsman, you'll always find someone to play the bagpipes. Alec McKinley played in the haggis and the New Year.'

Jack clears his throat. 'Ahem. Well, Irene was ill wi' malaria, an' wasna up tae a night oot ... an' o' course, there's the bra– I mean, the bairn. We canna stay late because she'll fall asleep an' we canna all fit in the Dodge, ye ken. It's tae small.'

Rob pushes his eyebrows up to his bald head. 'Why didn't you tell me? Just say the word, Jack, if you want an evening at the club. You can borrow the Buick. The child can sleep on the back seat.'

He turns to his wife. 'You don't mind. Do you, Helen?'

'Och, not at a'.'

Jack's bristles rush towards each other. He looks down at me with his frosty eyes. 'Weel, if ye're sure ...?

Mom sees Jack's look and signals me with her eyes, she nods her head to the door. I leave as Jack says, 'I canna ever remember missin' a New Year's Nicht, ye ken ...'

I'm in the glare of the sun, the crunch of the gravel under my sandals sounds extra loud. I don't know where to go or what to do. I walk around the garden, round flower beds and patches of grass. I wander past the kitchen and hear Hausa voices, the clatter of cutlery, the smell of roasting meat and curries, then I hear children's voices. I hurry to the sound. It's coming from a large swimming pool at the back of the club. Splashing and shouting. The water is choppy from tens and tens of bodies, children and their parents. I see a girl watching the splashers. She wears a red, wrinkled bathing costume. Her dark brown hair streams water down her back. She turns when she hears my footsteps.

We stare at each other.

'Hello. What's your name?' she says.

'Karin.'

She looks at me with fat black eyes. She has a short stubby nose and round cheeks. 'I'm Tansy.'

I'm shy. I can't think what to say.

'Where are you from?'

'Dorowa camp. And you?'

'Bukuru,' she says, 'that's halfway between Jos and Dorowa.' She lifts her chin and looks at the sky. 'My father is the minister of the Anglican Church.' She stops to look at me, then sucks in her breath. 'The first thing you should know about me is that my parents are missionaries – they are Evangelical Anglicans.' Her chest in its wrinkled red costume puffs itself up with pride. 'They're sitting over there.' She points to a man and woman sitting in deck chairs next to the pool. 'We're not High like the Roman Catholic Church, we're Low Anglicans but my father says it's better than being High because we don't speak dead languages like Latin or worship false idols.'

Her words are lost on me. I gape at her.

'What are you?' She peers into my face. 'What church do you belong to?'

I shake my head. 'Uh. I don't know. Nothing.'

I think of the 'Chrissakes' and 'Fer Godssakes' Jack says when he's irritated, but I'm sure he is not religious because he sneers at people who go to church. And Mom has a beautiful Bible with a white leather cover her father gave to her, but she says she doesn't believe in God anymore.

Tansy's eyes show curiosity. 'Nothing? Don't you go to church?'

I shake my head. Tansy rushes into a long speech about the Eucharist, the Liturgy, the Book of Common Prayer, the Litany. I think she sees me as a heathen like the pagan tribes living in this part of Nigeria. She carries on. High Mass. Lent. The 39 Apostolic Steps. I'm bored now. I see Tansy has a wide space between her front teeth. I wonder if it helps her to whistle.

Tansy stops. She sees me looking at her teeth. 'I'm going to school here soon.'

'Are you? So'm I. I can't wait.'

Tansy does not share my excitement. 'I expect it will be all right. In England we stayed at boarding school on weekends and holidays. I didn't like that.'

We eat together at lunch time at a small table away from the adults. There's bowls of ice-cream to cool the strong curry. Tansy eats everything on her plate, licks her lips like my kitten.

She leans towards me. 'Can you keep a secret?' she whispers, her black eyes fixed on mine.

'My Mom's going to have another baby. I'm nine, my brother's six and now we're going to have a baby brother or sister.'

'But ... how do you know?'

'Mom told me. My father planted a seed in her stomach. It's growing into a baby.'

'I thought seeds grew into trees.'

'No, silly. Not that kind of a seed. A human seed.'

I look for Mom. She always says if I swallow a pip, a tree will grow in my stomach. She's sitting across the room at a table with Jack, Helen and Rob. Two elderly people sit with them. They live in the house up the road in Dorowa. The lady has yellow curls round her head and the man looks really old, his legs are long and thin like grasshopper legs.

Tansy follows my eyes. 'Are your parents over there?'

I nod. I hope she thinks the old couple are my parents because Jack's face is red, he's talking loudly. He is not eating much, but he's drinking lots of whiskey. Mom's face is bent over her plate, her hair hides her face but I know she's got her wrinkled look, when the skin above her eyes looks like pleats.

'Which one is your father?'

I don't answer. I will never pretend Jack-in-the-box is my father. Mom says

I must pretend he's my father because 'your surname is Carmichael now'. But that's not true. And it doesn't make Jack my father. Mom doesn't want people to know she's been divorced; she wants people to respect her. So our old life must be a secret. 'People love to gossip and speculate,' she says. She squares her shoulders like a soldier and lifts her chin. 'Behind me is a life I never want to see again.'

I can't eat all my food. I push it around the plate.

'My mother says there are starving children in this country,' Tansy says. She pushes her face close to mine. She is very serious for her age. 'You should eat all your food.'

Tansy's mother calls her to go home when we're playing hopscotch after lunch. She has the same dark hair and gappy teeth. Tansy tells her I will also be going to the ATMN School.

'You must be so lonely on your own at Dorowa. You must spend a weekend with us when school starts,' she smiles down at me.

I wave goodbye as they walk away.

Jack burps sour whiskey fumes in the Dodge van on the drive home. Mom wrinkles her nose, she looks tired and her face sags. She sighs. Jack's face turns from happy hawk to cruel clown. He shoots angry looks from under his hoods at me.

But I don't care because soon I will have a friend.

> Never had he seen a lady so bewitchingly dark, not dark-complexioned for her skin was milky-pale, but with ebony-black tresses and eyes like two pools set deep in a midnight forest.
>
> Siward, shaking with pain and fever, raised his eyes and stared at this apparition, who was tending to him, until she returned his look. And Siward felt for the first time in his life as their gazes locked, a shock of knowing, of awakening, sharp as an arrow piercing his heart, and a hot sweetness stirred his blood.
>
> 'My name is Frida,' she said. 'Your men brought you to me to heal your wounds. Do not stir, young sir, lest you open up your wounds again. I have simmered samile, milfoil and bugle in white fruit wine to reduce the swelling and close the skin here,' she touched his arm, 'here,' she touched his cheek, 'and here,' she touched his chest.
>
> Siward, in another blood-rush, wished he had more wounds.

I call my kitten Frida like the dark lady in my Siward book. It was love at first sight from when Amos brought her to me. She sleeps at the foot of my bed and her clockwork purring puts me to sleep at night and wakes me in the morning. She grows quickly, changing from a fluffy kitten to a hungry, prowling cat. When a lizard or insect comes near, she spits and claws, she hisses, showing her spiky little teeth, her fur stands on end. She pats, paws and claws lizards and geckos;

she won't let them go, they try to escape her glittery eyes, but sometimes they lose a tail or a leg.

I don't eat in the dining-room with Mom and Jack anymore. I'm a thorn in his side, I hear him tell Mom. Mom brings my breakfast on a tray to my room or I eat in the gazebo sitting on a blanket, Frida at my side, waiting to lick the plate. On the blanket, I put down a cushion, all my *Beano* and *Dandy* comics, all my books and my Siward book. I sit in the shade of the reed roof and thick branches of bougainvillea, thick as a hedge. I have my own sanctuary away from Jack.

Mom sits with her embroidery all day. She bends over the material, her needle flashes in and out, pushed by the thimble on her middle finger. Flowers grow under her fingers. English flowers, roses, hollyhocks, violets, pansies and sweetpeas blossom on a tablecloth she is embroidering for a special visit.

Helen and Daisy are coming to tea. 'They took such good care of us when we were ill,' Mom says. 'I must thank them.'

On the day of the special tea, Mom sweats all morning in the cookhouse with Amos at her side. I stand at the other end of the table and watch Mom beat eggs, cream butter, mix flour into batter; she crumbles dough, then rolls it.

At the end of the morning, she spreads her finished tablecloth on the dining-room table, then sets down a round cake with lemon-butter icing, an apple tart made with tin apples, pumpkin fritters sprinkled with cinnamon sugar and lemon juice. Scones and *koeksisters* running with sticky sugar syrup. 'An Afrikaans treat,' Mom says. 'I'm sure neither Helen nor Daisy will have tasted this before.'

'My guidness, Irene,' says Helen. 'Ye've taken a lot o' trouble.'

'Wha' a feast,' Daisy licks her lips.

Mom's face has none of her worry lines, she smiles with her lips closed. Her eyes shine behind her black mascara lashes. She pours tea, hands around plates with slices of cake, pie and cream.

Daisy is almost twice as big as Helen. She has yellow-grey curls all over her head, like Shirley Temple. Her perfume takes my breath away. She wears big, white daisy earrings and strings of necklaces hang down onto her fat bosoms. Her face is covered with thick make-up like a mask; she rubs red stuff on her cheeks and mouth. She has plucked her eyebrows away and drawn thin black half-moon lines there. Helen is a little brown bird, like a wren, neat and small and quick. She cocks her head and looks at the table, Mom and Daisy with bright eyes.

Daisy bites into a dripping *koeksister* with strong teeth. Syrup drips down her chin. 'Och, look at me,' she says. 'Eatin' like a pig. My but these – wha' do ye call them? – cakesisters are divine – decadent, too, Irene.' She chews with her eyes closed. 'Mmm–mmm.'

Mom smiles and shows Helen and Daisy the embroidery on her tablecloth. 'Here I've used whipped chain stitch, here padded satin stitch and here, french knots ...'

Helen makes cooing noises but Daisy stops chewing, her eyes search Mom's work, she flips the corner of the tablecloth over to the wrong side, she peers at Mom's handwork at the back where a nest of hanging threads and rough knots makes an untidy jumble.

'The true test of a guid needlewoman,' Daisy says, 'is if the back is as neat as the front, if the embroidery looks the same.'

Silence. Mom stares at Daisy as if she can't believe what she's heard. Her face grows white, then two spots of red show on her cheekbones. She stands suddenly, scraping back her chair. She clatters cups, saucers and plates in her hands, piling them up. She rushes into the kitchen, her head high, making a tornado wind like Amos as she passes. 'Amos. Am-oos,' she shouts at the door. 'Come fetch.'

Helen and Daisy look at each other.

'Och, Irene,' Helen says, her voice sounds worried. 'Dinna be upset. Daisy means well – she's only givin' ye guid advice.'

'Aye,' Daisy wipes her mouth with a napkin. 'I didna mean tae offend ye. I was a sewin' teacher afore I came to this part o' the wurld. I'm sure if ye neaten these loose ends, yer needlework will be purfect.'

Mom stands at the door. 'Amos? Where are you? Come chop-chop.'

Amos comes running. His trips over his feet, he looks at Mom with anxious eyes red from standing over the fire all morning.

Helen goes to Mom, holds her arm and whispers in her ear. 'Dinna take on so ... remember ... can be verra lonely here ... we need tae give an' take ...' Whisper, whisper.

Mom's eyes stop shooting sparks, the ugly twist in her mouth straightens. I hate this look – as if the whole world is against her, everybody else is wrong and she's right. This look is like a donkey that throws his head back and won't jump when he comes to a fence, he digs his front legs into the ground. 'Your outraged, stubborn-mule look,' Uncle Dan used to say.

'I'm sorry, Daisy,' she says. 'Silly of me ... put so much work into the cloth ... I shouldn't ...'

'Tha's all right, luv.' Daisy pats Mom's arm, picks up her handbag. 'We'll awa' noo.'

They walk together through the front door onto the gravel.

'By the bye, Irene,' Daisy turns round, 'if ye're sae keen on sewing, I've got an aud sewing machine I dinna use anymore. I canna be bothered tae sew at my age. I'll send it doon wi' my houseboy. Ye can have it, if ye like.'

Mom makes a glad noise. 'Too kind.'

'Ye ken, Irene, I come frae sich a musical family, we all sang an' played an instrument ... even my sewing machine is a Singer ...'

Wha-ha-haaa. Daisy bends over, her mouth wide open. 'Aah-hah,' she laughs. 'Remember, Irene, we "cakesisters" must stick together.' She steps out onto the road, her loud wha-haas sound all the way up to her house. Helen walks in the opposite direction, smiling.

I hear Mom ask Jack one night, 'Did you always drink in the evenings, Jack, here at Dorowa, even when you lived on your own?'

I watch them from the dining-room, hidden from Jack. I took one of his magazines earlier to read. *Men Only.*

Smoke swirls in the yellow light of the lamp where Mom sits sewing. Jack's sour whiskey fumes are strong even though the fan whirs above him.

'Och, aye,' he says. 'Wha' else is there tae do in this God-forsaken place?' He looks at Mom with his smeary smile. 'Until you came, Irene, then we found plenty tae do, ey?' And he leans over and strokes her leg.

> When Siward was yet a boy on the threshold of manhood, his father, King Sveinn, took him to the mountain fastness of Rauddalsfjell behind Horstadt where the dwarves worked their smithies deep within their caverns. Gunnar brought Floki the blackbird on his wrist.
>
> 'My son,' said King Sveinn. 'We cannot dig down cliffs, cannot chain storm blasts. When the long winter is upon us, we have to venture south to warmer climes to survive. We cross the seas in our long flat boats, then like the old Vikings before us become creekers, penetrating strange lands. If foreigners will barter crops for our metal wares, we will do so, otherwise we will take what we need by force.'
>
> Snorri, a dwarf of great renown, brought a sword to King Sveinn. He beckoned and took them to the mouth of the cave away from the orange glare of the fires and the smoke to show them the sword he had wrought. Snorri said, 'Odin has ordained that this sword shall be called Brain-Biter.'
>
> After Siward's brave and crafty ploy in outwitting Halkell, thereby saving his life and the lives of his men, Gunnar brought the sword Brain-Biter to him. 'Your father would have wanted you to have this sword. Use it well.'

'We're a' goin' tae die,' Jack says in a loud voice.

I jump from the story to this hot, humid night where the fan pushes Jack's smoke round in circles. Here in the lounge, sitting on a pouffe at Mom's feet. Jack sprawls in his wooden chair. His eyes stare straight ahead. They scare me.

'Mom?' I ask. 'What's he saying?'

'Ssh,' she says. 'Don't listen, pretend you don't hear.'

Jack sees things we can't see. His hands claw at the armrests, he pulls himself upright. A Woodbine dangles, glowing red, between two yellow-stained fingers. He sits forward and looks down at his feet in disbelief. 'Where's a' this water comin' frae? Will ye look at this? Hell, but it's as black as a witch's curse … I canna see a fuckin' thing. Where am I? I dinna ken where the fuck I am.'

Mom's mouth tightens into a straight line, her worry lines are deep grooves. She says nothing, just pulls her needle through the cloth.

Jack half raises himself from the chair. 'We're listin' … I gotta get outta here. But am I below deck or above? Who are all these people rushin' past? God. Please help me off this ship, will ye?'

Jack shivers, his lips tremble, his false teeth chatter to each other. He puts his arms around himself and rubs them. Above us, the fan whirs to cool the hot night air.

'Aah. I'm gonna die.' Jack begins to sob, his shoulders shake, tears run down his cheeks. 'Oh, hell's bells, look at the size o' those waves, we're goin' tae drown, I tell ye. Oh God, dinna let me die … naw, let me see my hame agin …' He lifts his head and howls.Mom puts her hands over her face, rubs her eyes, then stabs the needle through the square of linen in uneven stitches. 'I'll have to pull this out tomorrow,' she says.

Jack rocks himself, tears fall into his mouth, he's moaning in his seat.

'I'm no coward, no matter wha' they a' say. I'm Jack Carmichael from Dorowa minin' camp, sweatin' day and night to produce tin fer the war. I hae a prescribed occupation, do ye ken wha' tha' is?'

He sways from side to side in his chair, 'Row, fer Chrissake, man, we'll be sucked under wi' the ship. Och, row, row.'

He waves with both arms, sits down and leans against the side of the chair, eyes peering out. Soon the hoods close and his breath comes out in whistling snorts. Mom's given up trying to sew; she sits with hands over her eyes, her lips move silently.

'Mom, what's wrong with him?'

'He's had too much to drink.'

'Why does he drink so much?'

Fear springs into Mom's eyes. 'Don't ask that. Never speak of this, Karin, do you hear me? I don't want you to bother your head about this. And don't ask questions and never-never tell anyone.'

She walks to her bedroom and returns with a small bottle of red nail varnish. She unscrews the lid and takes out the little brush and marks the levels of all the bottles of gin and whiskey. She screws the lid back on and looks at me with warning lights in her eyes. When she speaks there is a shake in her voice. 'If people know Jack drinks a lot, they will gossip about us, say nasty things. Tittle-tattles. You must keep Jack's drinking a secret. Just pretend it never happened.'

So we pretend. I look at Jack the next day. His face has its normal hawk look, his beak nose high, his eyes half-covered with their hoods. His hands jingle coins in their pockets and he struts around like a bird of prey in front of the servants.

He smiles and talks with the people at Dorowa as if he doesn't turn into a whiskey-drunk man at night, a man who sees things that happened long ago. Mom and I are good at keeping secrets.

Sometimes I hear sounds in the middle of the night, voices in their bedroom. Mom's voice. 'Don't touch me, Jack, I don't like being mauled when you're drunk … no, leave me alone.'

'I'll touch ye whenever I want, ye're my wife, ye frigid bitch, lie still …'

I lie awake staring into the dark, wondering what's happening to us. I wait until the noises stop before I sleep.

> Moonlight hung from the branches of trees like silver cobwebs. Siward watched from the trunk of an oak tree as Frida bent over some wild plants in a nearby copse. He heard her murmuring as she picked bunches of dew-damp leaves. Pall moved restlessly beside him, cracking some twigs with his great paws.
>
> 'Who goes there?' Frida spoke in a sharp voice. Siward stepped forward from behind the trunk. 'Do not fear, gentle lady,' he said. 'I will not harm you, but you are not safe outside the walls of the keep at the midnight hour.'
>
> 'I come to pick my medicinal plants when their properties are enhanced by the light and pull of the full moon in the dead of night …' She peered at him from the shadows. 'I am safe enough, close to my guardian's castle.'
>
> 'Let me stand guard while you pluck your leaves,' he said, blond hair hanging down his back, his face smooth and boyish except for the scar newly healed. He felt again the sweet rush of blood in his veins as he watched her lips murmuring the names of precious herbs like an incantation.
>
> Frida was conscious of the intensity of his look and understood how in such a short space of time Siward had become the beloved of the ladies at court.

Amos shouts, a cooking pot clatters onto the ground, feet thud towards me. Hands grip me under my arms, lift me, throw me into the air.

I fall heavily onto my hands and knees, sprawling on the gravel, my breath pushed from my body. As my book flies out of my hands, a streak of black rope falls in front of my eyes.

'Mamba, mamba!' shouts Amos.

'Machiji, machiji!' shouts Emoka.

My hands and knees are on fire, scraped and bleeding, tiny stones stick in my skin. I see Emoka run to Amos, a spade in each hand. A black snake zig-zags fast across the ground a few feet away. Amos and Emoka slice at the head of the mamba. It's a triangle head, a tongue flickers from its slit mouth. As the spade hits behind the head the mouth opens and it's black inside. I can see fangs. I can almost feel those fangs bite into my skin, feel the poison burn its way through my body. I look at the snake eyes. They glitter like black beads. My heart rattles in my chest.

A stream of blood shoots up as Amos' spade finds its mark, cutting the head from the body. Amos and Emoka stand back, chests heaving as they watch the snake throw its body from side to side as it dies.

Where I sat a few seconds ago, a chameleon with a swollen body lies stiff, its legs sticking up in the air. While I sat reading, the snake slithered along the branch above my head after the chameleon creeping on its prong feet, its tongue ready to flick its long coil at a fly when the mamba struck it as fast as lightning from behind.

I feel sick fear in my stomach. 'Ow-ow,' I cry from pain.

Mom and Jack come to the back door to see what all the noise is about. Jack's eyebrows shoot up, his mouth makes an O of surprise. His eyes follow the swinging of the mamba body. He runs his fingers through his hair, leaving tracks in his Brylcreemed helmet. His hands dig deep into his pockets, jingling his coins. Mom's hand flies to her mouth, her face is chalk-white. Every eye watches the windscreen-wiper swings of the mamba until it falls limp and still.

Amos and Emoka suck in lots of air through their wide nostrils and open mouths. Emoka leans on his spade, he is old and bent. His lips shake and his white woolly beard bobs as his chest heaves. Amos wipes sweat from his eyes.

Jack pulls his eyes slowly from the snake body, turns to the two Hausa men. 'Guid boy, Amos. You, too, Emoka. Weel done.'

Mom can't move, can't speak. I cry because my hands and knees sting and burn. 'O-ow.'

Emoka throws gravel on the pool of blood, shovels the mamba body onto the spade, carries it away to the back of the compound. As he picks it up and walks out of the shade, I see the body isn't black but really a dark green. I hear sounds of digging. He comes back for the mamba head and the chameleon.

Amos looks at Mom. The fear is gone from his eyes. He looks satisfied with himself, he puffs his chest out. Sweat runs on his face and neck. He waits, but Mom doesn't say anything.

'Medem.' He shuffles his feet in the gravel. 'Medem.'

He stares at her until Mom seems to wake up out of her shock. He points his finger.

'Medem mus' look out fo' dis chile. Dis chile mus' nevva sit unda dis tree. Dat be too, too much for danger. She mus' sit wid medem in de house or ova dere.' He points to the gazebo.

Mom moves towards me. Amos's eyes follow her.

'Medem, if dis Amos,' he touches his chest, 'if dis Amos no see dis snake in de tree wen I scrub-scrub de pot,' he waits, 'den dis chile – phew-ee – dis chile she be dade now like chamelyon.' He shakes his head, his lips wobble. 'Amos see dis snake goin' fall on dis chile, so chop-chop, I t'row de pot down an' t'row dis chile from de snake.' He lifts his arms and swings them. He moves his feet, waits.

Mom nods.

'Medem, if Amos not do dis t'ing, dis chile, she be dade now.'

Jack turns on Amos. 'Wha' is it ye want, Amos? Some dash fer yer quick thinking? Here ye are then.' He digs deep into his pocket, drops coins into Amos' outstretched hands.

Amos puts the coins in his pocket, and repeats, 'Medem, please, medem mus' look out fo' dis chile. Dis chile mus' nevva sit unda dis tree. Medem mus' watch fo' the chile.'

'Alright, Amos. That's enough,' Mom says, before lifting me to my feet and leading me into the cool of the house. I sit on the pouffe and moan.

'Shoosh, shoosh,' says Mom. 'Jack will hear you.' But I sob anyway.

She brings a bowl of warm water, cotton-wool, mercurochrome and tweezers. She crouches in front of me and begins to soak the cuts and grazes on my knees and hands with wet cotton-wool. She tweaks the little bits of gravel stuck in the cuts.

'Ow-ow,' I cry.

'Wheesht,' Jack's face glowers at me from behind Mom. 'Why is she greetin'? Only a few scratches an' ye'd think her throat has been slit. Will ye listen tae her?' He speaks to Mom as if I'm not there. 'Irene? What did I tell ye? Any cryin' frae her an' she'd be on the furst boat back tae Scotland. If I'd screeched like tha' in front o' my father, he woulda clouted me wi' the back o' his hand. Irene?'

Mom doesn't answer. She's too busy cleaning and mopping the blood and stones. The palms of my hands and my knees burn as if flames are licking them. I moan. Jack waits. I can see he's thinking. He lights a Woodbine, sucks on it, jingles his coins, then puffs a cloud of smoke out. He puffs and thinks as he watches Mom. His face looks sly.

'Did ye ken, Irene, tha' snakes are awfu' faithful reptiles, they mate for life wi' only one partner. Och aye, verra faithful. The dead mamba Amos has killed has a mate waitin' somewhere. A mate who will come searchin' fer it. Aye, it will come here an' if it should find the body of its mate wi' its missin' head, och weel, there's no tellin' wha' it might do.'

Jack walks up and down, puffing and talking, his hawk beak nose up in the air. 'Did I tell ye how a black mamba chased Rob Nesbit one day when he was drivin' doon the road in the Dodge? Eh, Irene? There he was, drivin' along, when he saw this black mamba racin' next to him on the side o' the ditch, its body was snakin' frae side tae side, goin' as fast the Dodge. Rob put his foot flat on the accelerator an' got the hell oot o' there, but ...'

Smoke gushes from his mouth as if it is a volcano. His words plant seeds of fear in me. 'Tha' mamba's mate could come creepin' in here one night, it'll find her bedroom 'cos tha's right next to the place where its mate was killed an' then ... when it smells the blood ...' Jack's face has his happy-cruel clown look as he tells me how the snake will want vengeance.

There's a picture of a rearing cobra with open hood and bare fangs on the cover of one of Jack's *Drumbeat* magazines. My heart shakes. I look at Mom. I whimper.

'Jack.' Mom blots red mercurochrome on my grazes. 'That's enough. You're scaring her.'

'Am I? Och weel, she'd better be on the lookout fer the dead mamba's mate, tha's all ...'

There's a knock on the front door. It opens and a man comes into the room. We stare at him as if he's a ghost. He's smiling a warm, happy smile that crinkles the corners of his eyes and cuts grooves into his cheeks, like long dimples. He looks like a Highlander, he's wearing a green and black kilt, the pleats sway as he walks towards us. His eyes smile and smile as he waits for us to speak. He pushes a long curl from his forehead, he doesn't put Brylcreem on his hair; its long and wavy and grows into his neck.

'Andy,' Jack says at last, his eyes under their hoods fixed in surprise on the man. 'Wha' a surprise. Come on in, come in.'

Mom stares up at him, her eyebrows lift into half-moons. She turns to Jack as if to say, 'Who's this?' She puts down the basin and stands.

'Andy, I'd like ye tae meet my wife, Irene.' Jack turns to Mom, his hoods are wide open, his grey eyes still shine with the excitement of the killing of the mamba and the snake stories he's telling. 'Irene, this is Andy Stewart. He joined us at Dorowa since we were last here ... an, o' course, ye came back later because of ...' He sends hate looks down at me. 'Weel, then ye've been sick.'

Andy Stewart stares into Mom's eyes and reaches for her hand. 'Irene, nice to meet ye at last. Ye've had malaria, I hear. Are ye better?'

Mom blushes. 'I feel much better, thanks, Andy, for asking.'

The three of them stare at each other in silence.

Andy looks down at me. 'An' who might ye be? Let me guess, the daughter o' the hoose?'

Jack's eyes shoot sparks, warning me to keep quiet.

'Jack! Ye're a sly, dark horse. Ye didna tell me ye had sich a charming family.' Andy's eyes run over Mom as if he wants to buy her.

My heart jumps. Does he know Jack's not my father? I hope so.

Andy bends down. I look at his groovy cheeks, see how his white teeth match each other, side by side.

'An' wha's yer name? Karin? An' wha's happened here? A wee accident mebbe?'

'A snake, a mamba ... well, it fell out of a tree,' Mom stutters. 'Almost fell on top of Karin ... but Amos managed to push her out of the way in time.'

'My guidness,' Andy looks at my cuts and scrapes. 'Ye've had a lucky escape, lassie. Nobody gets in the way of an angry mamba.'

Jack jingles his coins, waves his hand. 'Andy, take a seat. Wud ye like a drink?'

'Och, no, Jack, thank ye, no. Tae early fer me.'

Andy sits on the edge of a chair, his hands clasped on his knees. Mom carries the bowl of bloody water out of the room. I hear her call Amos to make some tea.

'Karin?' Andy leans towards me. 'Will ye be going tae the new school in Jos? I hear its openin' soon. Yes? Ye'll be glad to hae friends at last. Ye must be awfu' bored here.'

I nod. I can't take my eyes off him either. My badgirl voice says, *He's like a Viking with his long hair.* Mom would say, Don't stare, it's rude.

'Wha' do ye do all day?' His eyes look as if he's really interested.

I forget Jack is sitting in the chair nearby, my chest opens up. I'm nervous but I want to tell him about myself. 'I read a lot, I write stories, I play with my kitten and I walk with Mom in the afternoons.'

'Ye're a canny wee lass, I can tell. Yer mither an' Jack must be proud o' ye.'

Jack looks shocked. He never thinks of me except as a nuisance. He glares. 'Ye can go tae yer room the noo, leave us in peace.'

'Och, no, Jack,' Andy says. 'She's nae bother, leave her be.' He smiles at Jack and nods as if it's the most normal thing in the world for me to stay with them in the lounge. Andy talks about the habits of snakes, doesn't seem to notice Jack's sulky face.

Mom comes back into the room. I can see she's brushed her hair, put lipstick on her mouth. I can smell her lilies perfume. She looks pretty. Amos carries in the tray of tea, puts it down on the brass table. Mom hands cups of tea to Andy and Jack. Andy murmurs 'thanks' but Jack takes his cup in silence. He puts his lips to the cup and makes a slurping noise.

'I havena been tae well myself lately,' Andy says. 'I've had lots o' headaches ...'

Mom's blue eyes open wide as if this news worries her.

'Och, nothin' serious ... just my war wound playin' up.' He touches a spot behind his right ear. 'I hae a wee memento o' the war here, hit by Rommel's shrapnel, ye ken. Twinges frae time tae time.'

Mom leans forward in her chair. 'You fought in the war, Andy? I didn't know that. My brother was at Mersah Matruh.'

'Is tha' a fact? Weel, it's a wee world, we may hae bumped into each other. I remember there was a South African contingent nearby when I was at Mersa Matruh.'

'Mersa Matruh – Mersa Matruh. I'm sick o' tha' name,' Jack spits the words out. 'There was more to the war than Mersa Matruh.' He rattles his cup and saucer down onto the table.

'Ye're right, Jack, too much talk o' the war.' Andy stands, the kilt falls to his knees. 'Weel, I must awa' hame ...' He turns to the door. 'Och, before I forget why

I came. I wanted tae ask if ye are comin' tae the Robbie Burns Birthday bash at the club? In two weeks.'

Jack jumps to his feet. 'But its past January 25th, surely?'

'Aye. But we had tae change the date because Rex Niven wanted tae come an' he wasna here in Jos on tha' date. Ye ken, he's mad aboot Robbie Burns night even tho' he's no' strictly a Scotsman.'

'I wouldna miss yon fer the world.' Jack's mouth stretches into a big, wide smile. His hands jingle in his pockets.

'Guid, I'll see ye there then.'

Jack looks at Mom and me as if he wants to explode. He waits until the crunch of Andy's footsteps disappears down the road.

'Why do ye always have to carry on aboot the goddamn war, Irene? Can ye no think o' anything else to talk aboot? Eh?'

My knees are stiff and sore, the palms of my hand tingle. But I get up slowly from the pouffe and leave. I can hear Jack's voice behind me, '... and as fer yer child, I wilna have her sitting with us when we hae guests.'

It's dark. I lie under my mosquito net, listening to every creeping, slithering, scratching noise. I see grey shapes beyond the blur of the net. My heart bounces from side to side. My eyes can't stretch open, the lids are too heavy. I have to stay awake. I hear a tiny slither on the wall next to my bed. I push my nose against the scratchy net. It's only a gecko. I breathe again. Drums beat in the villages. My eyelids begin to close.

I'm screaming. I wake myself up in the middle of the night. I'm sobbing-screaming. I've been in a nightmare. I found myself trapped in the Dodge van with a mad Jack, who leant towards me and grinned with his cruel-happy clown face. A black Mamba plunged through the window, the forked tongue licking my face, the backward fangs ready to sink into the skin of my neck.

Jack's snores break the silence. I mustn't wake him. My heartbeat slows down. I dig my nails into my hands to stop myself from screaming. I'm awake until grey light shows at the window, until I hear the cock crow and the first bird call, then at last, I turn on my side and sleep.

Men are dressed up like some sort of animal. They run and skip, whistle and whoop. Jack and Andy turn their heads to watch them dancing and shuffling towards us. Bright cloth covers their bodies, wound round their shoulders and waists, stripes and dots in yellow and brown. Strangest of all, they're wearing shiny white masks over their faces. Masks almost like dolls' faces but with holes cut out for their eyes, their big, brown, staring eyes, to see. Eyes looking weird and wild in the shiny smooth white. They have caps with stiff broom bristles sticking up on their heads between cloth ears and hair like a horse's mane down the backs of their necks. They carry long rope tails ending in a little horse-hair brush over their arms. Sometimes they twirl their tails. They jump and crouch and run bending down, they slide and tip-toe to the thump of a drum. One man carries a drum hanging by a rope from his neck. Some wear gloves with long nails at the end of each finger. They click, whistle, stamp and roar behind their shiny white masks.

Mom's eyes open wide, her mouth sucks in breath, her hair sticks in black curls round her face. She puts a hand on her chest, reaches her other hand for Jack. He grips it.

'Och, aye, they're Ibibio. Nothin' tae be scared o'. They're play-actin'.'

Andy leans towards Jack; he has to speak loudly to be heard. 'Wha's that ye say, Jack? Ibibio? Are they no from Calabar down south?'

'They must be wanderin' minstrels, puttin' on a masquerade.'

'They look as if they're dressed up like leopard men,' Andy's voice is rough as gravel. His eyes shine like green chameleons. 'Is tha' no' banned?'

The Ibibio men and the yipping-clicking noises they make and their roaring, leaping-dancing make my eyes blur. The hot, hot sun digs like daggers into my eyes. I blink and rub them.

'Mom? I want to go home.'

Mom doesn't look at me, her eyes are fixed on the Ibibio men, but she lifts her basket of mangoes and paw-paws, puts her peacock-coloured cloth she's just bought on top. Jack leads her away from the market towards the black Buick parked in the shade of locust bean trees. Jack opens the back door, pushes Mom inside, then jumps in beside her before I can. Andy gets into the driver's seat. 'Come, Karin, sit in front.'

We drive slowly through the dusty streets, past the vet building where they make sick animals better, and the white church with the cross on the roof.

'Ironic, isn't it?' says Andy. 'Science, religion and superstition all living cheek by jowl in Bukuru.'

'Religion doesna belong here,' says Jack. 'This country is steeped in obsessions wi' spirits an' ancestors, sacrifices an' death.'

Air blows like a hot fan on my face and hair through the open window. Jack turns to Mom, tucks her hair behind her ear. He puts his mouth to her ear and whispers. Mom giggles. Her eyes shine blue as her peacock cloth, her cheeks are pink. She turns to Jack, he strokes her neck and kisses her on the lips.

I fold my arms on my chest and stare at the rows of cacti, the termite hills, the Fulani cows, little brown boys in rags carrying switches, Hausa women with heavy baskets on their heads. I've got angry red ants running in my brain, making my head hot. I hate Jack touching and kissing Mom. If I had a sword like Brain-Biter I'd cut Jack's hands off right now.

At home, Mom and Jack walk arm in arm into the house. 'Jack and I are going to rest now, Karin, so don't disturb us.'

I go into my bedroom. I hear Mom swish the curtains closed, then she shuts both doors to their bedroom.

I shut my door as well and climb under my mosquito net into my bed. My bed doesn't turn into the Viking flat boat called *Skidbladnir* right away, the mosquito nets do not become the wide red and white sail opening with the sea wind. I lie and listen to the noises coming from Mom's bedroom. The bed creaks, Jack grunts, Mom sighs, loud breathing, Jack groans, Mom giggles. 'Wait, Jack, let me do it. Sh-sshh.'

'Mmmh. Irene ...' Sighs, groans.

'Sh-ssh.'

> Siward rode into the wold with Gunnar, then stopped as Pall growled deep in his throat. He heard a horse scream, dogs yelp, saw sheep scuttle from a crashing amongst the trees, rushing back and forth in confusion.
>
> Gunnar shouted, 'Bear' and pointed. From the shadows of the oaks a lumbering white bear emerged. The two horses reared in fright, showing the whites of their eyes. Siward drew his sword, restrained Pall who, growling and baring his fangs, wanted to launch himself at the bear.
>
> 'Gisebert's bear has escaped,' Gunnar spoke through clenched teeth. Siward saw behind the bear, a dead horse, its back broken, a dismembered dog and a bleeding Karl from Gisebert the Fleming's household. This bear had gone berserk, maddened no doubt by being confined in a cage.
>
> Siward launched himself at the bear and drove his sword deep into its muzzle, praying to Odin all the while that his sword-thrust would find its mark. The bear dropped on four legs, his head sank, he keeled over, pulling Siward's sword from his grasp. Siward stared down at his foe. 'I am a champion, a slayer of bears; there is nothing I cannot do. I have nothing to fear.'
>
> Siward and Gunnar prevailed upon their horses to drag the carcass back to the household of Gisebert. The horses strained and pulled, snorting and sweating, rolling their eyes but brought their burden back to the castle-keep. The ladies of Gisebert's castle fluttered around Siward, praising his bravery and kissing him. 'You should be knighted,' they cried.
>
> Frida, watching from her bower, saw how vainglorious and conceited Siward had become.

Andy Stewart stands in the open doorway of the Yelwa Club, his body is black against the dazzling lights inside. Mom, Jack and I crunch our feet across the gravel towards him. The night is black and hot, the drums throb in the distance.

'Ye're here,' says Andy as we climb the steps. 'Welcome tae the Robbie Burns Birthday Night courtesy o' the Caledonian Society. Guid, ye wore yer kilt, Jack. But wha' aboot yer black jacket?' He looks at Jack's pepper and salt jacket.

'I'm no goin' tae wear any black velvet jacket, Robbie Burns or no. I'd feel a right fule.'

Andy smiles at Mom, nods at her dark red dress and tartan sash over her shoulder and across her chest. He leads us into the ballroom where the chandeliers hang, shining, tens and tens of little lights. Long tables are put together in the shape of a U. Candlesticks with many branches like the antlers of deers hold flickering candles.

Andy takes them to sit next to Dick and Daisy, then turns away to greet more people. I sit with a group of children at the window. There's a stage at the open end of the U. A lady plays the piano, a man in a kilt and a little black hat plays the bagpipes and another man plays the violin. Along the sides of the room, Hausa servants in white jackets and gloves, with little red skull caps, carry trays and serve drinks.

When everybody is seated, Andy Stewart brings in a tall man. His hair looks like a crown of tight waves running from his forehead. He wears a green and blue kilt, a black velvet jacket and a frilly white tie. Andy leads the man round the table. Jack stands and introduces Mom. 'This is my wife, Irene.' Mom smiles and lifts her hand. The tall man bends over it and touches Mom's fingers with his lips.

His voice sounds rich like a plum cake. 'Aah, dear lady, I am absolutely delighted to meet you and welcome you to our social gatherings at the Yelwa Club. And ...' his eyes run over Mom. 'May I say you are a most beautiful addition to our select little society? And, Jack,' he shakes his hand, 'greetings to you as well.'

Mom's face grows pink; Jack's hoods lift to show satisfaction in his grey eyes.

Andy takes the man back to the head of the table and speaks to Rob Nesbit who stands and raps a fork on the side of a glass.

'Ladies and gentleman, attention, please.' Rap-rap, tinkle-tinkle. 'Thank you. May I present the Toastmaster for tonight, Mr Rex Niven, President of the House of Assembly.'

People clap. Rex Niven bows.

'Good evening, one and all, and welcome to this most auspicious occasion, this birthday celebration of one of Scotland's greatest sons, our beloved bard, Robert Burns.'

Loud clapping and some cheers.

'It has often been said that God put the Scots people on earth to scatter around the world because of the gift he gave us – the gift of adaptability. The Scots can make themselves at home wherever they go. They know how to blend their traditions with local customs to leave a lasting legacy.' He raises his arm to point to an old couple sitting at his right. 'And what better example of Scots thrift and industry than Mr and Mrs McDonald, who run their own tin mine and farm and who have raised two daughters here ...'

A man stands and swaggers towards Rex Niven.

'Is tha' a fact? Weel, I hae heard it said ... although, by a Sassenach, ye ken, that the Scots are only industrious and frugal overseas. At hame they're shiftless and lazy ...'

People jeer loudly. 'Sit down.' 'Dinna talk nonsense!'

Rex Niven says in his loud, smooth voice, 'That may be, Angus, but for our purpose tonight, the Scots are assets wherever they may be.' He raises his glass. 'Without further ado, ladies and gentlemen, a toast to the Twa Lands, remembering our Robbie almost emigrated himself to the West Indies – May we flourish like lilies as the Bard said, though we're over the sea from Bonnie Scotland. To the Twa Lands. To Robbie Burns.'

People clap and clink glasses. They shout, 'Tae the Twa lands. Tae oor Robbie.' The piper walks up and down the stage, blowing a thin wail from his bagpipes. The people sitting below him begin to sing about a soldier, a brave Scottish soldier who fought and wandered far from home. He's seen glorious battles, told the stories of brave deeds but now he's homesick and sighing for the Scottish Highlands.

The Hausa servants carry in huge platters of food.

I hear Daisy ask Helen, 'Wha' aboot the haggis, Helen, how did ye manage it?'

Helen leans towards her, her eyes excited. 'Thank God fer the MacDonalds. They slaughtered sheep fer us and minced the liver, lungs and hearts ... we mixed the mince wi' oats, salt, pepper, cumin and cloves, then we boiled it in the stomachs of two sheep. They brought the haggis to the club to warm up fer the ball. An' the servants picked turnips and potatoes fer the chappit tatties and bashed neeps, ye ken.'

'An' they cooked the cock-a-leekie soup here?'

Helen nods; her face is pink with satisfaction. 'Och, aye, weel they just had tae boil the leeks an' chicken fer the broth.'

My stomach heaves at the thought of sheep's lungs, liver, hearts and stomachs. But the children are going to sit in the corner and eat chicken stew.

Rex Niven rings his glass. 'Andy Stewart will now address the haggis in the words of our bard.'

Andy stands next to Rex Niven. His black jacket has gold edges, his white tie frills under his chin, a gold brooch ties his tartan cape to his shoulder. His eyes shine green, his cheeks split into grooves as he begins.

'Fair fa' your, honest, sonsie face
Great chieftain o' the puddin' race
Aboon them a' tak yer place
Painch, tripe or thairm ...'

I don't understand a word he's saying but I love to watch his face as he's saying them. He looks so proud and alive.

There's a buzz of knives and forks clinking against plates, people chewing, talking, drinking, laughing. Eating that disgusting stuff cooked in animal stomachs. 'I'd rather drink whiskey,' I say to a red-haired boy. He says his name is Fraser. He's got freckle dots over his nose.

'Bet you wouldn't,' he says. 'Whiskey's foul. I tried to drink my dad's and it made me choke.'

I think how Jack swallows it as if it's cooldrink.

Somebody shouts, 'Bring oot the swords.' They cross two swords on the floor in the middle of the U. The pianist and the violinist play music you can dance to, stamp and twirl your feet to.

'It's a jig,' cries one of the McDonald girls. She springs to her feet and jumps into the four corners of the swords. Her feet flash, point and leap between the blades; she wears soft ballet shoes, her brown curls bounce, her kilt sways, one hand on her hip, the other over her head.

The audience claps and whoops.

Daisy stands and claps, her foot is tapping, she's strapped into a kilt and a red shirt. She looks as if she's going to burst. She moves to the dancing girl and says. 'Awa' wi' ye noo. Gie me a turn.'

The McDonald girl doesn't skip a beat, she dances out of the swords and claps as Daisy takes her place. I watch the floor shake as Daisy jumps and leaps and point her toes, but she's quick even though she is so big. 'Yee-ha', cries Daisy. Her yellow curls fly around her red face. She's huffing but she won't stop until Dick pulls her from the swords. 'Before ye have a heart attack,' he says.

One by one, other dancers take their place. The musicians play jigs and reels, the kilts fly as feet tap and point. Andy's the last dancer. He leaps over the blades, his kilt flying about his legs. His sporran jumps up and down, his long hair flops into his eyes, but everybody feels his joy. They clap in time to the music. A long, loud chord ends the jig. 'Andy, ye're the king o' the sword dance a' richt,' people call.

Hausa servants clear the tables, fold them away and line the chairs against the walls.

The musicians eat their food and rest.

An elderly man claps his hands and calls for attention. 'Will ye take a partner and line up fer the Duke o' Perth reel,' he shouts. 'C'mon all ye lads and lasses.'

Men choose their partners but Mom and Jack stay in their seats. I hear Daisy whisper to Helen. 'Will ye look at Andy Stewart?' Andy is bowing over the hand of the McDonald girl. 'I swear yon man has enough charm to melt all the wimmin's hearts here, young an' old.'

'Och aye. It's his bonnie smile and the tender way he has o' looking at ye.'

'Why, Daisy, are ye smitten?'

Daisy snorts.

Dick Fellowes catches Daisy's hand and pulls her onto the floor. Turning his head, he says, 'C'mon, Jack, on yer feet, show Irene how tae do the Hieland Fling.'

Jack looks sour. He shakes his head. 'I canna dance an' I'm no aboot tae learn now.'

'Are ye tellin' me ye're a dead hoofer? I've seen ye on the dance floor afore now, Jack Carmichael.'

The old man stands in front of the stage and calls out instructions. 'Ladies and gentlemen, choose yer partner fer the Hieland Barn Dance. Make yer bow – ladies skip across and round yer partner an' back tae yer line. Men, ye do the same. Ladies, skip sideways an' clap yer hands, men, do the same. Return tae yer partners, do the ballroom hold an' step-hop to the polka.'

Mrs Stevenson has an accordion strapped to her chest, the fingers of her right hand fly up and down the keys and her left arm squeezes the pleats in and out, the sound bellows like an organ in a church. The piper puts his bagpipes down and plays a little tin whistle.

The floor shakes; the dancers skip, hop and gallop sideways or round the room. The music makes you want to dance. I can see Mom's foot tapping. Jack looks bored, his arms are folded over his chest; a waiter brings him a glass of whiskey from time to time. His eyes show nothing.

A loud chord stops the dancers. In no time at all, the old man shouts 'Pick yer partners fer the *Wind that shakes the Barley*.'

Daisy comes over to Jack and speaks to him. Jack shakes his head. I hear her say, 'Och awa' wi' ye, Jack, I canna believe a Scotsman could ever give sich a sorry excuse.'

Mom says something to Jack. He frowns.

At the end of the Barley reel, Andy comes over to Jack and Mom. I hear him say, 'Are ye no' goin' tae dance, Jack? No? Weel, do ye mind if Irene has a turn? I need a partner fer the next dance. Is it not a fine knees-up we're havin', hey Jack?'

Mom says, 'Well, I'm not sure ...' but Andy pulls her onto the floor without listening. Mom doesn't know the steps at first, but after watching the other dancers, she learns to skip, tap and step-hop.

Jack leaves the room. When he returns, he stands smoking and watching Irene and Andy doing the polka skip-hop round the room. Mom is laughing. Her head is back and her mouth wide open. Mom loves this kind of running dancing. Her red dress swirls round her legs, her black hair swings. When the loud chord sounds, she and Andy do not come off the floor. They dance the next reel, the next jig. When Andy brings her back to her seat, I hear him say, 'I'll teach ye a strathspey next, Irene.'

She nods and falls on her seat. She turns to Jack, her eyes shine double blue. 'Oh Jack, it's such fun. Why don't you try? I'm sure you can do it.'

Jack's eyebrows look as if they are going to fly off his face. 'Will ye wheesht yer tongue, Irene? I canna dance an' tha's all there is tae it.'

A voice booms behind me. Rex Niven is swooping down on Mom, his hands outstretched. 'Aah, there you are. Dear lady, come and be my Highland fling. You don't mind, Jack?'

Rex Niven swings Mom back to the lines and bows low, his hand flourishes in front of his frilly tie and his tight hair waves bounce. Jack walks up and down, he's sulking.

Andy comes across and leans down to me. 'Ye're never tae young tae learn tae dance. C'mon, wee one, it's yer turn.'

Andy and I bow to each other. We hold hands and gallop sideways down the middle of the lines. His eyes smile at me, they're full of fun. He takes both my hands and swings me round. I laugh out loud with excitement. Then he lifts me in his arms as the couples do the polka side-hop round the room. I cling to his jacket and look into his face. I can smell his men's shaving soap, his sweat. His eyelashes are curly. This is how it must feel to have a father.

The music stops with long, loud notes. Andy sets me down. My eyes are level with the buttons on his jacket. He pats my head, 'Ye're a grand wee dancer.'

I run to tell Mom but she's still on the floor. Jack leans towards me and hisses, 'Ye little show-off. Bugger off back to the other kids.'

Jack heaves himself off his chair. Mom is getting ready to dance with Rex Niven again, but Jack pulls her away and takes Mom onto the floor. Jack's hoods are down, his eyes are little slits. He stares at Mom who helps him with the steps. Jack holds on to Mom's arms, jumps and slides out of step.

At the end of the reel, Jack leads Mom off the dance floor. He holds her arm and says something close to her face. Mom frowns and shakes her head. She pulls her arm away from Jack's hand. A moment later Andy Stewart fetches her to dance a jig.

I yawn. Fraser grabs my hands and we gallop sideways, round the dancers until we fall onto an armchair at the back of the room and lie down on it. I watch the dancers from the shadows. The music goes round and round, the colours of the kilts swirl and mix – the colours of heather, yellow gorse, brown streams, wild grasses, cold lakes, blood and stones. Round and round they go, the music, the colours, the feet. They're all mixing and circling into a whirlpool of colour and sound. I drift down down ... down into the whirlpool, fall into darkness and sleep.

Hurry, scurry. We're late.

I jump over small bushes and anthills. 'Look, Mom, look. Watch me.'

But Mom is walking-running, her straw hat hanging down her back, her breath panting through her open mouth, her hair sweaty. She's muttering to herself that she's forgotten the time, forgotten Jack's leaving for the evening shift at four o' clock and she has to prepare his chop-box for Obafemi to carry on his head down to the dredger. Our sandals skim through the dry bushes and grasses of the sloping hill behind the Dorowa houses. Behind us, the flat rock where we sat in the shade of the locust bean tree, and the gully where afternoon shadows are already staining the ochre rocks with purple. The gully where Andy and Amos say leopards roam.

'Amos will have cooked the curry,' Mom says. 'I just have to put it all together.' She sighs, her lips tighten into a red track. 'Thank God for Amos. I spent my childhood helping my mother in the kitchen, cooking and cleaning up for a large family and in those days all the washing was bleached, boiled, blued until it was white, then starched.' She's told me how her German mother had stood for hours in the kitchen, late into the night when everybody was asleep, and with an iron kept sizzling on the fire, ironed all the household linen, shirts, dresses and aprons. Obafemi does all the washing and ironing now as well as cleaning the house.

Mom shows Amos her way of cooking, all the slicing, dicing, peeling, chopping, then cooking the vegetables and meat with herbs and spices. She's stopped his slapdash way of preparing meals, shown him how to stir and blend ingredients in slowly. 'Let the flavours sweat into the mix,' she tells him. 'Take your time, Amos, you have all day. Obafemi does the cleaning.'

But here we are, rushing back so Mom can dish up the food and pack it carefully into the chop-box the way Jack likes it. I skip and jump as we run because Mom and I will be alone tonight. I'll be able to sit with Mom after supper, just the two of us. We run down through the banana grove up into the compound, past the round huts where Bola sits dangling her baby on her lap. Jack is waiting inside the kitchen door, dressed for work in khaki shirt and shorts, his sola topee already on his head, his foot tapping with impatience. His chop-box can't go in the Dodge van. The road is so bumpy, the food will spill. Jack wants Obafemi to carry his chop-box on his head to the dredger. Obafemi must leave at the same time as Jack so that the food will stay hot.

'Where the hell have ye been, Irene? The driver is waitin' in the front and ye're traipsin' around the countryside. Look at ye, wumman, yer hair is a' oer the place an' ye're sweatin' like a pig. Hurry noo. Get my chop-box packed. Ernest has been waitin' fer ten minutes already.'

He is impatient, hand jingling in his pocket, puffing non-stop on a Woodbine, sending clouds of smoke into the air.

Mom hangs her hat on a hook, brushes back her hair, and washes her hands in the pantry. Amos waits at the table, the wooden box with metal corners ready. He's already carried in pots of steaming rice and chicken curry. The curry smells make my mouth water. My stomach growls.

I sit on a chair and watch. Frida jumps onto my lap. A cushion of grey-striped fur, slit-green eyes, ears bent sideways and an engine purring softly in her throat. We watch Mom bend over the pantry table, her big hands spoon spicy-creamy curry onto rice in a white soup plate.

Amos shuffles his large, cracked-dry feet from side to side. He groans, he watches Mom's every move with panic in his eyes. He hisses in her ear, 'Medem, you mus' make chop-chop. Boss Jack, he be plenty angry, he be too hungry by now. Obafemi, he walk quick-quick wid de box on his head. But he no mus' spill de food. De food tak' me de whole mawnin' to cook. Boss Jack, he goin' shout Obafemi – "Why you be late, boy?" ... den ...'

'Yes, yes,' Mom says, her voice strains in her throat. 'Don't rush me, Amos.'

A drip of sweat appears at the end of her nose. She wipes it with the back of her hand, then wipes her hands on her apron. She slices cool cucumber and tomato and mango and onion and layers them in a small pudding bowl, covering it with a matching bowl. 'Careful now,' she murmurs, 'everything must be perfect.'

I watch and wait. When Obafemi leaves with Jack's food in the chop-box, Mom will dish up our supper. I can sit with her at the dining-room table. As long as I don't see Amos killing the chicken, I can eat the cooked meat. Frida's eyes widen, her whiskers quiver, the rumbling stops in her throat. With a loud cry, she leaps off my lap and wraps her body around Mom's legs, purring and meowing, frantically calling for food.

'Wait, cat.' Mom pushes Frida away with the side of her leg. 'Not now, wait.'

She puts a sparkling white tablecloth and napkin inside the chop-box. Amos hands her the covered bowls.

Obafemi comes in, his hands wind red cloth into a pad to put on his head. He watches the bowls of food, the knife, spoon and fork, and the bottles of Worcester sauce, chutney, salt and pepper go into the box with worry in his eyes. 'Medem, chop-box be too heavy. I mus' go now.'

Mom won't answer. She covers the bowls with a thick towel to keep it hot, tucking the sides down into the corners of the box. Amos jams the heavy lid onto the box and with a grunt picks it up, slides it onto his shoulder. Obafemi bends his knees so Amos can put it on his head. They settle it onto the cloth pad, Obafemi clutches the side of the box with one hand, balances himself with the other, then stands up and turns for the door, his eyes looking straight ahead like a horse with blinkers.

'Make quick, boy – Boss Jack, he be wait.'

Jack's face shows at the door, mouth angry-tight, eyes hard as bullets. Obafemi's eyes move to Jack, but his face and neck are stiff as a tree trunk. Amos' lips shake in his rush to get Obafemi moving out of the door. He sucks his bottom lip. 'Aa-uw. Boss Jack be wait-wait.' Obafemi stumbles, steadies himself with a hand on the wall. Frida sees the food leaving, screech-meows, slips between his feet, her eyes like green lamps lifted to the disappearing food.

'Mind the cat,' Mom cries sharply, her eyes swing from the box on Obafemi's head to Frida who runs between his feet. His big, bare feet stumble over Frida's body, twisting into a knot.

Jack shouts, 'C'mon, ye clumsy dolt, I dinna have all day.'

Everybody shouts at Obafemi. He loses his balance, his eyes show fear as his hand slips from the box and clutches at the wall, the box slides in slow motion. The lid comes loose, falls; the towel, plates, bottles tumble out, followed by sloshes of chicken curry in gloopy pools of yellow sauce. The box reaches the cement floor with a thud, echoed by a cat screech.

Silence. Everybody's eyes watch the pool of rice, curry gravy, pieces of chicken and then, like a tide, a dark red stain, spread on the cement floor.

'Bloody cat,' Jack shouts, his face red.

Mom shouts, her lipstick mouth twists in fury, her blue eyes open and staring, 'Obafemi! Why don't you look where you're going? Look at the mess.' Her eyes move to Amos to shout at him as well but Amos turns away, his face sulky, his chin shaking. He bends down, lifts the box and there underneath lies the still body of Frida, blood seeping from her ears, nose and mouth.

'Go,' he shouts at Obafemi. 'Go fetch de watta, de bucket, de mop.'

'No, no,' shrieks Mom. 'First get rid of the cat, it's bleeding all over the floor. Take it outside.'

'Obafemi!' Jack bellows. 'The bloody cat is dead, get it oot o' here. Hurry, get rid of it. Throw it ootside in the compound, chop-chop, behind the huts.'

I can't move. I can't speak.

Obafemi picks Frida up by her tail and runs, the body jerking, dangling, blood dripping in a trail to the door, Frida's sightless eyes, empty and staring.

'Don't,' I cry. 'Don't throw her out, she's not dead.' But not a sound comes from my throat. I'm stuck to the chair. I see but don't see the movement, arms, legs, angry faces. It's all a blur. Their angry voices grow faint. I can hear my heart banging in my ears.

Mom waits as Obafemi sweeps the food into a pan and washes the blood and gravy from the floor. Her nose twitches, there are two spots of red on her cheeks. Amos fetches more plates and linen, cleans out the chop-box. Mom fills the plates once more and repacks the box with shaking hands. I see Jack put a little silver flask in his pocket. The door of the Dodge van clangs shut. Ernest vrooms the engine and the Dodge races away in a cloud of dust.

I get up and run from the house. Out into the compound, past the cookhouse, past the fruit trees, past Bola feeding her baby at her brown bosom. Behind the huts. Here she is, face in the sand, my Frida. I squat down beside her and turn her gently. Her green eyes are tiny slits; dead-looking, drying blood mixed with gravel cakes her nostrils, ears and mouth. The tip of her pink tongue pushes through her tiny front teeth.

'Oh, Frida. Oh Frida,' I moan.

I can't leave her here. She will never be buried. I've seen how the pagan natives, called the Birom, run around the huts with bare bottoms except for bunches of leaves between their legs. They catch fat, lazy lizards unawares, swing them by their tails against the walls, killing them, then they cook and eat them. They roast them over a fire. I have watched those small bodies crucified on a stick, dripping fat and juices. They will do the same with Frida. The thought makes me shake.

I bend closer and see a movement under the fur of her chest, a small heaving. I run back to the house on rubbery legs, the breath jerking through my open mouth. I rush through the open door of the bathroom into its dimness. I blink and think what I'm looking for. I scrabble in the storeroom behind the floral curtain; inside I find an old cardboard carton, labelled Glenfiddich whiskey. I whip a towel off the rail, still damp from this morning's bath, fold it into a thin pad, put it in the bottom of the box, and then place it on the floor near the door. I find a smaller hand towel. Outside once more, through the empty compound, my heart knocks against my ribs, but I know what I am going to do. Save Frida.

I bend next to her still furry body and slowly wrap the towel around her head where blood has seeped into the ground, into her fur, then struggle, shaking, to pick up her heavy body. I stand slowly, holding her in my outstretched arms and stumble back to the bathroom. I put her down into the hospital box and fit her floppy head and legs into the square shape. I squat on my legs and watch her. She is still breathing. Standing on tiptoe, I pull a wad of cotton wool from the medicine chest, then dampen small balls under the tap. I pat the damp pads to Frida's nostrils, the corners of her eyes, the inner parts of her ears and wipe away steadily at the dried crust of blood and gravel. I worry that Frida won't be able to breathe so I work all the bloody sand onto the cotton wool. She's breathing easier as I wash her. Her face is damp and clean. I dribble a trickle of water onto the little pink triangle of tongue sticking out from between Frieda's teeth.

I hear Mom's shoes clicking towards me on the cement floor as I fill a saucer of water.

Mom's face has tram lines between her eyebrows, her mouth is tight as a zip. 'What are you doing, Karin? Jack told Obafemi to take the cat out and bury it. Why have you brought the pest of an animal inside? You know it's dead. Hurry up now, come and have your supper.'

Mom's voice gets louder. 'Did you hear me? I said come and eat. Now, before the food gets cold.'

'I'm not hungry.' I won't look at Mom, but I know her face has got its worst hate look, the look when she doesn't get her way, when I don't listen. I feel so bad when she looks at me like that, as if she doesn't really like me. I can feel a sob coming into my mouth, then I remember the running blood and curry mixture and I know I will be sick if I try to eat. Mom waits in silence, then turns on her heel and stomps out.

'No supper for you, then, Karin.' She throws the words over her shoulder.

'Frida's not dead,' I shout at her back. 'She's not.'

The next morning, I wake early and go to see if Frida is still alive. She's breathing. I run to the kitchen and bring her a saucer of milk. She hasn't moved in the night. I talk to her softly. I know that when people are in comas they can hear what is being said to them and they try to wake up.

I whisper in her ear, 'Wake up, Frida, wake up, drink your milk, get better, get stronger.' I dribble first water then milk onto Frida's protruding tongue, her tongue doesn't move, so I trickle milk down past her teeth. Is there a little swallowing movement? I am so busy watching Frida, whispering and stroking her body, that I do not hear Jack. His loud voice makes me jump.

'What the bloody hell do ye think ye're doin'?'

He stands behind me. His hair, stiff with Brylcreem and uncombed from the night, stands in spikes around his head. He wears only a pair of shorts and a sleeveless vest. His face is crumpled with sleep and a bad mood. 'Wha' do ye think this is? A bloody hospital for cats? Did I not gie orders for the cat to be removed? It's goin' to die anyway. Dinna waste yer time. Take it oot o' the house. I dinna want it lyin' around in the bathroom. Do as I say.' He fixes me with an evil stare.

My badgirl voice says, *Tell him no.* I stare into his hoody eyes. 'No.'

'Wha'? Wha' did ye say?'

I jump to my feet. *That's right,* my voice says, *tell him again, louder.*

I remember all Jack's nastiness, his cruel-happy face. The memories rush to my skin and make it burn with anger. My eyes want to burst through their sockets. My badgirl voice shouts in my head, *NO.*

'I said no. No. NO-O.'

I glare back at Jack, glare for glare. He's taken by surprise, he looks uncertain. He turns and walks. A moment later, I hear him shouting at Mom '... did ye hear that? That cheeky brat o' yours, shoutin' at me, disobeyin' me. I tell ye, Irene, if ye dinna curb that stubborn streak now, you will rue the day. She's nothin' but trouble an' she's goin' to boarding school not a moment too soon, otherwise she'll be on the next boat back to Scotland. Do ye hear?'

I hold my breath, waiting for Mom to reply. She doesn't.

'Irene? Did ye hear wha' I said? That brat o' yours will make ye cry one day.'

The next day Frida lifts her head a little, and I dribble more milk onto the pink triangle of tongue that laps in weak, small motions. She drifts in and out of consciousness, but slowly she recovers. She lost more than one cat life when the chop-box fell on her head.

> Frida sat at her window and pored over manuscripts and books the monks at her uncle's monastery had copied. When she was younger, they had tutored her in grammar, rhetoric, Latin poetry and prose. She had followed them round their medicinal gardens when she was small. She had planted her own herbal garden in a bower of the castle keep, within the bailey wall. She held a copy of Theophrastus'

Historia Planatarum on her lap, staring at the drawings. She lifted her eyes to look beyond the walls of the castle, beyond the monastery and the little town, to where the wold and the wood met the sky. Would she ever escape the court of her guardian or would she be doomed to live and die within its confines?

The face of the wounded Siward came to her inner eye. She recalled his feverish ice-blue eyes, flushed skin and long silky tresses. How intensely his eyes had gazed into hers as if she were an angel of mercy. 'Neither my uncle nor my guardian will decide my fate,' Frida said. 'I will not go into a nunnery or marry Halkell to suit my guardian. Neither convent nor suitor shall benefit from my banishing or my marrying.'

Every week news came to the court of Gisebert, news of Siward, of his beauty, his prowess, his songs, his strange adventures and wanderings. People spoke in awe of his sword, Brain-Biter, magically wrought by the dwarves, and how he asked Orm the Necromancer to consult the runes before he went on campaigns.

Frida turned the pages of her Historia Planatarum. Was there a love potion here? She would study the stars. A learned priest thought there was a connection between the body, the stars, planets and herbs. If Siward should return to Gisebert's Court then …

I sit half-hidden from Jack on the pouffe next to Mom's chair. I don't want him to see I have a *Men Only* magazine on my lap. Detective Sam Russell has been called to a crime scene in the Roxy Theatre. He leans over the body, looking for clues. 'Cor Blimey,' says the Constable. 'Someone took a dislike to him alright; he's been well and truly bumped off ...'

Andy Stewart leans forward in his seat. He's saying '... so wha' do ye think, Jack? Wha' do ye make o' this?'

Jack doesn't answer. I can't see his face but I know his hoods have come down. I can hear him suck on his Woodbine. The Woodbine makes a crackling sound. Amos moves slowly in the dining-room, packing away plates and cutlery after lunch. He's moving so slowly and quietly, I know he's listening. Mom's listening as well. But she's looking down at her knitting, knit one, purl one, her silver needles clicking fast. Her face looks peaceful and content, the way it does when she's working. She's pulled her hair back into a round ball on her neck so it doesn't get into her eyes when she's watching her stitches.

I look at Andy. His face is serious, no grooves, his eyes watch Jack. What's he been saying? I turn my head a little so I can see Jack out of the corner of my eye.

'Weel, Andy, we're a' rational human beings.' His eyes show he doesn't really believe this. 'An' we ken men canna change shape – wha' do they call it? – shape-shift. Say wha' ye like – it's a' superstition an' juju. This is a fact – Hausa men or men frae any other tribe canna change into leopards and go round terrorisin' the people in the villages.'

Andy nods. 'Ye're right, Jack, but how do ye explain the injuries on the woman?'

'Tell me agin, Andy. What marks did they find on the body?'

'The flesh had been scraped off her arm as weel as her face an' head an'...' Andy stops. He looks at me and Mom and clears his throat ... 'Parts of her body had been cut off.'

Mom stops knitting, she stares at Andy.

Jack pulls his hedges together. 'But, ye say, the so-called leopard paw prints didna look right, they looked as if somebody faked them?'

'Right. An' they found bamboo shoots with metal spikes stuck into the ends. So, it looked as if she'd been raked by a leopard's claws, but then how do ye explain the stab wound in the top o' her vertebra in her neck?'

Amos moves closer, he's dusting the chairs and the table. He stops and watches Jack and Andy. Jack sucks on his Woodbine until it shines fire red, then he stubs it out in the ashtray. The room smells of nicotine smoke and ashes. Mom tells Amos with her eyes to take the full ashtray out of the room.

Jack stands and pulls a magazine from a pile of *Drumbeat*. He shows the cover to Andy. There's a drawing of a man wearing a leopard skin on his back and on top of his head the dead head of a snarling leopard. His hands are pushed into the leopard claws and he bends over a frightened pagan woman lying on the ground. She's bare except for bunches of leaves between her legs. Black letters say: *Leopard Men Strike Again.*

'Ye see this, Andy, they discovered a secret society about four years ago in a place called Abak ...'

'Abak?' Andy thinks for a second. 'That's near the coast, isn't it?'

'Aye. The society called themselves The Long Juju. The members of the sect were cannibals. They used human fat to make a verra strong juju they called borfima. They believed if they rubbed this body fat ointment over themselves and ate body parts, they would become verra powerful and feared, rich as weel. An' it gae them the power tae kill their enemies.'

'But the District Officer shut the sect down, sent the perpetrators to jail, right?'

'Aye, they thought so at the time. But ye say this dead woman was found near her village just the other day?'

'Rob heard aboot it yesterday.'

Jack lifts his head and thinks aloud, 'This has a' the signs o' a cannibalistic killing.'

Mom shivers, a cloud passes over her face. 'Stop, Jack. I feel as if somebody just walked over my grave.'

Jack sees Amos shuffling his feet next to him. His hoods flap down. His voice growls in his throat. 'What do ye want, Amos? Why are ye hangin' around me?'

'Masta, I mus' go now to de village.'

'Wha' for?' Jack stands and pushes his face close to Amos's and sniffs. 'Have ye been drinkin' tha' foul beer o' yers?'

'No, Masta.' His lips push out, his eyes have spiderwebs of tiny red veins in the smoke-stained whites. He stares at Jack. The words tumble out past his rubber lips. 'Mus' fetch number two wife – she be alone in de village. Amos be too, too worried 'bout dis leopard.' His voice gets louder. 'Masta, Amos mus' bring number two wife to compound heah. I make de small-small hut empty for number two wife.'

'Ye've thought this all out, have ye, Amos? Two wives in one compound? Weel, it's yer headache. Make sure ye keep the peace. An' maybe yer new wife can do some work here.'

Andy stands. 'Yer number two wife? How many wives do ye need, Amos, to take care of ye? Tell me, is she young or old? Is she from here, a Hausa like yersel'?'

Amos spreads his lips across his cheeks. 'No sah. She be Fulani girl from Kano. She be plenty young. She goin' make lots o' chillen. Boy chillen.' Amos beams, his teeth flash.

Andy whistles. 'A Fulani, eh?'

Jack sits down, reaches for his cigarettes and says, 'All right, Amos. Be sure ye're back in time to make breakfast in the mornin', do ye hear?'

'Yassa.' Amos almost runs from the room, returns a moment later with a clean ashtray for Jack. 'T'anks, sah.'

Mom puts down her knitting. 'Amos, have you finished cooking the supper? Let me see. Andy, sit down. I'll make some tea.'

Mom follows Amos to the cookhouse. I hear their feet scrape along the walkway. Andy waits for Mom to leave, then turns to Jack. They've both forgotten I'm sitting on the pouffe, almost out of sight. 'Do ye remember yon Englishman from Bukuru? He worked at the veterinary training centre. His name was Wilson. Weel, rumour had it he went sorta native, became verra involved wi' a Fulani girl oot there. Caused a huge scandal.'

I watch Jack from under my eyelashes. He smiles his cruel-clown smile, his eyes have sharp nails in them, 'Is tha' so?'

'Aye. I've heard it said European men find Fulani girls verra attractive. Could be because o' their Jewish-Egyptian ancestry. Some Jews migrated into Senegal yonks ago. They hae verra fine features. This mixed blood makes them verra seductive.'

I'm bored. I go back to Detective Sam Russell. In the background I hear Andy say '... light-copper skin, verra slim ... not like Yoruban or Hausa wimmin ...'

Mom returns with a tray of tea. She sets it down on the brass table. She pours the tea and as she hands a cup to Andy, she says, 'What about Hausa women?'

'Nothin'. It's strange Amos has found a Fulani girl fer his number two wife, tha's a'.'

Mom's nose looks ready to twitch as she hands Jack his tea. Her lips twist up on one side. 'Hmmph. I hope there won't be trouble in the compound. Bola won't like a new young wife stealing the attention.'

'I wouldna worry aboot it. It'll be Amos' problem ... an' don't forget, it's part o' their culture. Polygamy, I mean.'

Mom sits and picks up her knitting. The purl one, knit one calms her down again. 'Still, I don't like their culture with their many wives, their superstitions and their cruelty. Horrible.' She shivers.

'Irene, I wouldna go walkin' in the hills until they've discovered wha's behind this killing.' Andy looks at Mom, his eyes look like the green in the stained glass church windows in Scone. His voice is soft and kind. 'But ye're right, Irene, let's hope wi' economic prosperity and education, their culture will move away from their old dark obsessions.'

Jack snorts. 'In yer dreams, Andy. The wimmin do a' the work in the villages, they farm an' brew the beer an' wait hand an' foot on the men. Why would they want change?'

Jack puffs his Woodbine, Andy sets down his cup and saucer, Mom click-clicks with her needles.

Andy's wearing shorts today. He says he's off to work his shift soon. He stands and walks through the door. We follow him to the Dodge. I'm thinking about the Leopard men and forget I'm carrying the *Men Only* magazine in my hand.

Before he steps into the driver's seat, Andy turns to say goodbye. 'Wha's that ye're readin'?' he takes the magazine out of my hand and bursts into loud laughter. I look at Jack. His hoods jerk up.

'Och, I see. *Men Only*. Is this wha' the wee daughter o' the hoose reads? My, my. Ye certainly hae a verra precocious child here. She'll outstrip both o' ye one day soon.'

Andy can't stop laughing; he starts the engine, waves and drives out of the compound, down the road in a comet of dust.

Jack's smile has turned off like a tap. His silence is scary. In the sun his skin looks yellow with wrinkle-tracks on his cheeks. He hasn't shaved this morning so the bottom half of his face has got a shadow of black dots. The magazine feels like a hot potato in my hand. I run inside and put it down on the brass table. Mom and Jack follow. The tightness in my chest is going to snap. My heart thunders like a locomotive. Mom watches Jack, her forehead creases into pleats, her eyes droop with worry. She puts out a hand as if to stop a blow.

'What the bloody hell do ye think ye're up tae? ... Ye sneaky brat ... readin' my books under my nose ... tae big fer yer boots ...' He grabs my arm and yanks me so my head snaps back. 'Did I say ye could read my books? No. Ye're tryin' tae make a fule oot o' me, aren't ye?'

His eyebrows make thick bristly question marks, his eyes shoot hate arrows and his mouth slobbers with words as he shakes me by my shoulders. My teeth rattle in my mouth and my hair swings over my face.

'Mom,' I yelp, waiting for her to stop him. Tears spurt from my eyes.

'This is a' yer fault, Irene. Ye nivver discipline this brat, no matter wha' I say.'

Mom and Jack stare at each other. Then her eyes wander from Jack to me.

'Mom?'

'Do I have tae remind ye I will send this child back tae Scotland as soon as there's a boat in Lagos? An' I will, Irene, if ye dinna stop her bein' tae big fer her boots.'

He turns and picks up the *Men Only* magazine from the table and throws it across the room. 'Ye made me look a right idjit in front o' Andy Stewart ... wilna stand fer it ... do ye hear?'

Mom snaps into life. Her cheeks go red, her blue eyes flame. She lifts her big hand and swings. The slap catches me on the side of my head and ear. She hits me again and again. All over, legs arms, backside, head. I don't know this Mom. She's forgotten it's me she's hitting. She screams, 'Do you want to go back to Scotland?' Slap, slap.

My legs and arms sting as if an army of bees has attacked them. 'Mom, don't. Mom, don't hit me.'

'Dinna greet like a muckle tawpy. Ye can greet in yer room. Awa' wi' ye.'

Mom pushes me from the room and marches me to my bedroom. She pushes me onto the bed. 'Crying isn't going to help, Karin, I don't know why you are so disobedient.'

My badgirl voice says, *Why can't you cry? Jack cries when he's drunk, Mom cried when she got divorced.*

Mom flashes me a last look. 'I'm disappointed in you. Just as well you're going to school on Monday.' She slams the door.

I curl into a ball and sob. My head aches. My legs and arms sting.

Badgirl says, *You'll never do this to your children. No, never.*

The smell of wood smoke drifts through the window. Amos clangs and knocks pots around as he cooks our evening meal before he leaves for his village. I will not be given supper tonight. The chug-chugging of the dredger comes from the river-bed. Andy Stewart is probably working his shift there now. I hear the baby cry and Bola's comforting shoosh-shoosh.

I cry into the pillow, tears soaking the cotton cover. I hear a faint scratch at the door. I open the door a crack. Frida pads in, her eyes dull; her little mouth opens in a silent meow. I pull down the mosquito net to shut out the world and make a tent. I lift a corner for Frida to jump. She turns her stripy body round and around. I pick up my little green book and slip under the net, hidden. Frida finally settles in a ball behind my knees.

The sun goes down, my room is dark. I don't switch on the light. I lie in the dark and listen to the drums. Boof-boof, boom-de-boom. My heart beats in time with the drumming. For the first time ever, I don't want to read. All I can think about is Mom. I see her swinging arms, her twisted red mouth, her eyes full of daggers. I'm disappointing to her. She said so. I see also Jack's smirky smile before he picks up his *Men Only*.

I'm not allowed to leave my room except to go to the toilet.

Amos brings my breakfast plate of eggs and chips. He looks at me with his red itchy eyes that he's always rubbing to get rid of the smoke. He knows I'm in disgrace. He must have heard them shouting. 'Missie, dere be more food in de cookhouse if you be hungry.'

After I've eaten, I tiptoe on eggshells into the dining-room and squint through the gap between the pillar and the wall. I can see half of Jack's head, the shiny helmet of greasy hair, and his ear. He's saying '... fer her own guid, Irene, ye hae to do somethin' aboot her precociousness ... I canna stand a bairn wi' flappin' ears ... why, in Godssake is she readin' my books when ye've bought her so many o' her own ...?'

*Blah-blah-bla*h, badgirl says.

I think he's hypnotised Mom. She doesn't say anything.

Mom brings piles of my clothes into my room, puts a brown suitcase on the table and packs it with enough clothes for a week. Her hair is pulled back from her face, tied up in a roll. Her eyebrows are two sharp lines above her eyes. She won't look at me. My heart aches. I want her to hold me tight and say, 'There, there, don't worry about old Jack.' I would give anything to be held in her arms now; a hug would melt my aching chest and tight throat. I want to hear Mom say she loves me, just once.

Instead, she says in a small hard voice, 'You're making things difficult for me, Karin. Jack is always complaining about your behaviour. I don't know what to do to keep the peace. You have to keep out of his way. Thank goodness you're going to school.'

I stop listening to Mom's worrying words.

Badgirl says, *You don't want to see Jack either. Who would want to be near his whiskey and cigarette fumes, his beak nose and hoody eyes?* I shut my ears to Mom. Tomorrow I will be leaving Dorowa. When I come home from school next Friday, I'm going to play at being The Invisible Child.

In the cold light of a morning in Scaldmariland, the wind blew straight from the North Sea and froze Siward and his men. Siward saw how the peasants, ill-equipped and out-numbered, had lured them into a bog. Their horses were sinking up to their knees in the marshy wetland, weighed down as they were by men in armour. The peasants grouped themselves in twos and threes around horses' heads and hacked at their necks with blunt axes to bring them down.

'Aoi! Aoi!' Siward roared the Viking battle cry into the teeth of the wind. 'To me. To me.' The men struggled to turn their horses from the marshes. Many dismounted and dragged their horses by the reins. When they gained the high ground, they looked and saw some of their comrades pulled from their horses and sinking into the mire.

Siward dismounted, threw off his chain mail tunic. He put his wolf's head on his helm and, filled with battle lust and fury, he turned Berserker. His men followed suit.

The air rang with wild cries and the clash of steel. Siward fought as one possessed, he fought with the strength of ten men. His eyes bulged in blood fury and the number of bodies around him grew. Brain-Biter turned red with blood. At last there were none left to fight.

There were wounds and gashes but Siward had not lost a man, and the peasants, having lost many, would not venture forth against them in a hurry.

My dream is filled with the sounds of battle, men shouting-screaming, clanging swords and horses' neighing, terrified by the smell of blood and the war cries of Berserkers as they murder and plunder across Scaldmariland. And there, amongst the foot soldiers are Mom and Jack, swinging their axes, their eyes shining with battle madness, shouting, 'Aoi, Aoi.'

Part Three

OUR FEET streak across grass and gravel, crunching and swishing. The ground falls away from us into a gully and we go tumbling down onto rotting mangoes soft as jelly. There are swings, jungle gyms, slides and see-saws. We're monkeys swinging from bar to bar, climbing, sliding.

Small Donald throws himself down the slide. 'This is ace,' he shouts. 'I'm going to be an ace pilot when I grow up.'

'No, you're not,' says Fraser, his hair the colour of orange fire. 'Cos I'm going to be an ace pilot.'

'We're brothers, we can both be pilots.'

'Let's play explorers,' says Hugh. 'I'll be Livingstone.'

'No, I want to be Livingstone,' says his sister, Ruth.

'You're a girl, you can't be a famous explorer.'

'Then I'll be Stanley.'

'No, you're too small, all the small ones have to be porters.'

'We could go exploring in the bush,' I say. 'There're no walls or fences.'

Beyond the school grounds lies flat bush to the horizon covered with boulders and ant hills like pimples. In the distance a small boy leads a herd of hump-backed Fulani cows. He carries a switch. He's alone in the emptiness with his white cows.

'We'll get into trouble,' says Tansy. 'Miss Hordern said we musn't go far.'

I think of Perth Academy. Red brick, three floors, tarmac playground, high walls. Mom says things are as different as chalk 'n cheese but I think this school is as different from the Perth Academy as Cadbury's chocolate bars are to yellow quinine pills.

Somebody shouts 'Tag!' and we race back to the school. It's a big white house with a stoep in front but the rooms have been turned into classrooms, dormitories and a dining-room. We're somewhere between Jos and the Yelwa Club.

We clatter, screaming, into the first big classroom and down the passage. A hand pulls my arm, stops me. I turn. Miss Hordern pulls me into her office, 'Karin, one word.'

She closes the door. Her watery blue eyes are steady and kind. They stare at me thoughtfully. 'I'm a busy woman,' she says. 'I simply do not have time to curb your wild enthusiasm so I'm going to give you work to do. You seem to have a lot of energy. I'm putting you in charge of the smaller children – make sure they're where they're supposed to be at all times.' She looks at her watch. 'Lunch is in half an hour. You'll just have time to round them up, see they wash their hands and take them to the dining-room. Off you go.'

She's not angry and she trusts me. I pull this feeling of importance into my chest and hug it.

Her face is long and thin and bony like a horse's. When she speaks her voice sounds like the voice of a radio announcer – low and soothing. A short brown fuzz surrounds her face. Bridget – Bridget Hordern. I say her name in my head. Bridge with a T on the end.

After supper we sit at the dining-room table in our pyjamas, listening to her read to us. Her large white teeth open and shut, letting out words in neat bites. Her lips stretch away from her teeth then close over them like curtains. Teeth open and shut, lips stretch and shrink. I could watch her all night.

She's reading to us from a book called *Puck of Pook's Hill* by Rudyard Kipling. An elf-creature stares at two children on the cover. Every so often she lifts her head from the page to look at us with her small blue eyes in their bony sockets.

At the end of ten pages, she leads us to our dormitories, the boys in one and girls in another. She waits until we climb in under the mosquito nets then says a prayer, 'Now I lay me down to sleep.' At the end, she switches off the light and says 'God Bless' and closes the door. The last thing I see is the shape of her body, thin and narrow, against the light.

After a minute, scurrying and slithering sounds as shadow children leave their beds and climb into other beds.

Tansy and Pammie climb under my mosquito net. 'Ugh. Macaroni cheese for supper ... and prunes and custard.' Pammie shakes her shoulders.

Tansy hisses, 'My father says there are starving children all over Africa, we should be grateful for the food we get.'

I remember the tiny children running after the train before Zaria, with their stick bodies and pot-bellies and huge staring eyes. 'They can have our macaroni cheese.'

'Are you homesick?' says Tansy.

'Yes,' says Pam, and 'No,' I say, hugging my joy to my chest.

'Mom says I must say my prayers every night if I'm homesick and He will make the days whizz by until Friday.'

I don't want the days to whizz, I want them to drag. I tell them there are no children at Dorowa and I have no brothers or sisters. Pam says her father runs the brewery at Barakin Mari and I should come and spend a weekend with them.

'Barakin brewery?'

'Where they make beer,' says Pam.

I can't ask them to stay with me. Jack would explode. I don't want my new friends to see Jack 'in his cups' ever. That's how Mom describes Jack when he's had too much to drink. Jack doesn't know how to talk to children. He embarrasses me.

There are no night noises here – no slithering snakes, no droning of Jack's voice, no drums. It's dark and quiet. The tight band round my chest is gone, I can breathe. I think about the day. Ernest bringing me to Bukuru where the school bus waits, then another long drive. A day of new things, surprises and the best surprise of all – Bridget Hordern.

Miss Hordern tells us about herself in her deep creamy-caramel voice. She comes from a family of teachers, her father was the headmaster of a school in Grantchester and her mother taught maths. 'Maths is more difficult than arithmetic,' she says. She was engaged to be married to a pilot who was shot down by a Fokker in the battle of Britain. The tip of Miss Hordern's nose gets pink as she tells us about her dead pilot and she stares into the garden for a second. 'England was full of war memories,' she says. 'I saw an advertisement for teachers in a school magazine, an opportunity to see the world. I applied, they accepted me and here I am,' she smiles, 'looking after you in this glorious sunshine.'

I love her quietness, she's always the same, she never gets angry or worried or disappointed. If something's wrong, she explains why and what you have to do to change it. She's like a long stretch of peaceful blue sky, or a pond that's always still.

'I want you to tell me about yourselves,' she says. 'About your lives, about your families, how you got here. There's blank pages on your desks, write your stories.' She looks at the smaller children. 'If you can't write yet, draw pictures of your families and where you live.'

Pammie, Tansy, Fraser and Hugh bend their heads over their pages and begin to write.

I think as fast as I can. But I can't think of happy things to write about. I see a field filled with mines and they all have D-words ready to explode in fear – divorce, drunk, drink, disappointment, dangerous, difficult, disappear, disease, dredger, drone, Dorowa, dad, death-camps, damn ...

The others are filling up their pages and I haven't written one word.

Write about the things you like, my badgirl voice tells me, *leave out the d-words.*

I write about adventures of long sea journeys, first, in a ship taking us to Scotland that once carried troops to war, then the shorter trip to Lagos, about the midnight-black ride in the express train to Perth, all the rocking-rolling motions of long journeys. About my first school where I learnt to read and discovered books. I write about Mom, how jerseys grow under her fingers, how she makes pictures with needle and silk thread. I write about Frida, her accident, about my family of books but mostly I write about Siward the Viking who lived in the ninth century, his beauty, his bravery as a warrior, his wolf-dog Pall, his sword Brain-Biter and his chanting-singing.

Not one word about my father or Jack.

Miss Hordern takes in our pages. 'I'll look at these later.'

She stands in front of the blackboard, a piece of chalk in her hand. 'I want to tell you about the system of schooling we'll be using here. It's called the PNEU system. Those letters stand for Parents' National Education Union. This system was started by a woman in the last century and is based on the home-schooling system she received from her parents. We want to train your minds in concentration, attention and recall.'

She writes 'recall = remember' on the board.

'But besides training your brains, we want to train you to have good habits. Habits are things you do every day so that they become second nature. You must think of this school as your home from home and because there are only 23 children here, we will be like a large family.'

We have a routine that marches like hands round the clock during the day. After breakfast we have lessons. Mrs Stevenson takes the small ones who are learning to read into another classroom. We have English grammar, writing essays, French, Arithmetic. Mrs Stevenson takes us for Ancient History and Music. I hold *From Ur to Rome* to my nose – it smells of paper-parchment, of nectar and spices and carries the mysteries of ancient cities and peoples in its pages.

'You're dreaming, Karin,' says Mrs Stevenson. 'Pay attention. We read a chapter every day, then we re-tell the story. It's called recapitulation. This helps you to concentrate and improves your memories. Then tomorrow you will write a short essay on what you remember today.'

Pammie nudges me and smiles. She's my new friend. I like her black hair cut like the man in the comic strip – Prince Valiant. She doesn't have brothers or sisters either.

Miss Hordern takes us on a nature stroll one afternoon. We carry glass jars, packets, tins and even a butterfly net. We walk bent over, looking for insects. Ants are easy, they're in the anthills. Miss Hordern says we can start our own colony.

She's set up a long trestle table in the main classroom under the window. 'Your nature table.' She puts a new nest of ants into a glass box like a small fish tank. We watch the ants scurry to and fro. One has escaped from under the glass and scurries across the table. A small boy, Adam, freckled with big gaps in his front teeth, squashes it before it can escape. 'Huh,' he says, 'motorized freckles.'

'Why'd you do that?' says Pammie. 'We're supposed to take care of the ants so we can watch them and learn about their habits.'

'I don't care about their habits,' says Adam. 'They're only ants.'

Mom's waiting at the market stall at Bukuru where the bus takes us. I'm nervous. She was still cross with me on Monday morning when I left for school. But now she's quiet, her smile is small and doesn't reach her eyes. She asks me about brushing teeth and washing hands when I'm bursting to tell her the interesting stuff.

I turn to wave at Tansy, Pammie and Fraser before I climb into the Dodge. Tansy's mom has heavy eyelids as if they're swollen with bee-stings, her eyes are like copper pennies in her sweaty face; she's wearing a tent dress, I can see a baby bump underneath. Pammie's mom is tall and thin, she smiles a bright beam in our direction, she also has a Prince Valiant haircut.

I sit next to the window in the Dodge as it jumps and jerks down the road. All the days at school have rolled into one. I try and sort them out to tell Mom. I start to tell her about Miss Hordern reading to us at bedtime, but I can see she's not listening. Her eyes stare straight ahead at the brown road but I don't think she sees the road; she's far away somewhere else.

Ernest drives at his usual frantic speed, the wheels bounce from ridge to ridge on the dirt track road. His black eyes watch the road for potholes, he chews on his stick with his white teeth, a fuzzy moustache decorates his top lip. We bump up to the top of the hill before the Dorowa mine. There below us I see the dredger in the muddy riverbank and I feel a knot in my stomach. I feel cold in the boiling heat of the cab. Mom sits still like a poker. She's vanished into her thoughts.

The house is quiet when Ernest stops the Dodge outside the front door. I wait in the doorway after Mom has gone in, but I can't smell whiskey or Woodbine fumes, Harry Lauder is quiet.

'Where's Jack?' I can hardly say his name.

'He's gone to see Rob Nesbit at their house, he'll be back shortly.'

My heart sinks. I was hoping he would be working the night shift.

My room is bare, it looks as if nobody lives here anymore. The tree branches outside make pools of waving green shadows on the walls and floor. My books and comics are stacked in square piles on the table under the window. I click open the locks on my brown suitcase and take out the book on top of my crumpled clothes. *Five on a Treasure Island*. The school has a whole room full of books, a library. We can borrow them at any time.

Frida comes running from behind the cookhouse at my call, meowing silently. Her voice engine has been broken by the chop-box falling on her head. Sometimes she makes a little croak like a frog. I pick her up and snuggle her to my chest. I open *Five on a Treasure Island* and begin to read, Frida behind my knees.

The afternoon darkens into evening. I read with my ears pricked, listening, waiting for the sound of Jack's droning voice, for the clink of glasses, the glug-glug of whiskey being poured. I hear voices coming from the cookhouse, Amos' and Obafemi's, the rise and fall of their talk, the savoury smell of supper.

Mom calls me for supper. She doesn't speak, her worry wrinkles are stuck on her face. She looks as if she's listening and waiting. When she hears the sound of the Dodge engine straining at the bottom of the road, her face crumples. We hear

Andy's voice, 'Do ye need a hand, Jack?'

Jack mumbles '... leave me alone.'

Andy appears in the archway to the dining-room. He crinkles a smile in his eyes and his grooves split his cheeks. His eyes are on Mom's face as if he wants to say something. Jack staggers into sight. His face is flushed, his lips hang loose. His eyebrows are sticking up all over. Mom sucks in her breath.

Mom rises from her seat. Jack looks round for his chair and almost falls. Andy's hand guides his elbow and he flops down. 'Sorry, Irene, I tried to remind Jack his supper would be waitin' but he would stay an' hae yet anither dram fer the road.'

Jack's eyes try to find Andy's face and end up staring at a spot on the wall past his shoulder. 'Sh-sit. Hae a drink.' He waves a hand to his whiskey bottles.

'Naw, naw, Jack. Yer supper's waitin' – it's cold by noo. Irene's been waitin'. I'm awa'.'

Mom stands and looks at Jack. Her face is white and her eyes dark. 'I can't believe this ...'

'Sorry, Irene,' Andy squeezes her arm.

Jack won't eat his supper

'Eat, Jack, you'll feel better,' Mom says.

'Wheesht, wumman,' his false teeth clack loose. 'Haud yer bletherin'.'

He leans towards his drink table and sloshes whiskey into a glass and slurps and swallows as if he's thirsty. Mom sits in the lamplight, picks up a piece of material the colour of gold and tries to embroider the stamens of a red flower, but she sighs and lets it fall onto her lap and turns her eyes on Jack. He's gazing at the ceiling through a fog of smoke.

I've only been gone for five days but I can see Mom has been busy on the Singer sewing machine Daisy gave her. She's been to Jos with Helen and Daisy and bought shout-bright African cloth. It has stripes and blocks and squares of tomato-red, parrot-green, sun-yellow and mango-orange. She's made curtains to hide the ugly window frames. Now she's sewing beautiful cushions to hide the ugly chairs. She's not making pictures of English flowers, she's sewing bright big tropical flowers like zinnias, cannas and hibiscus with long pointy stamens. Frangipani with waxy, creamy petals.

Mom decides to ignore Jack. She lifts the cloth and pushes the needle in and out with a thimble on her middle finger. Watching the rhythm of the needle, the way her finger smoothes down the cushions of colour, hypnotises me like watching a pendulum swing.

I sit on the pouffe next to Mom's chair, my library book on my lap.

Jack's eyes leave the ceiling and see me sitting there. 'An' where the hell have ye been? School? Aboot bloody time.'

He finds a spot on the wall above Mom's head and talks to it. 'Did I tell ye aboot the nights my father an' I went rabbit huntin'? No? Weel, every so often, on a Friday night my da an' I wud go into the country at Scone and shoot rabbits. This was the manly thing we did together – somethin' tae put into the pot. Aud Jock wud clean and oil the shotgun, I wud get an aud sack an' the torch an' off we'd go. But furst we'd stop for a wee dram at the Pig an' Whistle. The barman wud always complain because I was underage, ye ken, but ma father wud make short shrift o' him. "Do as yer bloody told, man, or I'll take ma business elsewhere." People who kenned my father called him Black Jock because of his temper and his loud mouth. One night we had two drams each an' by the time we got tae the fields, I was swayin' an' a bit tipsy. I used tae haud the torch fer my da, shine the light on the rabbits, so they were paralysed by the glare, their eyes wud shine like traffic-lights an' ma father wud shoot them – bam – between the eyes. But on this night when I was tipsy, I kept droppin' the torch an' the rabbits got away. Aud Jock had enough o' this after the third rabbit escaped. He turned on me an' socked me one on the jaw. I fell backward. Next thing, I felt the barrel o' the gun rammed into my forehead and peering down the barrel was Jock, his face as black as thunder. He put his finger on the trigger an' said, "If ye drop the bloody torch agin, I'll kill ye." Och aye, he was a violent man. He felled me many a time an' ma puir mither as well, the most silent, hardworking, faithfu' wumman ye ever came across. Uncomplainin'. Took everythin' as it came until one day she was sittin' at her tattin', a wonderful needlewoman, she was, Irene, like you, an' she just keeled over an' died.'

Mom's eyebrows crumple.

'I remember when I came hame from Edinburgh University and showed him my certificate that said cum laude. "Do ye ken wha' cum laude means?" I asked him. He looked at me as if I was some kind o' a fule and said, "Do ye think I'm an ignoramus, boy? 'Course I know wha' cum laude means. I also ken wha' summa cum laude means. Ye didna get that one, did ye?" '

Jack sighs.Unhh-uhh. His eyes grow red and watery. His lower lip shakes. I watch him in surprise. Jack's crying. Mom puts down her sewing and says, 'Jack?'

'Och, aye, I could nivver please ma father,' he says, wiping his eyes as his shoulders shake. 'I knew fer a long time afore he died, I knew my father nivver loved me. It seemed as tho' he did, but all he wanted was fer me tae achieve wha' he couldna achieve. Selfish aud bastard.'

Mom takes me to bed, watches me climb under the mosquito net. She stands over me and disappears into her thoughts. She lifts her hand and strokes her neck. 'Pops always called me swan-neck. I miss him,' she says. 'He was a kind man, a gentleman.'

'Who's that?' I whisper.

Mom and I are walking in the compound past the fourth hut when a girl comes out through the low door. Her cinnamon silk body glides past us. She leaves a smoky-earth smell in the air. She wears a cloth wound round her head, it looks like a bud about to burst open on the thin stalk of her neck. She has two bare pointy bosoms. My face gets red. I hang my head.

Mom doesn't answer. The end of her nose twitches. The girl sits at the fire next to Bola and her baby. She looks up at us as we walk to the back door. Her eyes look like the black olives Mom puts in salads.

'Who's that?' I ask again.

'It's Amos' second wife. I don't want any trouble in the compound.'

'Why would there be trouble?'

'Because no wife wants her husband to have a younger wife – Bola might treat her like a servant. There could be arguments.' Mom's face says storms are coming.

In the kitchen, Mom turns the filter tap on and fills two glasses of water.

I smell fumes, then the sound of Harry Lauder – 'Just a wee doch an' doris.' Jack is home from work. Mom smells it as well, her eyes close and she sighs a deep sigh.

I pour Oros into my water and take blocks of Cadbury chocolate from the pantry. I run out of the back door, into the bathroom and into my bedroom. I shut the door, pull down the mosquito net. Frida croaks. I lift her up and shut us into our cocoon. I'm standing on the rolling deck of the *Skidbladnir* next to Siward and Pall. The boat sits low in the water. I'm surrounded by the dark mystery of the sea, so huge, always moving in restless waves. We're on our way to another adventure – somewhere there's a war, or a quest, somebody's honour to uphold, a maiden in distress or special magic to find or omens brought by flying dragons or singing blackbirds.

Mom will bring me supper on a tray. I won't see Jack tonight.

> When Gisebert of Flanders saw his ward, Frida, daughter of his dead comrade-in-arms, Erik of Endor, often in the company of Siward Silk-Hair, the Bearslayer, he became enraged. He had planned to wed Frida to Halkell the Dane, thereby keeping her wealth for himself and adding to it the lands and fighting men of Halkell. He conspired with Sir Hoibricht, his nephew and noble knight, to send a message to Halkell saying that Siward planned to rob him of his bride and they should set a sum of money on his head and outlaw him.
>
> Gunnar came to Siward and told him of the rumours flying round the court of Gisebert, whispered from ear to ear.
>
> And so it came to pass when the moon was on the wane, Siward took Frida from her home to venture with him into the unknown. They climbed into a barge and rowed through brown, glassy waters, between green alders and reeds.
>
> Frida said, 'I have toiled and studied to master the art of healing. I have done nothing but good for those wounded and sick. All for nothing. I am but a chattel in the eyes of my uncle and guardian to be disposed of for their benefit.'

Siward saw the tears drop from her sloe-coloured eyes and wet her cheeks and made a silent vow to protect this proud maiden from her preying guardians.

Aa-ar-karh-karh. The sound is like a rusty saw, biting into the still blue air. 'There's a pied crow,' Miss Hordern shields her eyes from the sun with her hand and points to a black and white bird as it drops from the sky onto a branch of the locust bean tree, its bean pods hanging from the leaves like long purses. 'Can you see?' She passes the binoculars amongst us. When it's my turn I see the bird's black shape with its white collar and chest in the round lens that brings it close. 'The Hausas call the pied crow hangkaka,' she says.

Then her finger sticks up in the air again and shows a beige-brown bird with a long fan-shaped tail. 'Look – a piapiac,' she whispers although the bird can't hear us, it's some distance away flapping its wings to keep it in the same spot above the termite hill. 'Can you see? It has termites in his beak.'

She passes me the binoculars first; I hold them to my eyes with both hands. I can see the white termites trapped in its hard little beak. It's grinding its beak together and pushing the white wriggling termites down into its throat. Somebody takes the binoculars away from me but that's alright because the instant I see the piapiac's beak grinding away, I see Jack's mouth grinding out words on Sunday night, the night before I returned to school. 'Ye're a shlut, Irene, it's no wonder yer ex-husband left ye ... ye're a hoor an' a shlut ... watched the way ye look at Andy Stewart ... ye dinna fule me, Irene ... ye'd think butter wouldna melt in yer mouth wi' yer prim an' prissy manner ... but I ken different ...'

Jack woke me from my sleep with a waterfall sound of wee and his heaving drunk sighs – 'Och, aye' – his stumbling against walls and doors, pausing outside my bedroom door for a second, then I heard him bumping back to the lounge. I slid out of my bed and crept to the dining-room. I stood in the dark shadows behind the pillar and I could see them, Mom and Jack.

Mom's shaky hands covered her face. 'Stop, Jack, stop your lies ... leave me in peace ...'

'I'll no' stop, wumman, until ye tell me the truth. Tell me ye're a shlut an' a hoor ...'

'Karin?' Miss Hordern's hand shakes my arm. 'Come, child, you're dreaming. Have you got all your specimens?' Her small eyes take us all in in one sweep. 'If we return now, we'll have enough time to set our specimens up on the nature table and make drawings and write descriptions before supper.'

Miss Hordern shows us the differences between termites and ants. We make a list of them in our nature study books. Termites – beaded antennae, no waist, wings equal size, no eyes, eat wood. Ants – elbowed antennae, fore wings larger than hind, small waist, complex eyes, eat anything.

When I draw, I push all thoughts away, I forget Jack and Mom. The knots in my stomach undo themselves. I listen to Miss Hordern's calm, deep voice; watch her plump lips open and close over her teeth, biting out the words. I see her hands pick up specimens, hold them, turn them over, put them on the table in perfect, careful order.

I draw, I listen, I watch and think everything will be alright.

I hear sliding feet, voices shouting and balls being thwacked. I can hear Daisy's voice louder than the others. I stand up, step out from the gazebo where I've been reading, into the heat of the sun and cross the road. The crack and thud of tennis balls gets louder, I see the Fellowes dressed in white. Mom and Jack are also in white, playing tennis with Daisy and Dick.

I reach the court and climb up the umpire's chair.

'Oot o' the way, Jack,' Daisy grunts as she swings her right arm. Mom and Jack play tennis like scurrying rabbits, hop-hop here, hop-hop there, patting at the ball to push it over the net.

'Och, my guidness,' Dick says with pride. He stops to look at Daisy and her steely glare of determination. 'Weel played, ye Scots Boadicea, ye fightin' warrior queen.'

Daisy bounces on the balls of her feet, her white dress swirls around her strong knees, her white daisy earrings bob against her curls. Dick is like a grasshopper, jumping about on his long legs, his arms reaching everywhere.

'Come on noo, Jack,' Daisy bellows, going in for a killer shot. 'We hae them in oor sights. So, fire awa' if ye can.'

Dick and Daisy yell at each other and at Jack and Mom.

'Don't forget, we're playing agin' the Sassenachs,' shouts Dick.

'I'm no Sassenach,' Jack says, huffing and puffing, red in the face from trying to keep up with Daisy.

'Ye are fer the purpose o' this game,' Daisy says.

Jack bends forward, rocking from side to side and swipes at a high ball Mom has managed to push over the net.

I turn on the umpire's chair and see the Buick crawl up the road like a black beetle. It stops next to the tennis court and out hop Rob and Helen.

Daisy and Jack win the game when Daisy slams a ball into the corner out of the reach of Dick and Mom.

'Who wants to take us on?' calls Rob.

'We'll hae a go,' Daisy swings her arm, her eyes turning the Nesbits into Sassenachs. 'C'mon, Dick, time tae redeem yersel'.'

Jack and Mom sit, their heads following the ball from side to side as Rob and Helen take the lead. 'Och, weel played, Rob. Nice shot, Helen,' Jack claps his hands and smiles his false, oily smile. Mom's face looks washed out in the bright light of the sun. Her eyes look big and staring like a bushbaby's.

I hear footsteps on the gravel road. Andy is walking over, dressed in white shorts and shirts and old sandshoes without socks. His brown curly hair falls over his eyes. He arrives in time to see Rob hit the winning shot.

Rob asks, 'Would you like to take on the winners, Jack? You and Irene?'

Jack opens his mouth to say yes but Mom shakes her head. 'Sorry, I'm not in your class.'

Jack shoots a warning glint at Mom, his lips tight, eyebrows crouching.

'I'll play,' says Andy with a look at Mom's face. 'C'mon, Jack, let's take on Rob and Helen.'

'Make it a men's double,' says Helen. 'I'll sit this one oot.'

The men stride back onto the court. Jack and Andy versus Rob and Dick. Mom, Daisy and Helen sit below on the bench.

'Ye're lookin' kinda peaky, Irene,' Helen says. "I hope ye're no havin' a relapse after yer bout o' malaria.'

Mom shakes her head. 'This heat makes me tired, that's all.'

I can't see Mom's face but I know her eyes are blinking the way they do when she lies.

'But ... ye're frae a hot climate, Irene? Ye'd think ye'd be used to heat.' Daisy turns her head to Mom, I can see she's pushed up her pencil eyebrows. 'As fer mesel', I've taken to it like a duck tae water.' Then she stands and shouts, 'Dick Fellowes. Watch what ye're doin'. Ye're no holdin' yer racket properly.'

My head turns as the ball flies from one side of the net to the other. Andy swings wildly at the ball. Sometimes he hits the ball wide and it goes flying into the bush.

Jack tries to reach a ball Rob has hit into the corner behind him but misses and loses his balance. Andy is behind him in a flash and slams the ball past Dick at the net.

'Okay Jack, I've got it.'

I try to follow the scoring but can't make sense of the loves, the deuces and the advantages. Andy's eyes shine like green marbles in the sun, he's all over the court, his smiley grooves stuck in his cheeks.

'C'mon, Jack, ye can do it. Tha's the ticket. Keep yer eyes on the ball. Och, there ye go.'

The men finish their set. Daisy calls, 'Are ye men goin' tae hog the court all day? Gie the wimmin a chance.'

Rob and Jack come off the court and stand beneath me. I can see freckles on Rob's bald head. Jack's head is a few inches lower, one spike of hair falls forward. He lights a Woodbine and begins to cough.

Rob rubs a hand over his baldness. '... as I was saying the other night, Jack, I've always had a taste for politics ... I've been on the Plateau for twenty years, lived and worked with the Hausa and speak their language ... in ten years' time this will no longer be a British Colony ... independence ... Rex Niven ... his aide ...'

'Hmmm. I see. Och aye.'

Jack's voice is different, he sounds as if he wants to please Rob.

'... ATMN are looking for someone to manage Dorowa when I go ... I have recommended you ... You have a wife now ... necessary for a man in a position ...'

Rob's small eyes are sharp, the colour of sultanas, they stare at Jack without blinking. I think nobody can lie to Rob. There are little pouches of skin around Rob's eyes. He looks like a wise monkey.

'No, no don't thank me yet ...' he raises a hand. 'Rex likes to keep a finger on the pulse of ATMN ... he met Irene at the Robbie Burns Night ... as you know he has an eye for the ladies ... well, there it is. Are you up to the challenge, Jack?' Rob smiles at Jack but his eyes say, 'I'll be watching you.'

Jack harrumphs. His hoods are wide open. His hawk beak nose lifts. He jingles his coins.

'Let's regard this period before I go into politics as a trial one. I need to ease you into greater responsibility ... see how you cope under pressure ... need a good working relationship with the indigenous people ... colleagues.'

'Ye need have no fear, Rob, I'll do my verra best, ye can count on it.'

Rob nods as the others finish their set. 'Keep it to yourself for the moment, Jack, there's a good man.'

Jack looks at Mom sitting on the bench on the other side of the umpire's chair. She hasn't heard a word, she's lost in her thoughts.

Helen says, 'Fellowes, Jack, Irene, Andy? Wud ye like to come over tomorrow fer drinks? Aboot six?' She smiles at everybody.

I climb down from the umpire's chair and follow Mom and Andy to the road. He bends his head. 'Are ye alright, Irene? Ye're awfu' quiet.'

Mom smiles up at him, shows her square white teeth. 'Just a headache.'

They stand in the overhang of bougainvillea, their faces hidden. Mom leans up to him. They whisper.

I turn my head. Jack hasn't seen them, he's rocking on his heels, his hands deep in his pockets, concentrating on Rob. Dick and Daisy are far up the road, almost at their house. Helen has climbed into the Buick.

'See you tomorrow, then.' Andy touches her arm and crunches away over the gravel. Mom's eyes are dreamy.

The dark comes quickly, as if someone has thrown a cloak over the sun. Harry Lauder sings out of the gramophone, 'Roamin' in the gloamin'.'

Jack's 'ruminatin'. His eyes stare into space. He remembers something because his shoulders shake, his mouth opens and I can see his wet plastic teeth. He laughs without making a sound. 'Och, those were the days. Och, Harry Lauder, wha' a great man. I saw him at the aud music hall, wha' was it agin? The aud Pavilion. Every time he came tae Perth.' He shakes his head. 'I can see him noo on the stage, wha' a swagger he had, dressed in his kilt, his sporran in front an' his tam o' shanter on his head, carryin' his twisty stick. His stick made from a branch of the Hazelwood tree ... it grew like a corkscrew. He made a real Scots character oot o' Roderick McSwankey, tight-fisted and idiosyn ... idiosyncratic, wha'ever. Och, the jokes. Before he finished fer the night he'd point his arm at the audience an' shout "If ye can say it's a braw, bricht, moonlicht nicht ..." he'd put his hand up to his ear and wait fer the crowd to shout back "Ye're a' richt, ye ken".'

Jack leans towards me, cups his hand behind his ear. I look at him. What does he want? 'Go on, say it.'

I clear my throat and try to roll my rs and ggh the cht's. 'If ye can say it's a braw, bricht, moonlicht nicht, ye're a' richt, ye ken.'

Jack slaps his leg. 'Aye, Irene, I'll make a Scotswoman oot o' the bairn yet.'

I hear Jack laugh out loud for the first time. 'Waa – haa – waa – hee.' His eyes disappear into his hoods. His mouth stretches almost from ear to ear. Mom looks confused. She drops her sewing and stares at Jack.

'Och, I like my dram of an evenin', Irene.' His eyes are more yellow than grey tonight, he turns them on Mom. 'My father always said "Dinna trust a man who doesna drink." Aye, tha's wha' he said.'

Mom says, 'Time for bed.'

The tip of Mom's nose and her cheeks are pink. She's drunk two small glasses of sherry. Mom's sitting at Helen's upright piano, her big hands thumping up and down on the keys. Syncopation, she calls this piano playing which she learnt long ago when she was young. I don't know this Mom; she laughs out loud, her frown lines are smooth, her hair is loose down her back and curls stick to her cheeks. Her feet and hands thumping. Big loud chords.

'*I fell in love ... while stars shone above in Mexico ... dah, dee daa, daa. Ay yay yay yaaay.*'

Andy, Helen, Rob and Dick stand on either side of the piano, their mouths wide open, shouting-singing. Jack stands nearby, one hand jingling his coins in a pocket, the other holding his whiskey glass. Their shouting-singing doesn't sound anything like Ruby Murray. Mom's piano playing is nothing like Mrs Stevenson's.

Mom slows down and tosses her hair from her eyes. 'Sad to sa-ay ... we were parting ...' Then loudly again, the chorus. '*Ay, yay, yay, yaaay ...*'

I watch their faces grow redder, the singing louder and their laughter ready to lift off the roof. Jack tries to look happy, his fake smile stays stuck on his face. He's helping himself to Rob's whiskey.

'Anither ane, Irene, what can ye play?' says Daisy.

Mom pushes her hair back. 'Mmm, let me see, I haven't played for such a long time.' Rob brings her another glass of sherry. 'Perhaps this will inspire you.'

'Oh, yes, what about this…?' Mom's hands thump.

'Yeees,' they shout, 'we know this.'

They sing songs with baby words like Chatanooga Choo-choo and Chi-Baba, Chi-baba, chi-wa-wa. Daisy bends her elbows, moves her arms round in circles, shuffles her feet. *Wa-wa chi-baba, look at a baba …*' she bellows.

They're dancing now round in circles, as well as singing-shouting the words. Even Rob with his sharp, ginger-sultana eyes and his headmaster's voice, is shuffling, bending over as if he's a boogie-woogie train. Dick's grasshopper arms and legs turn like the wires on bicycle wheels. Andy's shaking his curls over his face, clapping his hands, bobbing up and down – *'Express train … choo-choo …'*

At last Mom looks round and sees me. 'Goodness,' she jumps to her feet. 'School tomorrow.'

'It's an acquired taste,' Bridget Hordern says. 'Don't you think, Kay?' She turns to her sister who sits at her right hand. We all stare at Miss Hordern's sister who is also Miss Hordern.

She's talking about mayonnaise. This is my first taste of this strange tangy sauce poured over the lettuce and tomatoes. My first taste of mayonnaise and my first sight of a bald woman. Well, almost bald. She still has short strands of brown all over, but there's more white scalp than hair. She'll soon be as bald as Rob.

'Mmmh,' says Kay Hordern. 'I acquired the taste almost immediately but then I like sour-tart tastes. I believe you were always the one with the sweet tooth, Bridget.'

I can't help staring at her. It's because … because she looks like a man. She looks like one of those men who live in a monastery, who wear long brown robes and sandals on their feet.

I don't like the taste of mayonnaise, it's too sour. I push it to one side of my plate. 'Yummy,' Tansy says. She eats everything they put in front of her.

All the children at the school fit around the long table in the dining-room as well as Matron Davies, Mrs Stevenson and the two Miss Horderns. Our teachers talk about the war and their memories of war – the raids, the bombings, the blackout, the destruction, the rations, the terrible winters, the losses. Everybody's lost someone. Except for Mom and myself. The war brought us someone, the war brought us Jack.

Fraser and Hugh listen to the war talk, their eyes wide. Fraser's eyes, the colour of grass in the dry season, shine. 'I say,' he says when he tells you something. I've discovered I'm not the only one without a father. Hugh is Matron Davies' son. He and his sister, Ruth, have no father. He was killed in the war.

'At least he died in the war,' Mom says when I tell her. 'That's a respectable way to lose a husband, not like divorce.'

Mrs Stevenson says, 'You children will have to rest before eurythmics this afternoon, your stomachs will be too full of all this delicious food.'

The Hausa servants are carrying in plates of apple pie and custard. Her voice sounds like gravel falling down a chute. My smoker's voice, she calls it. Her eyes smile all the time, her white hair jumps up from her forehead in a thick white mane like a lion's.

'Quite right,' Miss Hordern says. 'Would you and Matron Davies care to join my sister and I for coffee in my rooms while the children rest?'

Miss Hordern, Kay, is visiting us from England for a while. She's going to help children who are behind with arithmetic to catch up.

Matron Davies pulls her droopy lips back from her fallen-fence teeth and nods and Mrs Stevenson growls, 'I'd be delighted.'

'Kay? May I call you Kay?' Mrs Stevenson says. 'Two Miss Horderns is confusing. I haven't been home for seventeen years. Would I be shocked by what the war has done to Britain?'

'Will it ever be the same?' says Matron Davies. 'Two catastrophic World Wars – the cream of English manhood gone forever. We may never recover our old way of life.'

'Her husband was killed at Dunkirk,' Pamela whispers in my ear. 'She told my mother.'

'What's Dunkirk?'

Pamela eyebrows shoot up. 'I'll tell you later.'

'Gone but not forgotten, Matron Davies,' says Miss Hordern. 'As long as they are remembered, the dead are kept alive.' She's extra quiet and thoughtful for a long moment. I wonder if she's thinking of her dead pilot.

'The war has changed Britain forever, Mrs Stevenson, I am sure you would find it unrecognisable,' Kay Hordern says. 'We're bankrupt, our empire will collapse. Nigeria will become independent within ten years ... worst of all ... the Labour Government has changed the education system.'

'That's the first thing a new political party always does ... doesn't matter if the previous one worked efficiently ...'

We play the Postman game at the dinner table. Somebody thinks of a short sentence and whispers it into the ear of the person next to them. Each one passes it on by turning to the person sitting on their left and whispering what they think they heard. When the whispers have gone all round the table, the last one says it out loud.

'Matron Davies, you start,' says Miss Hordern. 'Now children, I want you to listen carefully and concentrate.'

Matron Davies bends her grey head to her daughter, Ruth, and whispers in her ear. Ruth turns and whispers in Donald's ear. We watch as the secret sentence passes from ear to mouth round the table. Tansy is the last child to have the sentence whispered in her ear.

'What is the message, dear?' Miss Hordern asks.

Tansy lifts her head. 'The lazy lizard died of fright.'

Smiles and sniggers.

'What? The lazy lizard died of fright?' Miss Hordern says. 'Is that the message you whispered in Ruth's ear, Matron?'

'No,' she says. 'It was "Can you sail a ship by night?"'

'What was Dunkirk?' I ask Pamela.

'You silly, don't you know? The whole British army was stuck on the beach at Dunkirk when the Germans were chasing them out of France. That's when Hugh's father was killed. The German pilots would fly their planes down low over the beach where the soldiers had nowhere to hide and bombard them with their bullets.'

'Oh, how terrible.'

Fraser says, 'They were sitting ducks, my dad told me.'

'Everybody in England who had a boat or a ship sailed across the English Channel to rescue the army stuck on the beach. Thousands of ships sailed for days and nights. I'm sure that's why Matron Davies chose her secret message.'

'I say, Dad says all those ships and boats sailing across the channel to rescue the British Army from the beaches saved the world from Hitler. Because those soldiers lived to fight another day.'

Tansy's brother Ben begins marching with a high goose-step, arms sticking out straight.

'If you think about it, if the British Army wasn't rescued at Dunkirk, Hitler would have conquered the world, everybody would be learning German now and saying "Mein Führer" and forced to read *Mein Kamf*,' Fraser says.

Hugh's face gets red and he hangs his head. His father wasn't so lucky, he wasn't rescued at Dunkirk. He's the oldest child in the school, ten years old. He only just remembers his father.

Ben's friend Connor says, 'I'd nivver say Mein Phoorer. Phooey. I'd be like William Wallace and fight tae the end.'

'My Dad read *Mein Kamf* and he said it was a load of rubbish,' Fraser growls. 'Hitler was a maniac.'

'Maniacmaniacmaniac ...' Connor chants until Fraser hits him on the head.

'Let's play Huns and Brits,' little Donald shouts.

The boys run off, arguing about who will be a Hun and who will be a Brit. They make sounds of diving planes and rattling guns.

'Come, Karin,' Pamela pulls me away. 'My mother would like you to come to our house next weekend. Would you like to come?'

'Of course!'

When Siward and Frida had arrived in Horstadt's fjord after fleeing Northumbria, he'd sent for Orm the Necromancer. Orm had shaken his bag of runes, pulled out a handful and arranged them in a circle on the ground. 'There will be a Great Death in Northumbria and its surrounding country,' he said. 'But Halkell and Gisebert will survive. They will not forget how you abducted Frida and made her your bride. Have Snorri make a suit of enchanted chain-mail and neither lance nor sword shall kill you as long as you wear hauberk and helm.'

Orm had leaned heavily on his stick, 'I will send Hauk the Eagle, my eyes, to scout the terrain near where you live when I sense approaching danger. When that time comes, you will dig the trenches and sharpen the bones ...'

The afternoon is hot and sleepy. The sun beats down in blazing waves. Everybody is resting, hiding from this draining heat. Jack and Mom lie on their bed behind their closed door.

Last Saturday when Pammie and I were talking on her bed, her Mom, Alice, came into the room and sat with us. She spoke to us as if we were her special, dearest friends. Her wide blue eyes watched us closely from under her Prince Valiant fringe. She spoke about important things, like being kind and always telling the truth.

'If I teach Pammie one thing and one thing only – that is to tell the truth always – well, then,' she smiled, 'I will have done my duty as a mother. There is nothing more harmful than secrets and lies.'

Mom comes into my room. She is wearing a white dress with blue stripes, a white belt and white flat shoes. Her black hair hangs in shiny waves, her eyes are tired. I feel a rush of love for her. I get off the bed and hug her. She smells of Drene shampoo and Lily-of-the-Valley. It worries me that Mom tries to hide the truth. The truth about the divorce from my father, and pretending that Jack is my real father. Anybody can see Jack doesn't behave like a father.

'I want you to get ready, Karin,' she says. 'Put on another dress, brush your hair. We are having tea with Helen Nesbit and we are walking over the field to her house.'

'Jack?'

'He's resting. He's working tonight.'

My heart does a little tap dance. I change quickly then follow Mom into the compound. We walk through the hot, dry stillness, rustle past the leafy branches of the red hibiscus bushes around the huts and slide down into the gully where the banana trees grow. Mom stops and puts a hand on my arm. 'What's that smell?'

I raise my head and sniff. It smells like raw meat, like blood.

Under one of the banana trees I see somebody has made a rough wooden hut with a roof of banana leaves. Inside the hut is a small clay figure standing on short fat legs like a dwarf. Her stomach (I can see it's a she) is enormous. Clay knobs make eyes, nose and a navel in the stomach. There's a slit mouth. Blotches of blood stain a rock at the feet of the figure, little streams run down the cracks in the stone.

Chicken feathers stick to the patches of blood. I remember the smell of Frida's blood mixed with chicken curry and want to vomit. I think of the juju skulls and feathers at the market in Lagos and my lunch returns to my throat, a hot sour taste.

I point to the shrine. Mom pulls in her breath and twists her mouth.

'Damn,' she says. 'Amos and his juju. I hate this. It's a fertility shrine. He wants children from his Fulani child-bride.'

She pulls at my arm, her face stares down at the shrine until we leave the gully. 'I must tell Rob about this,' she says. 'The Hausa servants are forbidden to practise juju here.'

Our shoes swish along the path trodden in the bush between Rob's house and our own. Our straw hats are little umbrellas shielding us from the fierce rays of the Nigerian sun. I squash down the sour taste in my mouth but my stomach feels sick. Oh no, I remember, I haven't brought my book with me. There's nothing to do while Mom and Helen talk. 'Mom.'

She stops on the path in front of me and turns her head.

'I've forgotten my book. You go on. I'll run back, then I'll catch up with you.'

I go back on my footsteps along the path, my body is soaked in sunshine. I slip-run down into the banana grove, turn my eyes away from the clay figure and the blood, climb up the other side, trot past the huts, the hibiscus bushes, and slow down when I get to the back door of the bathroom. I don't want to wake Jack. I tip-toe across the cement floor, my hat has fallen off my head. I'm half-way to my bedroom when I hear the noises. Mom's bedroom door is open. I'm sure it was closed when we left.

Cruump-thump from the bedroom. My heart stops. Soft moany-groans. I tip-toe extra quietly, holding my breath. I take hold of my book on my bed and turn back to the bathroom.

Jack is moaning a lot, he sounds as if he's in pain. I don't know what to do. Should I run and call Mom?

I slip very slowly to the crack between the door and the frame. I can see Jack's sticky, Brylcreemed hair bobbing on his forehead, his beak nose shiny with sweat and his open mouth letting out sighs and moans. His hoods are shut. He's rocking on top of something.

I turn my head. I can see the Fulani girl's black olive eyes looking up at the ceiling. Her cinnamon skin is shiny.

I hear a loud 'OOH, GO-OD' from Jack, followed by a sobbing 'aagh-aagh-aagh'. The bed stops creaking. Silence. I'm edging towards the door. As I reach it, I hear her speak in a soft voice, 'Dash, masta, dash.'

My heart is clanging like a bell in my chest. My legs are heavy jelly. I can't run fast enough to get away from the house. I tear into the banana grove, don't even notice the clay figure. I run along the trodden track, not seeing where I'm going. I look up and there's Mom walking up the gravel driveway to the Nesbit's house.

What will I tell Mom? I can't tell Mom anything. She might get angry, say I've made it up, it's all my imagination. I think what I saw is a secret.

'My guidness! Wha's wrong wi' the bairn?' Helen's smile disappears. She looks at my red, sweaty face and wipes my damp hair from my eyes. 'Sit doon. I'll get ye a glass o' water.'

I sit on a chair, my chest heaving. Mom stares at me, her eyebrows lift as if to say, 'What now?'

Helen brings me a glass of water, my hands shake so much I spill some water on the carpet. 'Steady, noo,' Helen holds the glass for me. 'Irene, are ye sure this child hasna had a fright?'

'Well,' says Mom, 'now that you mention it, we discovered a fertility shrine where the bananas grow at the bottom of the compound. I think Amos sacrificed a chicken there, blood and feathers everywhere. He's definitely practising juju. Perhaps you could mention it to Rob?'

'Mmmh.' Helen doesn't look convinced.

'And she forgot her book and had to run back to the house to fetch it.' Mom looks at me. 'I have a bookworm for a daughter.'

'Weel, tha's no sich a bad thing. Wha' are ye reading? *Siward Silk-Hair, the Viking*? Is it no awfu' boring?'

Ali, Helen's cookboy carries in a tray of tea and cakes. He puts the tray down on a centre table made of black wood and Helen pours.

Their lounge has thick carpets and soft couches, beautiful black wood chairs with thick material on the seats. 'It's ebony,' Helen says when she sees my look, 'made in the Congo.' The room is full of flowers and pictures and ornaments.

I sit still, my book open on my knees, thinking. My heart has stopped thumping. Jack has a secret. I saw it and now it's my secret as well. I pretend to read but my mind is racing round and round like a hamster on a wheel.

Helen goes to a cupboard and pulls out a record in a brown paper cover. 'I have a treat fer ye.' She puts the record on the turntable and moves the arm over. 'Hae ye heard o' the Luton Girls' Choir? No? Verra famous. Listen to this.'

She sets the arm down and after a few scrapes of the needle, the most beautiful silvery-gold sound pours into the room, so beautiful I want to cry. I wipe a tear from my eye before Mom sees. My scalp prickles. Tingles run down my spine. A waterfall sound of silver bells and flutes flows from the throats of schoolgirls – they must be angels – pouring their voices into a stream of silver and gold. I feel as if I'm drowning in this sound, my heart aches and tears prick my eyelids. It's so beautiful, I can't bear it.

My fear and worry pack their bags and leave as this sound covers me and carries me into my blue space. I close my eyes and disappear.

When the music ends and I have to come back. I hear Helen saying, 'Nae doot ye ken, Irene, wha' a dreamer yer daughter is ...' Helen's brown eyes are warm.

She smiles, 'If ye like this record so much, Karin, ye can come anytime an' I'll play it fer ye.'

The music plays in my head for a long, long time. I remember all the notes and most of the words. At home, I fill the dragon bath with browny-beige water, lock Mom's bedroom door and the back door into the compound. I lie in the warm water and wonder how I can leave here and go to Luton and try and join this famous choir. If I misbehave, would Jack live up to his word and send me back? Oh, dream, dream of escape.

> Siward and Frida lay hidden in the green-grass fen, the sea of reeds and the dark alder beds. They listened to the tramp of Halkell's men-at-arms as they passed close by. Frida had begged Siward not to confront Halkell with his Karls. 'He will strip me naked and burn me at the stake,' she cried.
>
> They were tired and anxious, having hidden and run for some days.
>
> Frida wiped her eyes. 'The stars told me I would have nothing but sorrow since first I saw your face.'
>
> 'Why did you marry me then?' asked Siward.
>
> 'Because I loved you. I love you still.'

I watch Mom from my doorway as she stands in front of the bathroom mirror. She's looking at herself extra carefully. We're going to the club tonight to see a play. It's called Amateur Dramatics. Helen and Andy are part of it because they belong to the Caledonian Society. Helen isn't acting, though, like Andy. She's a stage manager.

Mom's behaving funny-strange tonight. She's taken ages to bathe and dress. Now she's smiling at herself in the mirror, wetting a finger and smoothing her thin eyebrows, parting her lips and smiling, as if she sees someone else in the mirror. Her eyes still look tired but they shine with excitement. She brushes more mascara on her lashes to make them look longer. She steps back and smoothes her green dress over her hips and stomach. She pulls her stomach in. I turn away before she sees me.

I wait until I hear the wheels of the Buick crunch on the gravel outside. Jack's coughing again. It sounds as if he's trying to cough his insides out. His gravelly voice calls from the dining-room, 'Are ye no ready yet, Irene?'

'Coming,' says Mom, picking up her black beaded evening bag. She takes my hand and pulls me.

I can't look at Jack anymore without seeing him the way I saw him last Saturday. I've kept out of his way since – I've been at school. I only go into their part of the house when he's asleep or at work, but now I have to sit in the car with him. Mom pulls me into the back seat with her. Jack sits in front with Ernest.

Mom stares out of the window and Jack looks straight ahead. Nobody says a word on the long ride to Barakin Ladi. When Ernest turns round the island of cannas in front of the steps of the Yelwa Club and parks the car, I wait for Jack to lift himself out of the front seat and move away before I climb out. Mom sits in the back seat, patting her nose with powder and licking the curls around her cheeks.

People are wandering around the club with drinks in their hands, their voices make a humming noise as they stand and talk. I can see Rex Niven, the Nesbits and Dick and Daisy. And there's Pammie and her parents. Jack says, 'I'm goin' tae the bar fer a dram.'

In a minute he brings Mom a sherry. They sip in silence. *Jack sipping?* badgirl says.

I talk to Pammie in the corner. I can see Rex Niven watching Mom and Jack.

The ballroom is dark. The red curtains are closed. Mrs Stevenson plays music while we wait. A small lamp shines on her music sheets. Before they switch off the lights I read the programme. Jack doesn't come in from the bar.

The Voice of the Turtle by John Van Druten
Setting: An apartment in New York.
Time: A weekend in April 1943.
Three Characters: Sally, an aspiring actress, as American as
creamy vanilla milkshake.
Bill, an American Sergeant on leave from the war.
Olive, Sally's friend, a woman of the world.
Three Acts.

We can hear whispering and shuffling from behind the curtains before they creak open. The stage shows a sitting room, to the left, a kitchen, most of it painted on a backdrop; to the right, a bedroom. On the painted backdrop there's a window with skyscrapers in the distance.

Brenda McDonald plays the role of Sally who wants to be an actress. Her friend Olive is played by – it looks like but can't possibly be – Kay Hordern? She wears a yellow wig, stacks of make-up and her white teeth bite out words in an American accent. She's also wearing *trousers*. Under the bright lights their eyes look huge, their faces rosy – even Andy's.

Andy wears the brown uniform of an American soldier. He's on leave from the war and wants to go out on a date with Olive/Kay Hordern but she dumps him for another man. Sally has been dumped by her boyfriend, a person we never see. Bill/Andy and Sally/Brenda, both dumped, go on a date and get to know each other in the apartment.

They talk about themselves, their feelings, their fears and what they want and don't want. Bill and Sally recite poetry to each other. The actors walk and talk in a light brighter than the sun; I feel as if I'm watching their lives, made bigger and slower, through a microscope. It makes you wonder. Mom whispers, 'This is too sophisticated for you.'

In the end, Sally and Bill fall in love with each other. The curtain comes down on the two of them sitting on a couch, holding hands, looking into each other's eyes while a man on the radio sings, '*I would be your slave, if you would be my queen* …' Then the lights go out.

We sit in the dark, there's a hush, then there's a storm of clapping. In a minute the curtains open, all the lights go on, and the three of them, Bill, Sally and Olive stand in front of the footlights and bow. The audience whistles and thunder-claps.

Andy lifts his head from a bow, sees Mom sitting in the second row. His grooves show in his cheeks and he winks at her.

Mom comes into the bar, her frown lines are as sharp as knife blades. 'Jack, have you been in the bar all this time?' Her mouth is tight. 'I kept a seat for you. Why didn't you watch the play?'

'Wha' for? An' see Andy Stewart make a fule o' himsel'? I canna bear sich rubbish to begin wi'. Romantic nonsense.'

Happy, smiling people walk past the bar, talking, laughing. Pammie waves as she leaves with her parents.

There are invisible tight wires between Mom and Jack. They could snap at any minute. Mom's eyes lose their sparkle, the corners of her mouth droop and she looks as tired as I feel. She turns her head and sees everybody leaving the club. Andy is walking out with Brenda McDonald.

We wait for Jack to finish his drink as people talk and laugh and walk out into the night. My body is filling with heavy sinking sand. I can hardly move. I want to fall onto the back seat of the Buick and sleep forever, but Jack seems to be drinking extra slowly. He says to the barman, 'One more for the road.'

Mom's eyes shoot open, she opens and closes her mouth a few times. 'Jack, can we go now? Please. Karin is asleep on her feet.'

I watch Jack with sleepy eyes. His smile is sly, he watches Mom from under his hoods as if she's a rabbit he's about to catch in his talons. He's seen Andy winking at Mom from the stage and he's going to make her wait until he's ready to leave.

I'm too tired to think. My badgirl voice whispers in my head, *Tell her what you saw and heard when she was walking to the Nesbit's house.* But I'm too scared of Jack.

Jack drains his last mouthful of whiskey. We walk out into the night, our feet make loud crunches on the gravel. Ernest sees us coming and starts the engine.

The moon is a thin smile in the black face of the sky. The stars sparkle with secrets. Jack sits in front with Ernest and smokes like a chimney all the way home. The fumes choke me. I wind my window down to breathe the clean air. Mom sits on the back seat next to me, her hands rest on her lap. We drive in a silent car through a black night throbbing with drums.

At home I fall asleep to the sound of Jack's voice droning like an angry bumble bee. Drone ... drone ... drone.

Amos holds his baby between his knees, his lips spread wide and show his brown betel nut teeth. The baby's arms look like fat sausages joined to the cushion of her body. She wears a necklace of glass beads and nothing else.

'Jamilah. Her name be Jamilah.'

'Jamilah.' I take hold of her chipolata fingers and shake them.

'Dis baby, Jamilah, she be gawn walk chop-chop.'

I tickle Jamilah's stomach, touch her button nose and smile into her round brown eyes. She gurgles, showing four tiny teeth in her gums.

'By 'n by number two wife, Adia, be gawn make baby,' Amos says, turning his head to look at the Fulani girl sitting outside her hut.

I walk past her mat where she sits cross-legged. She threads beads onto a piece of string. Coloured glass beads spread out in front of her. She has finished necklaces and bracelets in complicated patterns. Her hair is tied into pigtails sticking up all over her head and decorated with bright beads. She wears necklaces and earrings, bracelets and anklets. She looks like an African doll, as if her face has been carved from wood.

I'm tired and bored. I can't wait to go to school tomorrow. Jack's in his sanctuary, sitting in a cloud of fumes. Mom's working in the garden somewhere. I drag my feet into the gazebo and sit on the low wall. What can I do?

I hear voices whispering. I move towards the sound. I part the leaves and petals. I can see bits of Mom and Andy Stewart a few feet away. Mom's crying, making soft sniffles. I see Andy's fingers rub her tears away.

He puts his hands on either side of her face. 'Irene. Irene.'

Whisper, whisper. Andy bends his head until it rests on Mom's, '... ye've had a raw deal ... comfort ye ... ye ken, I hae feelings fer ...'

Mom whispers, '... what will people say ...?'

'It's yer life, Irene ...' Andy's hands rub Mom's bare arms. Her long nose quivers. They stare at each other. Andy strokes Mom's hair. 'Anybody can see Jack has a drinkin' problem ... can see things are no guid between ...'

Mom drops her eyelids, her lips hardly open. 'What will Rob think?'

'... hope Rob's tae busy to notice,' Andy whispers in Mom's ear.

I move away from the bougainvillea. I don't want to watch this. I step out of the gazebo.

Jack's voice makes a loud sound in the quiet garden. His face looks out of the dining-room window. His mouth is a black hole. 'Irene? Where the divil are ye? Irene?'

I creep through the compound, over the cement walkway, into the bathroom, then my bedroom. I sit at my table and read.

Gunnar heard the rush of wings and, turning, saw Hauk descend at speed. He lifted his arm. Hauk folded his pinions and alighted with a rustle of feathers. He leaned towards Gunnar's ear and krr-krred. Gunnar nodded then, moving to Siward, spoke low in his ear, 'Hauk has seen a score or more of armed men on horseback approaching. They'll be here the day after tomorrow.'

Siward remembered the words of Orm – 'Dig pits and sharpen bones.' The men dug pits to the south and the east of the homestead. They dug swiftly, their arms strong from the work of rowing and fighting. When they were finished, Siward and Gunnar took antlers of red deer and the bones of their ribs, all sharpened to fine points and embedded them in the bottoms of the pits. They laid thin branches of willows over the the surface of the pits then covered that with strips of turf. Then a few hours before crow light, they armed themselves and lay in wait behind the pits.

Halkell's men came creeping silently, running bent over. Those in front fell into the pits and impaled themselves. Their comrades saw the trap they had fallen into and tried to aid the dying men. Great was their groaning until they died. Siward and Gunnar and the others held the remaining men to watch their slow dying then slit their throats. They threw their bodies in the pits to join those of their impaled comrades, then covered them up so that by sunrise there was no sign of what had transpired.

Siward took Frida and his men and all their goods and moved swiftly north. They found the horses of Halkell's men tethered a distance away and took charge of them. He settled Frida in safety with her nurse and a handful of men and left to join the JomsVikings on the *Skidbladnir.*

Amos brings me supper in my bedroom. Later, I hear Mom and Jack argue. Her voice is squeaky-high. It gets loud then soft. It sounds as if she wants to cry and scream at the same time. Jack is coughing and sneezing. I imagine snot and saliva splattering down his front. I don't know how Mom can look at him when he sprays goo like a baby.

'You can't go on like this, Jack,' Mom's saying. 'You drink far too much. Rob will see and you'll lose your promotion.'

'Wha' I do in the privacy of my ane hame, is nobody's business but mine. As long as I perform to the best of my ability at work, there is nothing Rob or anybody else can do. Do ye hear? An' if ye dinna like it, Irene, ye can find anither husband or go back tae where ye came frae.'

My stomach does somersaults, my supper slops around. I feel sick when I hear Jack's growling voice. I click open the locks of my suitcase to remind myself I will be going to school first thing in the morning. There they are. All the dresses Mom's sewn. A clean one for every day. The one with puff sleeves made out of lilac check material; the blue one with the Peter Pan collar and little rosebuds embroidered on it; the green and white striped. Mom's made these dresses out of some of her old ones. I feel silly wearing these dresses. The one I hate the most is a pale turquoise lace dress with a slippery petticoat. Turquoise lace. Uggh. It's torture for me to wear that dress. I can see the looks of pity on Tansy and Pammie's faces. Why won't Mom make me shorts and tops?

I climb under the mosquito net with Frida, my torch and Siward. I long for tomorrow. When my eyes get heavy, I switch off the torch and lie in the dark. The snakes slither off the branches and thud onto the roof. My stomach clenches into a fist to think that one of them might be the mate of the black mamba.

Tonight the moon shows through the black trees like a bony white face. Shadows of leaves and branches move on the walls.

Matron Davies carries in a surprise after lunch; a cake with pink icing and nine candles for my birthday. Miss Hordern lights the candles and says, 'I know it's your birthday on Sunday, Karin, so we thought we'd give you a little pre-party before you go home. Make a wish.'

I close my eyes. I make three wishes. One, the black mamba will never find me. Two, I'll join the Luton Girls' Choir one day. Three, Jack will disappear.

Miss Hordern leaves the room and returns with three small parcels.

She has wrapped a copy of *Robin Hood of Sherwood Forest*. Matron Davies has given me a hankie she's embroidered herself with teeny stitches. Mrs Stevenson has given me a square box of Black Magic chocolates. I can't speak I'm so happy. I thank them with my eyes. We eat the cake, every last crumb.

I carry my presents to pack into my case. Then I remember something with a whoosh of joy. I'm not going home this weekend. I'm going home with Tansy.

Mrs Roberts' stomach is as big as two balloons. Her belly button sticks out like the tied end of a blown-up balloon. It looks as if it's going to burst. She's squashed behind the wheel of their car when we arrive at the meeting place at Bukuru. Ben sits in the front with her, his eyes look huge behind glasses. He's reading a book called *A Guide for Young Stargazers*.

It's a short drive to the house next to the Anglican Church. The church has a white cross on the roof. The house next door is small with dark rooms. Inside the front door there's a wooden cross with a hanging Jesus on the wall. The rooms smell of musty books and burning candles, it smells the way I think a monastery or a nunnery would smell.

'My parents are teetotallers,' Tansy says as she leads me to her room. 'We don't have alcohol in the house. Mom and Dad only have special wine for Holy

Communion because they have to pretend they're drinking the blood of Jesus.'

We put our suitcases down. She stares at me with her fat black eyes. 'Mom says everybody else on the Jos Plateau drinks alcohol.'

I must never take Tansy to our house. Her mother would have a conniption fit if she heard Jack was in his cups.

Tansy's father looks like Snow White's Happy dwarf without the droopy night cap. He wears a stiff white collar round his neck like a necklace over his grey shirt. His eyes are blue sparkles behind his round granny glasses. He smiles all the time, even when he's talking.

We hold hands at the dinner table while Mr Roberts says grace. 'For what we are about to receive may the Lord make us truly thankful ... and bless our young guest who breaks bread with us.'

My shyness ties my tongue in knots. Jack shuts me up so often, I've forgotten how to talk to grown-ups. So I nod, say yes and no, thanks and please. Reverend Roberts asks about school and he listens to what Tansy and Ben have to say. Tansy's all fired up about the Sumerians and Ben wants to watch the night sky and find comets and stars. He would like a telescope. 'On our next long leave, I promise,' says Reverend Roberts. His glasses twinkle-shine in the candlelight as he looks at me. 'And what about you, Karin?' he smiles. His teeth are baby-size with big gaps. He waits.

I swallow my food and say, 'Umm, I like to read.'

'Good, good.' He nods. For a second he looks like a toy dwarf whose head bobs all the time. We stack our plates on the sideboard. Mrs Roberts carries in a big bowl of steaming plum pudding, then a jug of custard. She says she likes to cook for her family with her own hands. 'I cook our food with love,' her eyes shine like copper pennies in the candlelight. They light candles for every evening meal.

She reads to us at bedtime. She lowers her heavy body into an armchair with a sigh. She puts on her glasses and reads, resting the book on the bulging mountain of her stomach. She reads about Mole and Ratty and messing in boats on the river. Every so often she looks over the top of her glasses at us and says 'oh my' or 'fancy that' as if she's also enjoying the story. I watch her stomach as I listen, her belly button pokes at her cotton dress, then – I blink my eyes to make sure I'm not imagining it – I see a squirmy something wriggle and kick under her dress. The squirmy thing is trying to get out. I look at Tansy, but she's watching her mother's face and hasn't seen the wriggle in her stomach.

After Ratty and Mole, Tansy and I jump out of our beds and kneel on the floor while Mrs Roberts says a blessing prayer. When we say Amen and jump back into bed so she can tuck us in, she says, 'I hope your mother reads to you and listens to your prayers, Karin?'

I nod. I can't tell her that Mom doesn't believe in God anymore. Or she prefers to sit worrying and watching Jack drink whisky until he's in his cups. Instead of listening to my prayers, she listens to his droning.

In the dark I play back pictures of Tansy's mom this weekend – how she pants and heaves to get in and out of chairs, how her back hurts from carrying this heavy bulge. How she clutches her back as if to hold it up. 'I wish I could sleep at night,' she moans. I can see she's tired; her eyes have black half-moons underneath.

'Tansy?' I say in the dark. 'Are you asleep?'

'Mmm. What?'

'How will the baby get out of your mother's stomach?'

'The doctor at the hospital helps the baby to come out.'

'But how?'

'There's a special place where the seed went in and that's where the baby comes out.'

I think about the size of Mrs Roberts' stomach and the holes we have in our bodies. The baby can't come out of any of our body holes.

'Maybe the doctor cuts it out?"

'No, silly-billy. Go to sleep.' Tansy's voice is muffled. She's not listening, not caring.

I worry in the dark for a long time. The squirmy baby must be desperate to get out. I can't imagine being stuck in such a small space for so long, but I must have been. I'll ask Mom about how babies get born.

I tell Ernest to drive faster, I'm in a hurry to get home. The spinning wheels of the Dodge kick up a storm of dust leaving a tail like a comet behind us. Ernest likes to drive fast. He crouches over the wheel like a racing driver, chewing on his stick.

The minute I get home I'm going to ask Mom. I have to know.

Ernest brakes outside our house. He's skidded round the island of cannas in the front compound. I climb out with my suitcase, a cloud of dust settles on me.

I wait for Ernest to skid away, then I open the front door and wait. I smell fumes, hear Harry Lauder singing. *He's drunk again*, badgirl says. I pick up my suitcase with both hands, it bumps against my legs, and walk around the side of the house to the back door. I drop the suitcase on the walkway.

Mom's in the pantry, she's wearing an apron and a scarf tied on top of her hair. She's reaching up, washing the shelves with soapy water and a scouring pad. All the packets and bottles are on a table. Her face is dreamy because she's lost in work. She loves cleaning. Little beads of sweat sit on her top lip. She hasn't heard me come in. I sigh through my nose.

She doesn't turn. She finishes wiping a shelf dry. 'Karin. You're back.'

'Yes.'

'Did you have a good time?' Mom finishes drying and starts to wipe bottles of Worcestershire Sauce, HP Sauce and all the brown syrupy sauces that Jack likes. She wipes bottles of piccalilli, tomato chutney, pickled cucumbers, pickled peppers.

'Mom?'

She puts bottles in the order of the alphabet – allspice, aniseed, basil, bay leaves, cinnamon, cloves, coconut, cumin ...

'Mom? How are babies born?' The words burst from my mouth, loud and fast.

Her hands stop moving. She freezes, then – 'Oh, Karin, must you ask questions like that now? I want to finish cleaning the pantry before Amos brings in supper.'

As if he's heard, Amos clangs pots in the cookhouse.

'But Mom ...'

Silence. Mom's lips move. Dill, fennel.

I stare miserably at her back.

'They'll tell you about those things at school when you're older ... let me see, now ... ginger, ground chilli ...'

'Mom ...'

She ignores me, picks up a jar of picallili.

Get her attention, badgirl shouts. 'Mrs Roberts says you're not bringing me up properly. She says you're just dragging me up.' My own words shock me. Where did they come from? A whopping big lie.

Mom's eyes spin round; her mouth drops open, the bottle of picallili slips from her fingers and explodes on the floor. 'What did you say?' The colour is rushing away on Mom's face into two red spots on her cheeks.

'Uh, Mrs Roberts says you're only dragging me up.'

Mom's eyes blaze blue lazer-beams at me. I shrivel under their glare.

'Oh, she does, does she? I'll have to have a word with Mrs Roberts tomorrow morning.'

My throat sticks to itself. My stomach clutches itself in a row of granny knots. I want Mom to put her arms around me and say, 'Nonsense, nobody cares for you as much as I do. Silly Mrs Roberts.'

Jack shouts from the sitting room. 'Chrissake, Irene, wha's all that bloody racket? Must ye make sich a noise?'

'I'll give Mrs Roberts a piece of my mind ... just wait until tomorrow, I'll give her what-for.' Mom stares at the yellow mess of vegetables and broken glass on the floor. The smell of mustardy spices hits my nose.

I sit on my bed. I sag from a huge load of worries. I'm going to be sick. I can't read. I hear Mom and Jack arguing in the house. He stumble-bumps from room to room. I close my door quickly.

Mom carries in a tray with my supper. Then she brings an armful of clean clothes for the next school week. Her face is carved out of stone.

Mom's forgotten my birthday.

In the night I hear Jack emptying gallons of pee into the toilet, he wakes me up. Then I dream of angry faces shouting at me and lies like cartoon balloons coming out of my mouth. I try to close my mouth but I can't stop the whoppers. I dream of Mrs Roberts's stomach exploding, spraying everybody with blood, bits of stomach and baby pieces.

The bumping Dodge is a tumbrel. I'm Marie Antoinette on the way to the guillotine to have my head cut off. I'm a Roman Gladiator standing on the sand of the Colosseum, holding my sword up to Caligula, the Roman Emperor – 'We who are about to die salute you.' I close my eyes and see Siward's light-coloured eyes looking at me with disappointment. Only cowards lie. I hear Pammie's Mom saying over and over in my head, 'Always tell the truth.'

The sun's only just begun to climb the sky but already it's baking hot. I'm cold, as cold as I was in the freezing mornings going to school in Perth. The yellow school bus is waiting. Mothers and children are there with their suitcases.

I see Mrs Roberts straight away and so does Mom. She's just pushed herself out of her car, her stomach sticking out in front of her, covered in a dress like a tent. Tansy and Ben stand on either side of her. Tansy waves and smiles and Mrs Roberts turns her head towards us, a glad look on her face.

Mom steps out of the Dodge and makes a beeline for Mrs Roberts, her legs covering the ground in long steps. I pull at Mom's skirts and say, 'Mom, please ... Mom, don't.' But Mom brushes me off as if I'm a flea.

I can see Mrs Roberts is surprised by Mom's angry face, her smile shrinks and disappears. Mom stops in front of Mrs Roberts, puts her hands on her hips and says, 'How DARE you?'

Mrs Roberts waits, her eyes pop from Mom to me. I hide behind Mom's skirt.

'How dare you say I'm not bringing my daughter up properly? Who do you think you are? Who are you to criticise me ... you sanctimonious wife of a missionary ... only dragging her up? ... I'll have you know ...'

I stop listening. My heart shakes with fear and misery. *Mom, Mom,* I scream silently. *Stop.*

When she understands what Mom is trying to say, Mrs Roberts sends one hurt, horrified look at me. She opens her mouth to speak – 'But ... but ...'

Mom doesn't listen, she repeats all her words, over and over. 'I'll have you know ...'

She ends her attack with one loud 'NOW', spins on her heel and marches back to the Dodge.

Mrs Roberts stares after her with shock in her wide open eyes and hanging mouth. 'Mrs Carmichael, I assure you ...'

Her words fade away. Everybody stares at me and at Mom climbing back into the Dodge. I wish the ground would open up and swallow me whole.

I scrape my feet towards the bus, climb the steps and sink into the first empty seat. I hang my head then lean my forehead on the metal rail of the seat in front.

It smells oily-dirty. My stomach hurts. I hear children move past me to other seats. Nobody talks to me or looks at me.

This rotting-maggoty feeling won't leave my stomach. I am a rotten child. I sit rocking on a swing under the mango trees in the dip at the end of the compound. Ben runs down the slope towards me. He bends and picks up a rotting mango and throws it at me. It hits me wham-squish in my left eye. 'Yaah. Liar. Liar liar, pants on fire.'

Connor, Ben's friend, shouts, 'Yer nose is growing longer – I can see it growin' by the second.'

'Liar liar, pants on fire.'

Connor looks around. His face twists with glee when he sees the three of us are alone.

'Bloody bugger.'

Tee-hee. They snigger and run away.

My eye burns and waters. For the first time I don't want to be at school. I don't want to be anywhere. I think about the lies Mom wants me to tell – Jack's my father when he isn't. She hasn't been divorced when she has. Jack's normal, he doesn't drink.

When I'm not at lessons, I stay away from the others. I sit somewhere, on a rock, hidden by a tree, in the library, my eye waters and I hug my sick-rotty stomach. Miss Hordern looks at me with a strange glint in her eye, but I slip away to bed before she can ask questions.

I'm crying hot tears into my pillow, glad I'm covered by the mosquito net and the dark when I hear a rustle next to my ear. Pammie slides into the bed with me. She strokes my shoulder and my head. The feel of her warm hand makes me cry harder.

'I didn't mean to lie. It just came out.'

'It's alright,' she says. 'We all make mistakes.'

'But I've hurt Tansy and her family.'

'They'll forget about it soon. Tell her it was a mistake.'

'She won't listen.'

Mrs Stevenson is playing plinky-plonk on the piano. It's jumping music so we're crouching like frogs hip-hopping round the classroom. The playing changes to gliding water music and we're swans with long necks gliding-paddling on a smooth pond.

Another sound joins the running piano notes – a crack like a firecracker far away in the sky. Mrs Stevenson looks out of the window. The sky's getting dark. Giant purple black clouds rumble-tumble and growl over the sky towards our school.

When it's the rainy season I can stand in the garden and feel the rain coming every afternoon at five o' clock. It's as if invisible wires are whispering, 'The rain's coming.' It's almost like the air is trying to sing.

But today it's different, it's not rain, it's a storm.

The air crackles with electricity, the clouds boil, then lightning bang-flashes across the sky. Zigs and zags and sheets.

All of us, teachers and children wait at the window. We shiver in the cold. Fat heavy drops of rain thud onto the ground and the tin roof. Fat-splat heavy drops. Then the noise turns to banging. The drops of rain have turned into balls of ice.

The garden, green and gold and red not long ago, is thick with white hailstones. Our eyes pop at the sight of a winter garden. 'It's magic,' a small girl cries. The white cold stones crash onto our roof. We can't hear each other. We wait and stare. Then after a long time, someone or something waves an unseen stick that signals stop and the hailstones settle. The clouds roll onwards and the lightning vanishes.

We push open the door and step out onto a carpet of hailstones – scrunch, scrunch. Our feet sink ankle-deep into the icy piles of stones.

Mrs Stevenson picks up a stone and holds it with both hands. 'In twenty years of living here I have never seen a sight like this.' She waves her arms. 'Take note, children, of what you see. One day you can tell your grandchildren you saw hailstones the size of rocks, big enough to kill a cow, on the Jos Plateau in 1950.'

'Mmm, remarkable,' Miss Hordern's teeth are chattering with cold.

Matron Davies catches her breath in her throat. 'Aah, it's like home, just.'

The boys pick up hailstones and throw them at each other. Pammie, Tansy and Ruth try to build a snowman by piling stones high but it looks more like a pyramid. I pick up a ball of ice, my hands ache with cold. Everybody drops their ice balls and blows on their hands. The branches of trees and flowers have been bashed by the wild wind, rain and the hailstones. The flowers are flattened, the tree branches hang slanty. The sun shines with a pale light when the last of the storm clouds disappear into the blue. Later the hailstones melt and sink into the ground. The garden has a layer of melting ice, it looks fresh and clean-washed like a new slate. The air smells like rainwash.

We're sitting at the table in an ice-cream cone of light, waiting for Miss Hordern to read.

She's silent and her pale blue eyes blink a few times.

'Today is October 15th,' she says. 'My fiancée-pilot, Malcolm, died on this day ten years ago. He died fighting in a Spitfire during the Battle of Britain in the sky over the southern parts of England.'

She licks her lips and her throat swallows. I think she is trying not to cry. 'The average age of those pilots was twenty-one, and their life expectancy was eighty-seven flying hours. They stopped the Germans from invading our island. Millions of us owe our freedom to a handful of brave, true-blue young men.'

She opens a book and clears her throat. 'I'm going to read a poem in honour of those men. This poem was written by John Gillespie Magee when he was nineteen, which is also the age he was killed in a training accident. It is the most famous poem ever written about flight and is the official poem of the Royal Canadian Air Force and the Royal Airforce. It is called 'High Flight':

> Oh! I have slipped the surly bonds of earth
> And danced the skies on laughter-silvered wings;
> Sunward I've climbed, and joined the tumbling mirth
> Of sun-split clouds – and done a hundred things
> You have not dreamed of – wheeled and soared and swung
> High in the sunlit silence. Hov'ring there
> I've chased the shouting wind along, and flung
> My eager craft through footless halls of air.
> Up, up the long delirious, burning blue,
> I've topped the windswept heights with easy grace
> Where never lark, or even eagle flew –
>
> And, while with silent lifting mind I've trod
> The high untrespassed sanctity of space,
> Put out my hand and touched the face of God.'

Miss Hordern sighs and shuts her lips.

Adam cries out, 'Miss – Miss Hordern, I'm going to be a pilot.'

'Shut it, Ad,' says Fraser, his ears red.

'I am, too, I'm going to be an ace pilot.'

'I hope you never have to fight in a war.' Bridget Hordern's lips lift to show her teeth standing straight as sentries.

'Miss, Miss, why do they call them dogfights?'

'Have you ever seen dogs fight? They circle round and round each other closely, then dart in. That's what those fighter planes did – those, Hurricanes and Spitfires, Messerschmidts and Fokkers – zooming round and round each other.'

Miss Hordern's face is pink, her eyes shine. 'I'm going to write this poem on the blackboard tomorrow and you can copy it into your essay books. Use your dictionaries if there are any words you don't understand.'

When we've climbed into bed and Miss Hordern stands in the doorway of our dark dormitory, framed by the light behind her, she says our 'Now I lay me down to sleep' prayer then calls 'God Bless.' In that second I think she looks like an angel. I lift my head and call back, 'God Bless.'

Frida's croaky meow close to my ear wakes me. I don't want to wake up. Something's bothering me. I remember we're driving to the Yelwa Club late this afternoon in the Dodge for a grown-up supper and dance. I'll be stuck in the hot cabin of the Dodge with Jack for an hour. But it's not the thought of the drive that's bothering me. Then I remember. Before I fell asleep I read in my Siward book –'And Siward knew his end was near.'

I sit up, pull the mosquito net aside and open the book at page 518.

> Siward drank much mead at the midday meal, then lay down to sleep, forgetting to set guards to keep watch. He dreamed of all the men he had killed and seen being killed in battle until it seemed as if his whole life had been a stream of killing and dying with interludes of tranquil happiness with Frida. He woke with a feeling of heavy doom.
>
> All at once through sleep-slowed eyes he saw above him the fierce grim visage of Halkell and the sinister face of Sir Hoibricht. He saw ten other knights crowding at their elbows and knew he had been trapped; for once he had not been watchful.
>
> He sprang to his feet. Brain-biter and his enchanted armour were out of reach. Instead he took up his double-bladed axe. A knight rushed at him. Siward's axe clove his helm and lodged there. The end came swiftly. Five lances cut through his body.
>
> Siward clawed for a shield and threw it in the faces of the knights bearing down on him. 'Odin,' he shouted and fell dead.
>
> Hallkell stepped forward, looked down at his fallen foe. He growled, 'Outwit Halkell once but never twice.' He pushed aside Siward's long yellow locks and severed his head from his body in one savage stroke.
>
> They set the head of Siward on a spike above the hall-door as a warning to all who would cross Halkell.

I put the book down and howl. Tears pour out of my eyes, my nose swells and my mouth screeches. Snot and saliva pour down my front.

Mom comes running. 'What's the matter? Karin?' She peers at me with anxious eyes.

I can't speak. I can't stop my tears or my heaving chest.

Mom waits. Her eyebrows fold impatient arms. Her face is a blur.

'He's dead.'

'Who's dead?'

'Siward.'

'Oh. Is that all? Heavens, Karin, you had me worried for a minute.' She hummphs. 'Really, what a commotion over nothing. It's only a story. Siward wasn't real, he was just a person in a book.'

'He WAS real. He's real to me. He really lived and ... and now he's dead.'

'But,' says Mom, 'he died a long time ago.'

'I don't care. I only found out about it now.'

Mom stares at me. I moan and shake.

'I'll bring your breakfast on a tray. Come, cheer up. It's a beautiful day and you'll see your friends at the club tonight.'

'I can't eat. How can I eat when Si-wa-wa-ward is de-ead?'

'Wha' the bloody hell is wrong wi' her noo? Why is she greetin 'agin? Irene?' Jack shouts from their bedroom.

Mom's eyes get big. She shakes her finger at me, 'God, Karin, shut up. You're putting Jack in a bad mood and we don't want that, do we?'

'I don't care,' I moan.

He's always in a bad mood. So what? badgirl hisses.

'You only think about yourself. You're so self-indulgent.'

'How could they cut off his head? How are they going to bury him?' I choke on my gasping sobs.

'Karin, dear God.' Mom's getting mad. 'How should I know? Read and find out.'

She marches out and returns with a plate of greasy eggs and chips on a tray. She turns and walks out, her mouth tight and angry, her frown set like glue.

I put one chip in my mouth. It tastes dry as dust. I can't eat. I can never, ever read my Siward book now that he's been killed. I won't finish it.

Mom forces me to eat a cheese and cucumber sandwich at lunch time. I have to drink water to swallow it down. I wander round the compound. I keep seeing Siward's head stuck on a spike above the hall door, his fine hair sticky with dried blood, his mouth gaping open and the lids drooping over his unseeing eyes. Why did they behead people in the old days? Why was there so much killing? Miss Hordern says more than sixty million people were killed in the last war that ended a few years ago. I can't imagine how many tens and hundreds that is.

Bola's rolling sticky fufu balls then dipping them in a stew and feeding her baby girl. She crawls around on her fat knees, only sitting when Bola puts a ball in her mouth. She chews and swallows then opens her mouth and flaps her arms for more.

The Fulani girl, Adia, sits behind the fourth hut on a mat. She's sifting tiny seeds into the neck of a calabash, then puts a cork in the neck. She shakes the calabash from side to side, the seeds inside make a shoosh-shooshing sound. It's a peaceful sound. She stares at my red, swollen eyes and down-turned mouth, then holds out a bead bracelet. For a second our hands meet. I look into her chocolate brown eyes with their curly lashes. I wonder what it would be like to be her. She can't read or write. She has nothing except her mat, her beads and string. She has to obey Amos and Bola. I feel sorry for her.

The minute I feel pity, I feel better. My sadness gets lighter. I move towards the gazebo, picking up Frida on the way. I hug Frida's furry cushion of a body. Her eyes are green slits, she purrs like the Dodge stuttering up the hill. I bury my face in her fur and listen to her stuttering purr; my heart still hurts when I think of Siward and how he was killed. I sob into Frida's ear.

Mom's standing in the bathroom doorway. She's rushing. 'Hurry-hurry,' she says, her hair's rolled in curlers all over her head. She's rubbed white pancake stuff on her face to make her skin smooth. 'Jack has finished bathing. I want you to bath now, Karin, and get ready to go to the club. We have a long drive.'

I drag my feet across the gravel, still holding Frida.

'Don't dawdle,' Mom grabs Frida, pushes her out of the door and closes it. She switches on the taps, the geyser groans as the brown water gurgles out. 'Karin, get moving. I have to bath as well.'

I climb in the dragon's belly and wash with soapy brown suds. I feel dreamy and tired. I want to lie on my bed in a ball with Frida and think.

I wander into my bedroom to dress. I can't find my sandals. Where are they? I leave the bathroom through the back door. Mom will be furious if she finds me walking barefoot after my bath. I tip-toe to the dining-room and find them under the table. I bend and push the strap through the buckle. Someone calls my name.

'Karin. Karin,' the voice whispers. I'm not sure who it is. I tie my buckle and push the other strap in its buckle.

'Karin?'

This is strange. This must be Jack's voice. But he never calls my name. I finish putting on my sandals.

'Karin.' His voice is louder now. 'Come here.'

I walk slowly into Mom's bedroom. The curtains are half closed. The room is dark. The bathroom door is closed. Mom's running bath water. Jack is lying on his bed, he's dressed in his vest and shorts. His black chest hairs push out of his vest, they're wet and curly. His forehead and beak nose are shiny-sweaty, his eyes glitter under their hoods. He watches me come to his side of the bed. He wets his lips with his tongue. He smiles. His hand is moving up and down in the opening of his shorts. He looks down at his hand, then looks at me. He wants to show me something. He licks his lips. He looks down again, I follow his eyes. He's pulling something down there. I don't know what it is. I think it could be a little snake. Maybe he wants to show me a little snake between his fingers. Is it the mamba snake?

He pulls the snake up and down. His eyes never leave mine. He licks his lips over and over. A soft grunt comes from his lips. I want to cry out but then I see it's not a snake, it's something red and swelling bigger with a black hole at the fat mushroomy end. Jack's hand moves so fast now it's almost a blur, he grunts and moans softly, his eyes look as if they want to burn into mine.

I look at the bathroom door. Can't Mom hear? I don't know what's happening. What does he want? My heart bangs against my ribs. Thump-thump. Jack's tongue licks his grunts out. Unnh, Mmnh.

His hoods lift up, his eyes open wide, he looks as if he's going to explode. His body jerks, his eyes close, the swollen thing shoots gooey stuff out of the black hole onto the hairs on his leg. The air leaves Jack's mouth in a long hissing sigh. Sssss-ssh.

Uh. I gasp, I turn and run – out of the bedroom, through the dining-room into the kitchen and out of the house. My mouth sucks air into my body, my heart thumps extra loud in my ears. I run into the gazebo and crouch down next to the wall so nobody can see me. I shake. I put my hands over my eyes to shut out what I've seen. Then I put my hands over my ears to shut out the sound of Jack's voice.

I hear Mom's shoes on the gravel. She's calling me. I don't answer.

I look up. Mom's face stares down at me. Her frown lines are as sharp as her voice. 'What are you doing here? Hurry. Jack and I are waiting for you. Ernest is here with the Dodge. But we'll come home in the Buick so we can stay late.'

I can't move.

'Karin. I'm waiting, don't make me angry.'

My badgirl voice says, *Tell her you don't want to go.*

'I feel sick. I don't want to go.' This is not a lie. I do feel sick.

Mom looks at me. 'Where do you feel sick?'

'In my heart.'

'What? What does that mean? Really, Karin, I won't let you read books anymore if you behave like this. There's nothing wrong with you. It's just your imagination.'

'My stomach feels sick too.'

The Dodge horn hoots. Blaar-blaar.

Mom grabs my hand and pulls me out of the gazebo and drags me to the Dodge. Jack sits in the cabin next to Ernest. He doesn't look at Mom and me. She climbs in next to Jack. I sit sideways on Mom's lap so my back's to Jack. I can't look at him.

Ernest rips up the dust with the wheels, leaving clouds of sand behind us. It's hot. I can feel Jack's breath on my neck. Mom's wearing a red silk dress for the dance. She moves me around on her knees, she doesn't want her dress to wrinkle. I hang onto the end of the dashboard.

I try to sit like a feather on Mom's lap, I take in little sips of air. I can see Mom's face in the side mirror. Her lips flatten into a thin line and her brows knit to each other. I'm extra careful not to move, I stare at every bush and tree and cactus, every donkey and cow as if I've never seen them before.

Mom hummphs out a heavy sigh, 'Karen. Sit on Jack's lap, please. You're heavy and you're wrinkling my dress.'

I pretend I don't hear. I hang onto the dashboard.

'Karin.'

My badgirl voice whispers, *Tell her why you won't ever sit on Jack's lap again. Tell her about his snake-worm thing that grows big.*

But I can't. I know Mom won't believe me. She will just say it's my imagination.

She puts her hands under my arms and tries to move me onto Jack's lap. I slide off her lap and crouch on the floor of the cabin, my legs bent double, stuck next to my chest.

'Fer Chrissake, leave her,' Jack's voice is cold and hard.

The floor of the cab is uncomfortable and bouncy but I don't care. I put my chin on my knees and my arms round my legs.

When the Dodge stops, Mom opens the door and I tumble out. My legs ache. Before Mom can say anything, I run away. Into the garden, past people and children. I run to where the garden ends and look out at the empty bush, just grass and termite hills. I find a big rock and sit there next to a fat lizard. Nobody looks for me.

The sun is sinking fast, it's painting the bush with bits of gold. As the sky gets darker, the sun gets redder. I picture everybody sitting down to eat. Jack, Mom, Rob and Helen, Andy, Pammie will be there. I have to think out my thoughts and pretend nothing is wrong. I have to hide the shame. Jack has tricked me into another secret. I have a horrible feeling in my stomach, as if acid is burning my insides.

The sun blinks over the horizon like an angry red eye and disappears. The shadows stretch and grow long. I leave the lizard and walk back to the clubhouse. The windows show bits of red sky and behind the red, gold lights in the ballroom. I can hear voices, people laughing in the distance, music playing; but the garden is still, waiting for the night. The shadows swallow everything in the garden. Insects begin their cricking-creaking.

Pammie's waiting at the top of the steps. 'Why didn't you eat supper?' she says.

'Not hungry.'

Mr Stevenson has put up a canvas screen at the end of the stoep. He's loading big reels onto a projector on a table. Chairs are in rows next to the ballroom windows. Children and grown-ups who don't want to dance sit down.

'Come,' Pammie says.

We sit next to the windows. If I turn my head, I can look into the ballroom. It's full of people talking, waiting for music on the gramophone. A man's voice sings one note with thumping drums: *'Like the beat, beat, beat of the jungle drums in the heat, heat, heat of the night'*. His voice swoops into a song, *'Only you, you are the one ...'* People put their arms round each other and sway to the music. Mom's dancing with Rex Niven; his arm is round her waist, the other holds up her hand. His perfect waves roll back into a sea of glued hair. All the men are wearing suits and ties. Mom's red dress swings away from her legs and floats. She looks like a gypsy with gold hoops hanging from her ears, a wide gold bracelet on her wrist and her eyes big and shiny. Her black hair is loose down her back. She's smiling up at Rex Niven.

'Your mother's flirting,' Pammie says.

I can't see Jack.

Mr Stevenson starts rolling the reel, the projector hums. Black numbers flick onto the screen backwards – 5, 4, 3, 2, 1, 0. Then the screen is blank white. A circle shows on the screen and in it the head of a roaring lion, then MGM PRESENTS – MRS MINIVER.

An orchestra plays film music. Lists of names scroll down. Inside, the dance ends on a long note – 'Da-ay'. Rex Niven takes Mom back to her seat and bows. Andy Stewart brings Mom a drink. People walk past. I lose sight of them.

I can't see Jack.

'What are you looking at?' Pammie says. 'The film's starting.'

I pull my eyes back to the story on the screen. There's a family called Miniver who lives outside a small village on the banks of the river Thames. Mr Miniver has a boat he sails on the river and he has bought a new car. Mrs Miniver is going to have a rose called after her at the village Flower Show. They have three children, the oldest son has left Cambridge University to become a pilot in the war. He meets the young niece of the lady of the Manor, Lady Beldon. At first they don't like each other but then 'they're falling in love,' Pammie whispers in my ear. The orchestra plays sweet violin music.

I love the way the family talk to each other; their voices are low and loving, kind and gentle. They call each other dear, darling, dearest all the time. They are never angry.

The music changes. Horns and dark scary sounds with drums. The Spitfires take to the sky.

I look into the bright light of the ballroom. Rob and Helen swing past the window. Rob towers over Helen's small body dressed in a satiny green gown that shimmers and changes colour under the light. Rob's round sultana eyes smile down at her. Daisy and Dick jump around, locked in each other's arms, Dick on grasshopper legs and Daisy on her tree trunks. They circle the dance floor twice as fast as other dancers, as if it's a race.

There're Mom and Andy. They talk and laugh as they dance. Mom's head is bent backwards to look into Andy's eyes. She nods and laughs at everything he says. Andy's grooves cut up his cheeks.

'Watch the film,' Pammie pulls my arm. 'It's more interesting than boring old dancing.'

I can't see Jack.

The Minivers' son marries Clare, niece of Lady Beldon. They marry in a hurry because of the war. Mr Miniver takes his boat into the English Channel to help rescue British soldiers from Dunkirk. I see him at the wheel of his little motorboat, sailing down the river Thames, down to its mouth then into the English Channel, over wild, choppy waves to Dunkirk. I feel anxious for him, but also amazed at his bravery. The son fights in his little Spitfire chariot in the sky.

Then I hear a man's voice from the ballroom singing dance music, he sings about love, swooning love, music so tender, nights of tropical splendour. I'm stuck in a dream-like trance, everything is winding down slowly. I see Andy pull Mom closer to him in slow motion. There's no space between their bodies. Rob smiles from his monkey eyefolds when he passes them. Daisy and Dick turn and wink. Round and round they go, lost in each other, lost in the music.

I see Jack in the doorway.

He's looking for Mom, his hawk-beak nose juts from side to side.

My stomach ties itself in a knot. Rat-tat-tat. There's an air raid over England. The night sky is dark grey, lit by streaking lights and firework explosions. Bomber planes zoom over the village like metal birds of prey. Mrs Miniver sits in the underground bunker with her husband and children. She reads from *Alice in Wonderland* to distract them. The air raid ends and the siren sounds the 'all-clear' but Mrs Miniver reads to the end of the book, reads how Alice, when grown up, would keep the simple and loving heart of her childhood.

Inside the ballroom the music has stopped. People drift off the dance floor, talking, arm-in-arm.

Jack's disappeared.

The summer sun is gone and Mrs Miniver and her daughter-in-law drive home in the dark. They can't switch on the car lights because of the blackout. All around them there's gunfire, explosions and screaming bullets. When she stops the car outside the house, she turns to Clare and finds she's been shot. Mrs Miniver drags her into the house where she dies. It's so-o sad. I can hear Pammie sniffing.

The funeral takes place in the old village church. The mourners can see Spitfires returning to the sky through the gaping big hole in the roof. You can hear the drone of their engines.

Choppy dance music comes from the gramophone. Dum-de-dum. Mom's spiky black heels tap out the steps.

Jack's in the doorway. He looks funny with Mom's red sequin bag hanging over his arm. Andy's arm turns Mom round and round. She swirls away from him, her skirt rising like red flames up her legs. Their bodies bounce back to each other, Mom's hair swings into Andy's face. They laugh. Their legs step in and out of each other, their cheeks stick together.

Jack's body snakes from side to side, he finds Mom and Andy amongst all the dancers. Mom and Andy stop their dance and look at Jack. Their eyes are wide in surprise. Jack's hand jerks Mom's arm, he pulls her from Andy towards the door, with a force so great that her head swings back.

People stop dancing to watch. Rex Niven's eyebrows shoot up to his waves of hair, Rob steps forward, a worry frown between his eyes, Helen raises her arm, Andy's mouth is open, his feet are stuck to the floor, but Jack ignores them all.

He drags Mom from the ballroom. Even the Hausa servants watch them leave the club.

Andy rushes to the door. I stand up and try to call Mom but my throat is stuck.

'Where are you going? What's wrong?' Pammie cries as I begin to run after them because it looks as if they are going to leave me behind. Jack pulls Mom so hard, her feet in their high heels trip on the gravel.

'Jack, Jack, you're hurting me.'

'Shut up.'

Ernest sees them coming towards the Buick and shoots out of the car to open the passenger door. But Jack is moving faster than I've ever seen. He yanks at the back door, flings it open. 'Get in, ye feckin' Jezebel.'

I run to the car, my feet crunching.

Jack shoves Mom into the back seat with one arm then at the same time slams the car door hard so the metal scrunches onto metal like the crack of a train door.

I hear Mom scream. Jack opens the door again and Mom drops her hand from the door hinge. She holds it on her lap, crying in pain.

Ernest opens the other back door, takes my hand, 'Sit quick, Missie.' It's so dark I can only see the white's of Ernest's eyes and his teeth.

Mom's hair hangs over her face, she sobs. Jack sits in the front, slams the door, Ernest climbs into the driver's seat. Slam, slam.

Ernest vrooms the motor, the wheels chug backwards, then Ernest turns the wheel and we leave the Club. I turn my head and see Andy's dark shape against the bright light of the doorway, staring after us.

We're on the dirt road taking us away from the Club. We are in a cave of dark night. Only the car's lights beam a small track of gold on the road ahead and the thick clumps of bush.

Jack turns his head to look at us. 'Wheesht, wumman, haud yer greetin'. I hae nivver in my life been so humiliated. Carryin' on like a strumpet wi' Andy Stewart on the dance floor. An' everybody watchin'. Ye'll never see the insides o' a dance floor agin, I can tell ye that.'

Jack sucks on his Woodbine as if he's sucking in air, the tip glows bright red. I can see Ernest's eyes in the rear view mirror.

'I'll be the laughin' stock. What were ye thinkin'? Ye dinna hae a brain in yer head, wumman ... no wonder yer fursst husband left ye ...'

On and on the hate words pour. Jack doesn't take a breath, he never runs out of words. He sucks in the red hot fumes of his cigarette and blasts them out on Mom. His mouth is like the barrel of a gun – his word bullets hit Mom. Rat-tat-tat. She holds her bleeding hand on her lap, sobbing softly.

I can smell her dark blood seeping onto her dress. I try to hold her other hand but it is cold and lifeless.

Ernest drives slowly for once because he can't see far ahead, the beams from the car's headlights only shine on a small stretch of road. There's no moon tonight. Apart from the patch of gold in front of the car, there's only a dim, green glow from the dashboard and the red tip from Jack's Woodbines as he chain-smokes, lighting the cigarettes from tip to tip.

Jack looks around at the darkness outside. 'Stop,' he says. 'Stop the car.'

Ernest brakes, Mom moans as the car jolts her hand. Jack lifts his head to listen, he unwinds the window. 'I canna hear them,' he says. 'I canna hear the drums.'

He's right. There's only the sound of the Buick's engine purring in the silent dark.

Jack turns to Ernest, 'Ye've missed the turn-off. We shud be hearin' the drums by noo.' He lights a new Woodbine from the end of the old one and throws it out of the window. 'Turn the car,' he says. 'We'll hae to go back. Careful noo, Ernest,' Jack turns his beak towards me. 'We dinna want tae spend the nicht oot here when the bush is crawlin' wi mambas an' cobras an' leopard men.'

I see the leopard men, the juju men, the spitting cobras, the lightning-quick mambas jumping out at us from the dark.

'Mom?' I howl.

'Och, Ga-awd,' cries Jack. 'Do I hae to put up wi' a screechin' brat as weel as a wailin' wumman who makes an exhibition o' hersel' on the dance floor?' He squeaks high in a woman's voice pretending to be Mom, 'Och, Andy, do ye like ma dress? Och, Andy, ye dance so-o weel. Och, Andy, ye make me feel so randy.'

Mom weeps. I swallow my fear into a big ball in my throat.

Ernest changes gear and turns the wheel so we can go back. He reverses the Buick into the donga at the side of the road. We slide backwards, the wheels spin in the loose sand. It seems as if we are going to drive all night then Ernest shouts, 'Boss Jack. Boss Jack. I hear dem. I hear de drums.'

Above the purr of the engine and the crunch of the wheels comes a faint boom-boom.

Jack stops ranting. Mom lies against the door of the car, her eyes closed, her hand curved on her lap. I sigh with relief.

We've driven forever but now the sound of the drums doesn't leave us. The Buick crawls forward in the dark. It climbs a little hill in the road and, when we get to the top, we see the lights of the dredger blossoming like a Christmas tree below us. Its chugging joins the booming drums.

At home, in my bedroom, I pull the mosquito net under my mattress into a cocoon. Frida's waiting, her little pink tongue shows in a silent miaauw. I'm holding her warm furriness close to my chest. I listen to her thin rumble, close my eyes and bit by bit, my bed becomes the *Skidbladnir*, rolling and skimming the crests of the waves, her orange sail opens upwards with a cracking sound and the ship bounds forward, we're sailing into the deep night on the heaving black sea, sailing into the other world where Siward waits ... then I remember, he's dead, his head hanging on a spike and I can never go into the other world again.

Part Four

'FRESH AIR, digging, and skipping rope had made her feel so comfortably tired that she fell asleep.' Bridget Hordern closes the book. Our magic hour's over.

Ivy grows over a gate on the book cover. A girl holds an old-fashioned key; a robin looks down on her. She's about to enter the secret garden.

I wish I had a key to go into another place away from Jack and Mom. I can't look at him ever again. At home I sit in my room with the door closed. Pammie has not invited me to her house since that night at the club. Jack sulks all the time, he glares at Mom and me. He won't talk to Mom. She sits in her chair looking in front of her as if she's seen a ghost. She has a big bandage on her thumb and she holds her hand on her lap as if it hurts.

I sigh and drag my feet across the floor.

'Karin, come here for a moment, please.' I turn. Miss Hordern holds her arms out to me. I walk towards her and feel her arms lift me sideways onto her lap. She winds her arms round my body. I slump against her bony, flat chest.

'You've been quiet for some time, Karin, not like your usual self. Is something wrong?'

I stay silent. I can't find words to tell her.

'Is something wrong at home?'

Hot tears fall down my cheeks. I want to tell her but I can't. I feel red shame burn my face. My chest heaves. Mom would kill me if I told anyone. I sit like a dumb doll, staring down at my brown feet as if I've never seen them before.

'All right, Karin. Remember you can talk to me whenever you want. Off you go.'

She squeezes my arm and pushes me gently off her lap.

I climb into bed. Miss Hordern's fuzzy hair shines gold in the doorway. She folds her hands in front of her and closes her eyes. 'Now I lay me down to sleep. I pray the Lord my soul to keep ... Amen. God Bless.'

Tomorrow I will be back in Dorowa.

Mom's lost her thumb nail. Her thumb looks strange, like a bald head.

'Is it sore?' I touch the scars where the nail used to be.

'Numb.' Mom closes her eyes. She doesn't want to think about Jack slamming the car door on her thumb.

Whoosh. Someone rushes down the walkway. Scrrf-scrrf. Feet scrape on the cement. I see a blur of brown and purple through the open door. A woolly head without a skullcap. 'Boss Jack! Masta!' A thick, loud voice shouts. It sounds like Amos. 'Bo-oss Jack. I mus' speak wid you.' His eyes have spider webs of red, they look through Jack as if he can't really see him. They look brown and red beside the white paste covering his skin. His brown lips shake and shiver.

Jack finds his voice. He points the red tip of his cigarette at Amos, 'Get ootta here, Amos, yer're drunk. Ye've been drinkin' yer awfu' beer agin. Get the hell oot o' here.'

I don't know what Amos is shouting, he's shouting in Hausa. He comes close to Jack and swings at him with his fists. Jack steps back, his hoods spring open in shock, his grey eyes stare at Amos. 'Wha? Wha' do ye think ye're doin'?'

Wham. Amos' fist lands on his chin. Bam. Amos' other fist hits his ear. Jack stumbles back. His mouth hangs open. He doesn't seem to know what to do. He lifts a fist and tries to punch Amos, but he bends sideways and comes at Jack with his fists swinging like windmills. One hits Mom on the chin, his other arm knocks me back so I crash against the fridge. Amos' feet leave the ground as he hits Jack on the back of his head. Jack stumbles forward, knocking against the table with the water-filter canister on top. He loses his balance and slides down against the legs of the table. Amos hits him again. Jack grunts and sinks to the floor, looking up at Amos with dizzy eyes.

Mom grabs my arm, 'Run for help.'

I run through the house, onto the driveway. I meet Andy Stewart sprinting towards our house. He's heard the shouting. He pushes past me into the house, into the kitchen. He gets there as Amos lifts his foot to kick Jack. His eyes are crazy-red, foam is coming out of the corners of his mouth. His lips, his head, his body shake. His eyes never leave Jack's face.

Andy takes Amos' arms and twists them behind his back. He shakes Amos so his teeth rattle together. He pushes him out of the kitchen. He shouts in Hausa, then 'Hae ye gone mad? There'll be hell to pay fer this. Shut yer gibberin' mouth and stop this madness.' He pushes Amos down to sit on the walkway.

Andy's frowns make thick tracks on his forehead, his eyes shine like fog lights as he stares at Amos. His chest heaves from running and pushing. Amos looks like a balloon that's been pricked. The fight and the fury have whooshed out of him. He holds his head in his hands, tears smear the white paste on his cheeks. He chews his lips.

Andy sees a movement in the cookhouse and shouts, 'You. Boy. Go run to big boss Nesbit's house. Tell him bring the Dodge chop-chop.'

Obafemi creeps out of the door, looks at Amos' bent-over body and runs to the back of the compound on slow legs. We listen to the thud of his feet. Jack hauls himself up and comes to stand near Andy. He rubs his jaw. His hoods fall. He doesn't look at Andy. He pushes his greasy hair out of his eyes.

'Bastard took me by surprise. He stayed in the village last night – he didna arrive in time to cook breakfast. Drunk as a bloody coot on his stinkin' poison beer.' He bends down and peers into Amos' face. 'Ye've ... cooked ... yer ... bloody ... goose ... this ... time, ye ... cunt. When the police are finished wi' ye, ye'll never drink anither drop o' beer agin.'

Amos'eyes blink shut and make brown circles in the white mask of his face. He moans, 'Amos mus' do work. Boss Jack need Amos for cook food.'

'Ye should hae thought o' that afore ye lifted yer fists to me.'

Now Jack's looking at Amos' face as if for the first time. 'Wha' the bloody hell is that stuff on yer face?'

Amos is silent, more tears roll down his cheeks.

Andy pushes Amos' leg with his shoe. 'Have ye smeared borfima on yersel', Amos? Eh, is that what ye've done? Ye've been to the juju man and bought this hocus-pocus cream, haven't ye?'

Emoka and Bola wander from their huts, they watch us from behind the cookhouse, their faces poking out, eyes worried. Amos doesn't turn to face them, he's slumped forward, his hands holding his head as if it's too heavy to hold up.

'Ye thought the juju stuff would make ye brave an' strong, did ye?' Andy sneers. 'Did ye just want tae scare them or did ye want tae hurt Boss Jack? Kill him maybe?'

We hear the drone of the Dodge in the distance, a comet of dust moves up the road past the dredger. It comes close, slows for the corner at the bottom of the road then rushes up the hill. Its putter-stutter stops outside our front door.

Here comes Rob now, a sunhat sits on top of his bald head, his sultana eyes see everbody waiting and he stops with a look of surprise. Mom, standing in the doorway, her nose twitching, her face white. Jack's hoods hide his eyes, he jingles coins in his pockets. Andy watches Amos. Amos shivering, his shoulders hunched, his hands covering his face.

Rob pushes his hat back, rubs his baldness. 'What's going on?'

They all speak at once.

Dried foam sticks to the corners of Amos' mouth. 'Boss Rob ...'

Jack opens his hatchet mouth, 'This bloody bastard ...'

Andy points his finger, 'I heard him shoutin' ...'

Mom's shaky, screechy voice, 'He hit me on the chin when I came into the kitchen ...'

Rob holds up his hand. 'Whoa. One at a time. Jack?'

'I saw straight off he was fightin' drunk, full o' beer. He came screamin at me, punched me to the floor.'

Amos bursts out, 'Boss Rob, sah. Dis be de trutt. Somet'ing happen wid Boss Jack an' numba two wife. Somet'ing make Amos plenty angry.' He jumps to his feet, fire starts to burn in his eyes again. 'Mastah Rob, sah. I see numba two wife got dash. She got t'ree shillin' in her han'. Yassah.' He stabs his finger at Adia who's skulking-lurking behind the cookhouse.

He chokes on his words, 'I say for her – where you get dis dash? She say – Boss Jack, he gib me dash. I say – whefo'? She hide her face.' Amos turns his face sideways, looks down and covers his face with one hand. 'Mastah Rob, I know whefo' Boss Jack gib her dash. Boss Jack, he make jig-jig wid numba two wife. Yass. I know dis. He make jig-jig wid her.'

Rob Nesbit's mouth drops, he turns his eyes on Jack.

'Ye lyin' black bastard,' Jack shouts. He has a white line around his mouth, his face is grey. 'Ye'll go to prison fer lies and assault. That Fulani girl shoulda stayed in the village. Nothin' but trouble, wantin' dash all the time.'

Rob sighs hard. Woo-oof. He stares at Amos. I can almost see thoughts rolling round his bald head. He scratches it.

'Amos, I can smell you've been drinking all night. Then you come here and cause trouble. If you thought you had a complaint, you should have come to me first. Now it's a matter for the police.' He shakes his head. 'We'll have to drive to the police station at Bukuru. You can all make statements there. Boss Jack will have to decide whether or not he wants to lay a charge against you.'

He turns to Andy and Jack, 'I need you all to come with me as witnesses. You, too, Obafemi. Bring Amos and put him in the back of the truck.' He sees Bola standing next to the cookhouse, her baby on her hip. 'Amos, tell your wife to pack all your belongings and walk down to my house. The Fulani girl as well. Wait for me at my house. When we return from Bukuru, I'll take them back to the village.'

Bola listens to Amos, then turns slowly and drags her feet in the dust to her hut. I see how torn-shabby her clothes are, how the baby is dressed in rags.

Amos watches her walk back. He looks at the trees and the donga. His eyes wake up, but Rob sees his interest and says, 'Don't even think of it, Amos. You won't get far. Let's move.'

Amos pushes Rob's arm away, his lower lip juts out. He walks between Rob and Andy to the Dodge and swings himself up into the back of the van. Obafemi climbs in after him. Jack climbs into the cab with Andy and Rob.

Mom and I watch the Dodge drive down the road and turn.

'Mom?' I say, but she lifts her hand and says. 'Not now, Karin, no questions. I don't know what's going on. I'm as confused as you are.'

I'm watching Bola and Adia leave the compound carrying all their bundles on their heads. Bola's baby is tied up in a blanket on her back. I can see her head and little feet sticking out. Their backs are straight, their eyes look ahead with their heads held high to balance the heavy bundles. They're on the narrow path leading to Rob's house. I'll never see them again. Their shadows stretch out in front of them as the sun falls in the sky. Nothing lasts.

I know Amos spoke the truth. I saw Jack rocking on top of Adia on his bed. Was he making jig-jig with her? If that was making jig-jig, then he was doing it. I could have told Rob that Amos was angry because Jack was rocking on top of Adia. I could have saved Amos from prison, but who would believe me?

Amos let the fire go out in the cold stove in the kitchen. Mom sticks her head in the dark, smoky room. The pots and pans sit on the shelves, bent and buckled by Amos' rough scrubbing.

'No ... I'm not going to try. What for?' Mom wanders back to the pantry-kitchen, slaps a board on a table and cuts bread. She bangs a sandwich on a plate next to Jack.

He lifts his head. 'I'm no' hungry.'

'Suit yourself.'

Jack smokes in his chair. The radio pours sounds of soft music and low voices into the quiet room. He drinks one glass of whiskey then more. He stares up at the ceiling, ruminating. Then he folds his arms around himself as if he's hiding a secret behind them.

Mom fidgets. She twitches the curtains, peers into the dark. She plumps up cushions, she rearranges the mirrors, bottles and brushes on her dressing table. She straightens the bedspread, shakes the pillows. She stands back and looks at the bed, walks round it. She shakes her head, rubs her cheeks, covers her face with her hands.

I fold myself into my cocoon bed. There's no noise in the compound, no smell of cooking ground nut stew, no voices talking round the fire. No giant shadows thrown on the mud walls by the leaping flames. I remember how ugly Amos' face was, how smeary with white paste, how red his eyes, how his words slobbered through wet lips. I smelt his sour breath when he breathed on us. How his nostrils opened to the size of small caves so he could suck in more air.

He's smooth and round like a brown seal and walks quietly in his sandals. His feet are not cracked and dry like Amos'. His skull cap is always white, he wears a jacket shirt, also white. His eyes always look down. I never see into his eyes. He listens to Mom without saying a word, then does what she asks perfectly. His name is Ali. Helen Nesbit sent him to be Mom's new cookboy.

Ali works like a machine, he cooks meals without burning the food, his chips do not drown in oil, he scrubs the pots quietly. He's gentle and silent.

Mom likes Ali. Her face becomes less cross as the days go by. She loves the way his brown hands work. The shelves in the pantry have lines of herbs, spices and sauces in alphabetical order, the gleaming glass containers of sugar, coffee, flour and cereals all match. The fridge sparkles white when you open the door.

Mom's found someone who likes neat and clean as much as she does.

'Remember, Karin, singing is all about breathing,' Mrs Stevenson smiles. She looks like Brahms when her nose and chin bend to each other. She's shown me a photograph of Brahms when he was an old man. 'My favourite composer,' she says. 'Do you know why, Karin?'

I shake my head.

'Because his music tells us about the tenderness of unrequited love. Poor Brahms knew a thing or two about unrequited love – you won't understand this now, but when you're older, listen to his intermezzos.'

She's teaching me to sing 'The Magnificat' for the nativity play. She sounds the notes on the piano and I sing them. I learn the notes without the words, then, when I can remember them, I put the words in. She teaches me to listen to the spaces – intervals, she calls them – between notes so that my voice can land on the right one. She tells me when to sing loudly or softly, when to hold onto a note.

'Hold your diaphragm in, Karin,' she pushes her hand below my ribs. 'Imagine there's a column of air going up into your throat – then the notes will float out on your breath.'

She plays the first note then stops. 'You'll be singing "The Magnificat" a capella – that's Italian for "in the manner of the church or chapel", in other words, you'll be singing without the accompaniment of an instrument.'

She nods but doesn't touch the piano keys. Now I will really learn the notes. 'Let's begin ... The Lord has magnified my soul ...' She sings with me, her voice sounds like a growly bear. We sing it over and over. I can sing it in my sleep.

This is the day, the moment has come. We're crowded in the library, struggling into shepherd's costumes, angel costumes, sheep costumes. Pammie wears a long white dress belonging to her mother with gold cardboard wings tied on her back. Her halo is gold cardboard tied with elastic onto her forehead. It keeps slipping down onto her neck. She's supposed to be the Archangel Gabriel.

Fraser is Joseph in a striped dressing-gown and a red wool beard and a broom with a hook on top. 'I look stupid,' he says.

Adam, a shepherd in a brown sack, hoots, 'I hope Mom and Dad brought their camera.'

I'm wearing a blue tablecloth with a gold belt. Mrs Stevenson has just put a white scarf over my head. The scarf makes me hot; I feel my cheeks growing red. I'm nervous and excited.

Outside, in the front classroom, are tens and tens of parents, family and friends. They've listened to our poetry – 'Horatio on the Bridge' – watched our eurythmy; they've looked at our nature table, our art and our exercise books.

Miss Hordern comes to inspect our costumes. Her face is pink. I can see she's pleased. 'Ready children?' She looks around at the sheep and their shepherds, the Three Wise Kings, Tansy, Hugh and Ben with gold cardboard crowns and carrying calabashes of Gold, Frankincense and Myrrh. 'I almost forgot,' Miss Hordern says, wrapping a white shawl round a plastic doll and putting it in the manger, a wooden fruit box from the market.

Mrs Stevenson bends to whisper in my ear. 'I'll be right behind you, I'll play the first note on the piano then you can begin. Can you sound your note?'

I have the note in my head. I make a 'mmmh' sound for her. She nods. 'Let's go.'

My heart leaps and bucks and makes so much noise in my ears. I hope I can hear myself sing. Mrs Stevenson's told me how to control my stage fright. 'Pick one person in the audience and sing to that person.'

I want to sing to Bridget Hordern. She's not in the room, but I'll look over everybody's heads and pretend she's there.

I kneel and put my hands together as if I'm praying. I close my eyes. This is soppy but I have to do it. I hear Pammie's bare feet shwish across the floor. They stop in front of me. I wait. I know she's lifting her arms and looking down at me. Her voice sounds squeaky, 'Hail, Mary, full of Grace, I bring you tidings of great joy ...'

She finishes her speech. I stand, still holding my hands together. In a quick look I see Mom's face, her anxious eyes, Alice, Pammie's mother's smiling eyes. She gives a little nod. Oh no, I see Tansy's parents near the front. Tansy's Mom looks at me with two copper penny eyes beneath her beestung lids.

'Breathe,' Mrs Stevenson whispers behind me. I gulp in air.

She sounds the note on the piano. For a moment I think I've gone deaf then I hear the note in my head and open my mouth, '*The Lord hath magnified my soul and my spirit*' – interval, a small jump – '*hath rejoi-ced ...*'

I hear my voice sound through the room. It's shaky at first then I think of Miss Hordern and I can feel it sounding stronger. I'm not the Virgin Mary, though. I'm a monk in a brown robe singing in a cathedral and I send my voice soaring to the top of the pointy arches of the roof. It's going to be okay. Now I'm singing to the dead Siward as well, only his head is still on his shoulders and he's listening with a smile, looking at me with his ice-blue eyes. I'm singing the last section now: '*For behold from henceforth, all ge-e-ner-a-tions shall call me blessed*' – I'm in the home stretch and feeling confident so I sing a little ornament on the 'a'.

I hear a cough and a stutter and a squeak as a car door opens outside. I lose my place, the last notes rush out of my head as I see Jack's feet, first one then the other, land on the gravel. He pulls himself up with one hand on the Dodge door and stands rocking.

Don't let Jack come in.

But he lurches up the steps and rattles the door, his beak nose pressed up against the glass panes. I feel Mrs Stevenson's eyes on my back. She plays the notes on the piano but I can't sing because this huge frog is stuck in my throat.

I don't want to open my mouth in case I sing kwaak, like a frog. Jack's swaying in front of the door. Nobody sees him except me. The moms and dads think I've broken down because I've lost my nerve. Jack rattles the handle, he doesn't know whether the door opens in or out.

People's heads turn. Old Mr Stevenson sits nearest the door. He stands and opens it. Jack almost falls into the classroom. His hair stands up in stiff spikes. There's dried spit on his chin, not-so-dry snot down his shirt. He walks like a baby trying to balance on his legs. Step-wobble-lunge. He's looking for something and when I try to sing 'Holy, Ho-o-oly is ... His ... name', Jack points his finger and wobble-walks towards me. Pammie sees him, her blue eyes pop out of her head.

Mom's head shoots round, then she turns back and closes her eyes. Everybody's looking at Jack now. I hear whispers and mutters and sniggers.

'Wheesht.' He spray-spits saliva from his mouth. 'Dinna shing sush holy shit. Naah. Shing wha' I tell ye.' He bends forwards, almost falls then rocks on his feet. His eyes fix on a spot above my head. 'Wha'd I teash you? Hey, c'mon, shing.' His eyes struggle to find me, they squint. Then he lifts his head up and bawls, 'Jus' a wee Doch 'n Doris, jus a wee wifie ben ...' His voice cracks on 'wifie'.

I hear Mrs Stevenson get up from the piano stool and walk to the door behind her.

'Biddie. Biddie. You'd better come quickly,' she calls to Miss Hordern. They whisper in quiet explosions.

Jack wobbles towards me, his mad grey eyes fixed just above my head. 'Whashat? Ey? Whad I teash ye?' He tries to find his ear with the cup of his hand but misses. 'If ye can shay ish a braw bricht moonlicht nicht, ye're a richt ...'

He spray-spits a small fountain, he begins to sneeze. Wet waterfalls rush out of his mouth, his body shakes with the force, then his false teeth leave his gums in a rush. Sss-plat.

Mrs Roberts feels wet spray on her face then pulls away as Jack's teeth land at her feet, grinning up at her.

'Dear God.' She wipes her face with a hankie.

Miss Hordern, holding her timetable in her hand, comes out of the passage. The look in her eyes is fierce, her mouth opens but no words come out. Reverend Roberts stands and looks up at Jack. He says in a loud sermon voice, 'Mr Carmichael, this will not do. This is unseemly behaviour for children to witness ...'

'FUCKORF.' Jack's mouth has fallen in like a collapsed cave. His lips suck the words out. He shakes off Reverend Robert's hand as if it's a mosquito.

Nobody moves, nobody speaks. Jack swivels his eyes around then opens the cave of his mouth and shows gummy stalagtites and stalagmites.

'Jack. Jack.' A voice speaks as if to a baby. It coos and soothes. Mr Stevenson is at Jack's elbow. His old eyes look up at the wreck of Jack's face. 'I've got an idea. Nothing to drink here. Why don't we go to the club and we'll sing there and have a dram. Eh? What do ye say, Jack?'

He bends, and with a handkerchief, scoops Jack's teeth into his pocket. He puts his hand on Jack's elbow, turns him towards the door and leads him out, talking all the while. 'Ye like Harry Lauder, then, do ye, Jack? I remember when ...'

We watch Mr Stevenson lead Jack to the door towards the Dodge, open the door and push Jack into the cabin. Ernest starts the motor and they crunch down the gravel drive.

People turn back to the stage. Miss Hordern steps up. 'Right, shall we continue with the nativity play? Mrs Stevenson?'

Mrs Stevenson plays 'While Shepherds Watched their Flocks by Night'. The sheep, shepherds and Joseph shuffle around me and Pammie. Miss Hordern tells the story as we go along. Matron Davies holds a glittery cardboard star high on a pole. The Three Wise Men follow it. They sing 'We Three Kings of Orient Are'. Miss Hordern's deep voice sings with them.

Fraser leads me to the tomato-box manger, pushes me onto a chair, then hands me the doll wrapped in the shawl.

Mrs Stevenson plays loud chords. Audience and children sing together, 'Hark, the Herald Angels si-ing ... Glory to the Newborn King ... peace on earth and mercy mi-ild, God and sinners reconciled'.

I stare at the china doll in the shawl, its painted face and empty eyes. My ears are ringing, my face is hot. I look at the doll's stupid face and shake.

Mom stands in front of the window, her arms folded over her chest. I'm home at Dorowa for the holidays. My report in its brown envelope sits in my case. I haven't shown it to Mom. She hasn't asked to see it. Her face is flour white, she has black half moons under her eyes.

'Now, Karin, listen to me,' she begins, 'never ever talk about what happened at the nativity play. I don't want to hear about it from you or anyone else. Least said soonest mended, my father always said.'

Mom doesn't pay attention to her own instructions.

I'm lying on a blanket in the gazebo, my head on a cushion. Frida lies next to me curled into a ball, her tail wrapped around her nose. On a tray there's a glass of Oros and a slab of Cadbury's chocolate. I've brought home a book called *Twenty Scottish Tales and Legends*. I'm lying on a carpet of leaves and moss between huge roots of ancient trees. The roof of the gazebo is a canopy of leaves. I hear Mom's voice. She's talking to Andy Stewart.

'... so ashamed, so humiliated. I can't bear to see Helen and Daisy. What will they think? I suppose they heard about Jack's appearance?'

''Fraid so. But Irene, gie them a chance. They probably feel sorry fer ye ...'

'I don't want anybody's pity. Can't stand that.'

'Dinna look at it like that. They probably want to help ye.'

'I'm a grown woman ... don't need help.'

'Ye're gonna need support sooner or later, Irene, if Jack continues tae drink the way he does.'

'It's like being a prisoner in my own house. I can't go out or have anybody here ... I'm lonely.'

'I wish I could help ye ...'

'God, no. I don't want to give them another reason to gossip.'

The Dodge rattles into our driveway, then stops past the house under the locust bean tree. Rob blasts the horn three times. He steps outside the cabin and waits for Jack.

They stand face to face in the shade of the tree. Rob takes his pith helmet off and rubs his head up and down and round and round. He lifts his arm, points his finger at Jack, waggles it in Jack's face. Jack stands, his hands deep in his pockets, doesn't speak.

Rob kicks stones with his boot, kicks the wheel of the Dodge then gets in the driver's seat, slams the door and roars off, leaving a cloud of dust to settle around Jack.

Mom watches from the window. When Rob drives away, she turns and walks into the kitchen, opens the fridge door, slams it so the bottles rattle. She goes to the kitchen door and shouts, 'Ali. ALI.'

Mom attacks the bougainvillea round the front windows with the garden clippers as if it were a double-edged sword. Clumps of scarlet flowers and leafy boughs fall under her vicious clipping. Emoka follows her, raking the clumps of scarlet and green leaves into a pile, then lifting them on the spade into the wheelbarrow. His chest heaves and he rests on the spade from time to time because it seems as if the pile of clippings will never end.

When she finally throws down the clippers, the beautiful bougainvillea looks like scraggly eyebrows.

Inside, Obafemi sits in front of rows of silver cutlery and bowls, wiping Silvo onto them. Then when it dries to a milky crust, he rubs the silver until the shine hits you in the eyes. Ali cleans the cold stove and hangs the pots and pans in order, then he lights a fire to cook.

Jack is at the dredger.

Everybody's busy. Busy, busy, busy. 'The Devil makes work for idle hands,' Mr Roberts said in his sermon. The house is quiet and clean and orderly.

Jack's in his bar-sanctuary, sweat pouring down his face, he mops the wet away with a handkerchief. He slurps his whiskey with loud noises and lots of ice cubes. I like the way they clink-bump against the glass. He burps and says, 'Och, aye.'

When this happens for the sixth time, Mom turns on him. 'You're a disgrace. Look at you, drunk again. How could you drink after making such a spectacle of yourself?'

Jack doesn't answer. It's as if Mom hasn't spoken. He lifts his beak nose and stares in front of him.

'I can't hold my head up at the club or at the school again,' Mom says, her right hand holding the sewing needle as if she wants to stab him.

Jack's hoody eyes look at her as if he doesn't know who she is or what she's talking about.

'Go on then, stonewall me,' she says. 'You can't stonewall me forever.'

Jack's fingers shake as he tries to write. The nib of his Waterman pen scrapes over the pad of Basildon Bond. Instead of his rows of slanty, even letters, the nib leaves a trail of black zig-zags. He frowns, puts the pen to paper and scrawls a straggly J.

Mom carries a vase of yellow chrysanthemums and scarlet zinnias to put on the table.

'Jack?' she says 'What are you doing?'

Jack puts down his pen, rubs his eyes and forehead. 'I dinna ken,' he mumbles. 'I canna think – I hae a headache. My fingers feel numb.'

'Perhaps you should take an aspirin and rest on your bed.'

'Aye, I think I will.'

Jack puts the palms of his hands on the table and heaves himself up. He hasn't shaved, hasn't rubbed Brylcreem in his hair. It hangs over his eyes. He looks like an old man. He disappears into the bedroom on shuffly feet. I hear the springs creak, hear him sigh, 'Och, I dinna ken wha' the matter is.'

He snores for a few hours and he doesn't get up in time to go to work.

'Irene,' his voice rasps. 'I dinna feel I can get through my shift. Get a note down to Rob and let him know.'

Ali comes swooping down to the kitchen door. He calls from the kitchen, 'Missus Carmichael.'

He gives Mom a letter. 'From Boss Nesbit.'

He waits as she reads. 'Mmh. An invitation to supper at the Nesbit's house. All right, Ali, you can take an answer later.'

'Irene? What's goin' on?' Jack's voice is thick with phlegmy-goo. He looks up at Mom from his chair, his eyebrows standing up in two spiky bushes.

Mom hands him the letter. 'The Nesbits have invited us for dinner at their house on Robbie Burns's birthday.'

He reads it and looks at her. 'An' ye dinna want tae grace their house wi' your presence?'

Mom's two red spots show on her cheeks. 'No, I don't. I can't face them.' She doesn't say 'because of you' but I can see those words flashing from her eyes.

'We'll go. Ye dinna say no to Rob Nesbit.'

Daisy's perfume takes my breath away, it's so strong and sweet. Her laugh makes me deaf, her waa-aagh-aaghs beat against my eardrums as she pokes me in the side with her elbow. She's dressed in a red cotton dress and giant red flower earrings bob amongst her curls.

Mom sits on my other side, quiet and still, dressed in black with a gold stripe. Rob sits at the end of the table and opposite him at the bottom end, Dick. Jack sits at Rob's right hand, then Helen, then Andy.

Helen's eyes shine in the candlelight. 'Irene,' she says, 'ye'll be glad tae hear I've no cooked the haggis tonight, just the cock-a-leekie soup and the chappit tatties and bashed neeps wi' the roast chicken.'

Mom makes a mmh-mmh noise. She and Jack say nothing. Jack sips his whiskey and either looks up at the ceiling or at Rob.

Rob walks to the sideboard, opens a bottle of champagne with a loud pop, then fills every glass at the table. He stands behind my chair. 'You can have a few drops with us tonight, Karen.' He drips the liquid into my glass.

He sits in his chair and clinks an empty glass with a spoon. We look at him. 'I have an announcement to make,' he says. 'I have news that will affect all of us. Helen and I are expecting a child.'

Eyes open wide, mouths drop. Aagh. Everybody speaks at once.

'Och, tha's great news.' 'Congratulations.' 'Guidness me!' 'Blow me over wi'a feather.'

Dick springs to his feet. 'A toast fer Rob an' Helen.'

'Tae the wee bairn. May all yer troubles be little ones.'

They clink their glasses. Helen smiles at Rob then at each of us.

Jack says nothing.

The houseboy carries in the bowls of cock-a-leekie soup. The smell of creamy chicken blocks out Daisy's perfume. I'm starving. I lift the spoon to my mouth and swallow the warm, salty thickness.

Dick asks, 'So, Rob, how will your baby affect the rest o' us at Dorowa?'

Rob swallows his soup. He says he has been planning to go into politics for a long time to help the process towards Independence. 'I know this country like the back of my hand ... so I should, I've been here almost twenty years ... I've been talking to Rex Niven ...'

Daisy puts down her spoon. 'Unhh-hunhh. So how will the baby change yer plans?'

'Wait, Daisy ...'

The houseboy carries our bowls out and brings in platters of roast chicken and lamb and dishes of mashed potatoes and turnips.

Rob turns to Jack, 'How long have you been here, Jack?'

Jack says nothing. He looks as if he hasn't heard the question. He stares at the ceiling for a long moment.

Cat got your tongue, badgirl says.

Rob frowns, he rises to fill the glasses. 'It's going to be a complicated process to put a complicated system into place ... three regions, west, east and north, here, where we are ... each to have their own government, Lieutenant-Governor, Executive Council and House of Assembly.'

'I canna remember ...' Jack's voice sounds dreamy and his words are slow.

'Hey? Never mind, Jack. Now where was I ... ? Oh yes, there was talk of Rex Niven being the first President of the House of Assembly here in the north and he's asked me to be his assistant ...'

Rob cuts the chicken. Helen hands round the plates.

'What I'm trying to say is with a baby on the way, I don't know if I can commit to staying in the country for the duration of the process.'

'Aye, havin' a bairn changes everything,' says Helen.

'What do ye mean?' Daisy asks.

'Weel,' says Helen, 'I dinna want tae be one o' those parents who only see their children in holidays, ye ken.'

'But we hae a school here now ...'

'Aye, but it's still a boarding school. And only three teachers. It's just a matter of time before Bridget Hordern gets married.'

My heart skips a beat. Miss Hordern can't get married. The school wouldn't be the same without her.

'An' it must be awfu' lonely here without children. Isn't that true, Karin? Do ye no miss yer friends when ye're at Dorowa?'

I nod.

'Rob,' says Dick, his forkful of chicken and tatties halfway to his mouth. 'So tell me, how will your havin' a baby affect us at Dorowa?'

'I won't be going into politics, I can't make such a long commitment. So you'll be stuck with me here at Dorowa until Helen and I decide it is time to take our child home.'

'Oh, weel,' says Dick. 'Tha's no' sich a great change fer any o' us except, mebbe fer ...' He looks down the table at Jack.

'Jack?' Rob says. 'Do you have any thoughts about this? Any comment?'

Jack's eyes are smoky grey and dull, two holes in his face. He looks bewildered. After a long pause he says, '1940. When I furst came here. 1940, that's aboot it.'

Jack doesn't seem to have heard his promotion has slipped away from him, but Mom's nose quivers.

I hear Dick clear his throat, hear Rob's sigh and Andy asking Helen for the mint sauce. I'm tired of grown-up talk. I want to go home, snuggle in my cocoon and read the book Andy gave me for Christmas. *Little Women*. I wasn't interested in the story in the beginning, then I discovered Jo March is a tomboy and a writer and I think it will be a different kind of adventure. Andy has written on the first page 'Christmas, 1950. With love from Uncle Andy'.

A noise pulls me from my thoughts. I look at Mom, she's making a gasping noise in her throat. Everybody is looking at Jack. He has dropped his knife and fork. Clang. His eyes are rolling backwards in his head, his mouth gapes wide, gurgling, his face has gone as grey as his eyes. He's twisting out of shape, with his head lolling and his body falling sideways. Foam comes out of the corner of his mouth.

'My dear fellow,' Rob jumps to his feet. 'Are you ill?'

Daisy put her fork down, Dick swallows and says, 'Wha's wrong wi' Jack?'

Jack's body begins to shake, he falls off his chair slowly, sideways.

What now, badgirl says, *what's he up to now*? My heart bumps. Jack-in-the-box is out of control, his springs are falling apart. He lies on the floor, arms and legs jerking. We can't move, we're statues in a child's game.

Helen is the first to leave her seat. She kneels at Jack's side, turns his head sideways, loosens the buttons of his shirt. 'Get me a cushion for his head, quickly, Rob,' she says.

Everybody's standing, looking down at Jack. Helen says, 'Looks as if he's havin' a seizure o' some kind. Has he ever had a fit, Irene?'

Mom shakes her head, her nose has stopped twitching, her eyes are frightened.

Dick and Andy kneel down and try to keep his arms and legs still, but Helen says, 'Leave him, it will stop soon.'

We watch as Jack's body jitter-judders on the carpet. I think of the black mamba weaving his long rope body from side to side, trying to stay alive. I think of the words I don't want to remember – making jig-jig.

Jack's making jig-jig, badgirl says. My cock-a-leekie soup burns back up my throat. I swallow hard. Tears come into my eyes.

Then the shaking stops and Jack lies still, like a rag doll, grey and sweaty. Helen puts two fingers on his wrist. 'It doesna look guid,' she says.

Rob has one hand on his hip, the other rubs his head, he has monkey folds on his forehead as well as round his eyes. 'Right,' he says. 'Dick, find Ernest and tell him to bring the Buick round to the front door. Andy, you and I will have to drive now to Jos with Jack. We have to get him to a hospital as soon as possible. Daisy, you and Dick must take Irene and the child home and stay with them until I get back. Irene,' he turns to Mom, 'I'm sorry, my dear, you cannot leave Karin alone. Go home now, then Ernest can drive you to see Jack tomorrow.'

Andy and Rob pick Jack up, sling his arms round their shoulders then drag him to the Buick. They put him on the back seat, the same seat that's probably still got Mom's blood from the night when Jack shoved her in and slammed the door on her thumb.

Mom, Daisy, Dick, Helen and I stand in front of the house and watch the red lights of the Buick crawl towards the road out of Dorowa, past the dredger then into the distance over the hill. The dredger looks like a silent ship lit up on a dark sea.

'What is making jig-jig?'

We're playing Roman soldiers, huddled under our shields, in a tortoise shape, creeping towards a pretend enemy. I throw in the question because we can't see each other's faces.

'It's when you dance.'

'No, it's not. It's Pidgin English for ...'

'Shut up, Adam.'

'No, I won't, it's when a man puts his thing in the woman's hole ...'

'ADAM.'

'... and jiggles it.'

'How do you know ...?'

'It's how they make babies.'

'I read it in Dad's medical book.'

'It's penis and vagina ...'

'That sounds like Latin ...'

'You're all horrid and rude,' Tansy's voice squeaks like a little pig. 'I'm going to tell my parents.'

'Sissy. Prissy-sissy. Run and tell Mumm-ee and Dadd-ee.'

I break away from the tortoise and stand up. I don't want to hear anymore. I run to the swings under the mango trees and throw myself onto the seat, jerking it into motion. I don't want to know about this.

I won't think about it.

I push the swing higher and higher.

Everybody at school's forgotten about Jack and the nativity play because they know he's in hospital.

I will never think about jig-jig again. It's vomit-making, sick, sick, sick.

I'm swinging so high, I can see the sky above the trees, I bend my knees and make the swing go higher, soon it will make a full circle, then I can push myself off the seat and fly up, up into the burning blue.

'Irene,' says Rob.

I'm hiding behind the pillars in the dining-room and can't see them but I know he has pulled a chair close to Mom's.

He makes a rattly cough to clear his throat then ummh's and aah's. 'I'm so sorry, Irene, this is not easy for me to say. I'm afraid I have bad news. I took the liberty to speak to Dr Dunleavy at Jos Hospital on my own, never dreaming the news would be so dire.'

I can hear Mom breathing. The silence hangs like a heavy blanket. I can hear the rustle of paper after a while. I think Rob must be reading papers.

'Can I see ...?' Mom's voice is faint.

'I think it will be easier for me to tell you in simple language first then later you can read this and look at the X-rays. I'll repeat what Dr Dunleavy told me.' He breathes in lots of air, then huffs it out. 'Jack has lung cancer. It is advanced, in stage four, and it's aggressive. The cancer has metastasised into the brain and that caused the seizure. The tumour in the lungs is the size of a tennis ball, the tumour in the brain is inoperable.'

Mom sucks in air.

'Irene. I'm sorry. No, don't get up, you look as if you're going to faint. Can I get you some water? No?'

Pause.

'The doctors can do nothing more for Jack. They're going to send him home soon. They say he only has a few weeks left.'

Mom cries, 'He's going to die?'

'Yes, Irene. Helen and I will help you every step of the way. Helen will come every day to care for Jack in his final days and to help you.'

Mom's sighing and moaning. Rob says, 'There, there.' Then, 'I have to go, Irene, I'm needed down at the dredger but Helen will come up later. And ... Irene? I think it would be best if you try and prepare Karin for Jack's death.'

I hear Rob getting to his feet, then his footsteps leave the house, crunch over the gravel, then the Dodge door slams. I wait until the sound of the engine has disappeared down the road. I creep into the lounge. Mom's crying, her hands cover her face, her shoulders shake. I wait for her to look up and see me but she doesn't. I move closer and put my hand on her arm.

'Mom? Mom?' I give her a little shake. 'Mom? Is Jack going to die?'

She shakes her head and takes her hands away from her face. Her eyelashes are stuck together with tears. 'Not now, Karin. I don't want to talk about it now ... I can't believe this is happening.'

I leave Mom and wander out into the compound. The shade under the mango trees is dark green. The sun shines in such bright patches of gold, the light hits my eyes like a dagger.

When I blew out the candle on my birthday cake, I only wished Jack would disappear. I didn't want him to die.

Jack's smells are gone, the voice of Harry Lauder doesn't whine from the record player. No more *roamin' in the gloamins*. The house smells of lavender polish and Silvo. Obafemi kneels on little cloth pads on the cement floor, brushing it to a dull red shine, whistling through his teeth his happy working song, 'Nhyeh-nenhey-nheey.'

I'm watching Mom watching Emoka working in the garden as he weeds and rakes round the clumps of daisies and zinnias. Mom sighs a long shaky sigh as if she's just stopped crying. She pushes her hair from her eyes and moans, 'I won't have a place in the world.'

Emoka leans on his rake and rubs his back, his white speckled beard bobs as he chews his betel nuts. He works slowly but the garden always looks cared-for, watered and raked. The flowers shoot up blotches of red and purple, orange and blue.

I want to tell Mom her place is with me, wherever we are, but something about her sniffling silence tells me she won't listen. She's tens and tens of miles away in her thoughts.

Emoka puts all his tools in the wheelbarrow and pushes it to the back of the compound. We hear the slow squeak-creak of the wheel.

There's a knock at the front door. Andy's voice sounds, 'Irene? Are ye there?'

She clears her throat. 'Here. I'm in the dining-room.'

He comes into the room, his head poking forward. Mom lifts her droopy eyes, the corners of her mouth when she sees him.

He sits at the head of the table and reaches out and takes her hand. He tut-tuts when he sees the snail-trail of tears on Mom's cheeks. 'Irene, I heard the news from Rob – I canna tell ye how sorry I am.'

Mom's bottom lip trembles, she tries to smile but sniffs instead. 'My life's in ruins again. I don't know how I'll get through this.'

'Ye're not alone. We'll all help ye, Rob, Helen, Daisy and Dick and mesel' o' course.'

'I don't know what I'll do when ... Jack's gone.'

'Dinna think aboot it the noo. Take each thing as it comes along ...' He squeezes Mom's hand and talks softly.

I wander into Jack's old sanctuary and swish my hand through the dahlia petals in the vase on the brass tray next to his seat. His bottles, glasses and ashtrays are packed away in the pantry. I squeeze past the tray and look at Jack's books and magazines. I can almost feel Jack's breath on my neck, hear his voice blasting my eardrums, 'Wha' the bloody hell do ye think ye're doing?'

Badgirl reminds me, *You can do what you want now, stop creeping around.*

I pick up a small red book, it fits easily into my hands. *Greenmantle* by John Buchan. I sit down where I can read and see Mom and Andy at the same time.

Andy's voice murmurs like the sea at night, '... I have tae tell ye, Irene, I've been at a crossroads ever since the end o' the war. At furst I was gung-ho, fightin' fer freedom an' all that stuff, but when I was in the thick o' battle in the desert an' saw my friends, all young, die horrible deaths, I thought – this isna wurth it. It was all so senseless. Why did so many men have tae die to get ownership o' the land where they fought?'

I look up. Mom's staring into Andy's eyes as if she's hypnotised, they're holding both each other's hands now. She nods her head and says, 'Mmm-mm.'

'It was only when I heard about the death camps in Europe that I understood the war had to be fought ... we couldna allow such evil to exist ...'

Mom shakes her head.

'... an' when I heard of Himmler's decision, announced in a public speech, mind, to kill every Jewish wife and all the Jewish children so they wouldna grow up to be avengers, I decided I would nivver bring any child o' mine intae this world ...'

Andy stares at Mom's sewing basket as if he's never seen such a thing before.

Greenmantle is about war. Jack's books are all about crime and war although he's never fought in a war. One of the characters in *Greenmantle* has my father's name – Peter – and he's a Boer who hunts elephants in the Congo. I haven't thought of my father for a long time. I wonder if we would still be living in the big house with the rose garden in Cape Town if he and Mom hadn't got divorced.

My bare feet kiss-kiss the cement floor, I can wander from room to room without Jack's hoody eyes snaking at me, without his mouth turning into a wolf's snarly fangs. The chirping-creaking noise of the cicadas and the crickets, the kwaaking of frogs and the slithering of snakes don't sound scary tonight, they sound almost friendly. The night sky is purple-black like bruises and mysterious with a bright-white moon shining behind curtains of clouds. I find some Cadbury's chocolate in the pantry. Mom doesn't see. The rich, sweet blocks melt in my mouth.

'Irene, Irene, I'm so glad we never, ye ken, did anything beyond a wee cuddle an' a kiss ...'

'Oh, I know what you mean...'

'... we woulda felt sae guilty noo ...'

'Shoosh, Andy.'

Mom looks at me curled up, sucking the melt-in-the-mouth Cadbury's. It's my idea of heaven – reading and eating chocolate. Would sailing to Valhalla in a dragon boat across a night sea sky feel the same? I fall asleep in the lounge.

Mom's voice wakes me. 'That's not true, Andy, how can you say ...'

'It is true, Irene, ye're a neat freak. All you care aboot is yer clean hoose an' appearances. I'm wondrin' if ye can let yersel' go and fall madly, deeply, wildly in love ... ey, Irene? Do ye think?'

Mom's brought a bottle of sherry to the table and they're swallowing the dark red-gold stuff as if it was water. Mom's crying and laughing, she's sad and angry. She looks like a wild gypsy. Her hair is a tangle of curls, her blue eyes are wet with tears, her mouth is soft and twisted.

'I can be different with the right man ...'

'Aah, but who wud that be? A knight in shining armour? I'm no sure o' mysel' either ... too much war ... it's unsettlin' ...'

They stop speaking. They drink and look at each other.

I wake in my bed the next morning. Mom's tied up her hair and put on a clean dress. She's bent over the sewing machine Daisy calls Singer and it whirr-whirrs, its needle click-clacks, setting down tens and tens of stitches, all the same, in exact rows.

The Buick crawls up the dirt road to our house.

I'm hiding on a low branch of the mango tree. The sun hangs straight up in the middle of the sky. Its heat soaks into everything; flowers, gravel, leaves, trees. They lie back and bake. Outside our front door, the passenger door swings open. Rob steps out. Ernest joins him at the back door; they open it and, bending down, pull out two arms, then the body of a shrunken old man. He's wearing striped pyjamas and a blue and red dressing gown with big teardrops on it. He totters on shaky feet, held up by four strong arms and they disappear into the house.

I drop from the tree and run into the house after them.

The old man's hair hangs in thin grey threads on his forehead. No Brylcreem. His skin is grey-yellow and saggy, his eyes are holes in their sockets, his mouth is an old man's mouth, puckered like a purse. Only the nose tells me it's Jack.

Mom takes two steps towards him then stops. She holds out her arms. 'Jack. Jack.'

Jack lifts his head, he raises one hand like the Pope about to bless the crowd. He uses Mom's words, 'Not now. I'm tired, verra tired ...'

Rob jerks his chin to the bedroom, 'Shall we?'

Mom rushes in front of them. She throws back the covers on the bed and watches as Rob and Ernest lower Jack slowly onto the bed, take off his dressing gown and slippers, then lift his legs and settle him onto the pillows.

Rob takes two bottles from his pocket. 'These are his pills, Irene. I think one is morphine, not sure about the other. Give him one of each every four hours. He had a dose two hours ago ...'

Mom nods. Her eyes search Rob's baldy dome and the monkey folds round his eyes as as though looking for something to take away her fear.

Rob takes Mom's arm after she pulls the curtains together and leads her out of the bedroom. He says, 'Helen and Daisy will come every day to help you give Jack a bedbath, rub ointment onto him so he doesn't get bedsores. Help you with bedpans and feeding and help you carry him into the sitting-room when he's strong enough. Now, Irene, I don't want you to worry too much. If you're lonely or scared, one of us here at Dorowa will come and sit with you ...'

I watch Jack as he lies in bed. He's so still. He looks like the stone knight in armour lying on top of the tomb in the church in Scone. Mom sits with her eyes fixed on the floor, her hands dangle like doll's hands at her sides. She's gone into her thoughts, she's locked in a little cell like a nun, she's suffering and brooding.

Something cold comes into Jack's room. The curtains are half shut. The sun is fire-hot outside, but in the corner of Jack's room is something extra cold. I think it's a spirit or a shadow. I think it's Death and he's waiting for Jack. I think he bends over Jack and sucks the life out of him with his hollow mouth, he follows Jack with red otherworldy eyes. Death has a smell – a mouldy, old smell like soil buried deep in a cave.

Helen and Daisy come to help Mom look after Jack every day. Helen gives Jack a bed bath and rubs ointment on his back so he won't get sores from lying in the same spot all the time. They put clean pyjamas on him and half carry half drag him to the sitting room. They stick cushions all around him, then cover his knees with a blanket.

Death shrinks into the corner when Daisy and Helen are there. He waits with his arms folded. I think Mom can feel him as well. She won't sleep in Jack's bedroom anymore. She gets Ali and Obafemi to set up a camp bed in my bedroom.

I used to long for Mom when I slept on the floor in Lizzie's bedroom, or when I was smaller and we lived in the flat above the Main Road. But now I like to have a room to myself and my bed with its cocoon of nets becomes my sanctuary, my ship, my reading and writing place. Mom won't let me read as long as I want. She switches off the light. She moans in the dark. It reminds me of when I was very small and I would watch Mom in bed, crying and talking to the wall.

Helen cuts slices of cake. Daisy pours the tea. She holds a cup to Jack's mouth and he sips, his mouth sucking on the edge of the cup as if it's a baby's bottle.

'There, there, Jack, ye must be thirsty – take yer time.'

Helen puts cake on a fork and puts it in front of Jack's mouth. He shakes his head.

'Is he no eatin' Irene?'

Mom shakes her head.

'I'll get some Ovaltine fer Jack. Get Ali to cook up some chicken broth. It's fine if he's on a liquid diet.'

Mom switches on the radio. They listen to the BBC news. A man's voice says the Rosenbergs have been found guilty of espionage in New York and have been sentenced to death. The Rosenbergs are traitors, the law says.

'They surely wilna put a women to death in the electric chair,' says Daisy, her voice sounds like a needle scratching on a gramaphone record. 'Nivver. I don't believe sich a thing.'

'What if she's innocent ...?'

'I think she was dragged into selling secrets to the Russians by her husband.'

'Those puir children ... have to live wi' the reality o' their parents bein' electrocuted.'

'There's no peace even though the war's been over for more than five years.'

'Aye, but it's a cold war the noo and the enemy has changed.'

They turn their attention on Jack. 'What do ye think, Jack?'

He sits with his head hanging over his chest, not listening. His hoods are almost covering the grey of his eyes.

'Do ye want tae get some rest Jack?'

He blinks.

They pull him onto his feet, grab each of his arms and wrap them round their necks, then put their arms round his body and they shuffle Jack along on tiny steps back to bed.

Doof-doof. The drums sound across the compound. The compound is like a risen cake cooling after a day baking in the oven of the sun. Jack sits in his chair, his hands on his knees, his eyes have come to life, they look around as if he's searching for something.

Mom holds her embroidery cloth up to her eyes, but her needle doesn't stab the material. Feet crunch across the gravel outside. Mom puts down her cloth. A hand knocks on the open door, then Andy steps into the house. He looks at us sitting like dummies on our chairs, then he crosses the floor, pats Mom's shoulder and stands looking down at Jack, 'Och, Jack, wha' a skunner.' He bends his knees, sits on his haunches so that his face is level with Jack's. He covers Jack's hand with one of his own. Jack's eyes flick to Andy, his stubble chin lifts off his chest.

Mom's eyes are like shady pools watching Andy. 'I'll make some tea.' She disappears into the kitchen.

Andy talks to Jack as if he's a sick child, 'It makes my heart sore tae see ye like this ... just the other day we were playin' tennis ... ye're still a young man, too young fer cancer ...'

Jack watches Andy's lips. I don't know if his brain understands words anymore. Does his brain know he's dying?

Mom brings in the tray. Her hand shakes as she pours tea in a cup and gives it to Andy. He dribbles the tea into the saucer and lifts it to Jack's mouth. 'Come, Jack, yer mouth looks dry. Drink some tea.'

A shudder moves Jack's body. He pulls away from Andy and scrabbles at the saucer. A thin grunt comes from his lips. 'Naw ... naw ... do-it-mesel'.'

Andy won't stop. He dribbles tea into Jack's mouth, waits for him to swallow. Jack's apple moves up and down in his throat as it pushes the tea down. Andy wipes Jack's mouth with his handkerchief, talking all the while in his nanny voice, 'There, there Jack. Is tha' better? Aye, it is, yer mouth's no' so dry ...'

Jack turns his head, spills some tea, then huffs a heavy sigh out of his mouth. He closes his hoods.

'How are ye goin' tae get him intae bed ...?'

'I don't know ... he wouldn't let Daisy and Helen take him to bed earlier.'

'I'll gie ye a hand, ye'll nivver manage on yer own.'

They go to Jack, each stretching out a hand. 'Jack,' says Andy in a louder voice. 'Come. We'll put ye tae bed.'

Jack's hoods flap open. His eyes spit snake poison at them. His hands hold the armrests; they claw and pull forward until he sits on the edge of his seat. His mouth grunts – gnhh-gnhh. He leans forward, looking at the floor, then he drops off the chair. His hands and feet scrabble at the floor like a weak swimmer. He huffs and grunts until he wobbles onto his hands and knees. He swivels his face up to look at Mom and Andy. Nonsense sounds come out of his mouth, 'Gnnh-grmhh-gnsh.' He moves one hand, then one knee. The other hand and knee follow. He crawls like an ant over the cement floor. I jump to my feet. I begin to understand his gnhhing and grmming, he's saying, 'Dinna ... let ... any ... man ... in ... my ... hoose ... agin.'

Andy and Mom bend over the crawling striped pyjama body of Jack. 'Jack. Jack. Let us help you.'

He stops his frantic scrabbling-crawling for a second, turns his fixed staring eyes at them and grinds a choked sound through his false teeth, 'FUUUCKORF.'

They follow his ant's progress into the bedroom, inch by inch to the bed. Heaving and panting, he claws at the bedspread, pulling at sheets and blankets. He gets the top half of his body onto the bed and lies there face down gasping for breath.

'Fer Godssake, man,' Andy bends, takes hold of Jack's legs, lifts him sideways and flips him over onto the bed like a flapjack.

Red spots spring up all over Jack's face. His eyes shoot hate arrows at them, then he turns his head to the wall and closes his hoods.

Mom's face is worried-scared, Andy's face is shocked. They stare down at Jack for a moment, then creep out of the room. I think the shadow figure of Death moves closer to Jack's bed; his red eyes are greedy, his arms unfold themselves and stretch towards Jack's body.

'School started last week.'

I wait for Mom to say, 'Why didn't you say so? Of course you must go back to school. Let's pack your suitcase.' But she doesn't. Her eyes don't really see me. I don't know what she's thinking. Obafemi's ironing Jack's pyjamas and sheets in the kitchen. I smell hot clean cotton. Mom looks around her as if she doesn't know where she is.

I wait until Daisy and Helen come bustling in. They bring sunshine and kindness with them. Daisy has a bunch of spiky yellow and lilac dahlias; Helen brings Horlicks and a bowl of chicken broth.

'Let's open the curtains in here a wee bit,' says Helen. 'Jack can see the trees and the blue sky.'

'*Blue skies shine at me ... blue skies make me hap-pee*,' sings Daisy, her voice sounding like peaches and cream. '*Only blu-ue skies do I see ...*'

Jack turns his grey face to them, lifts his hoods.

'Let's gie ye a wee bit o' a shave today, Jack, comb yer hair.' Helen fills a bowl with warm water, gets Jack's shaving cream and razor.

I go into my bedroom while they're busy. I find my suitcase under my bed and pack my books into it, open my drawers and find clean clothes.

They've propped Jack up in his chair in the sitting-room; they've stuck cushions all round him so that he can sit without falling sideways. He smells like hot iron, shaving cream and Brylcreem. Daisy's carried in a tray of tea and macaroons. 'Here, Jack, drink some tea – I'll help ye ...'

'Daisy, I'll put yer tea on the table, sit, take a minute ...'

'Och aye, shall we put on the radio? No news though ...'

Mom's putting clean sheets on Jack's bed.

'Aunt Helen? Aunt Daisy?'

'Karin, do ye want a macaroon ...'

'School started last week. All my friends are back at school.'

They stare at me. 'An' why are ye no' back at school as weel?'

Mom joins us.

'Irene, why have yo no' sent Karin back tae school? I'll send Ernest wi' the Dodge in the mornin' ...'

'But then ... I'll be alone here at night if Karin goes back to school.' Mom's angry with me, I know, her nose is twitching, two pink spots flower on her cheeks.

'Nonsense. We'll take turns to spend time wi' Jack in the evenin's. Rob and Dick an' Andy as weel.'

Helen turns to me, 'Tha's settled then, Karin, ye'll gae to school tomorrow.'

'Is your father very sick?' Pammy stops sucking on her bullseye to ask me.

'He's not my father,' I say it before I remember I'm not supposed to.

Tansy, Hugh, Fraser and Pammie stare at me. 'Who's he, then?'

'He's my stepfather.'

They think. 'Did your real father die in the war?'

'No. They're divorced.' I say the unpleasant truth. The sky doesn't fall on my head.

Fraser's freckles stand out against the white of his skin. His brown-yellow eyes watch me, they're sharp and interested. 'Where is your real father? Do you ever see him?'

My tongue goes into knots. I only know my father's name – Peter van Zyl. He lives in Cape Town. My father doesn't want girls. I can't say any of this.

'Well,' says Fraser. 'I bet your real father wouldn't turn up drunk at your school's nativity play.'

I nod, but I don't know if my real father would even come to see my school's nativity play.

'Jack is going to die,' I say.

They huff their breath out through teeth made black from sucking bullseyes and liquorice sweets.

'What's he going to die from?' says Pammie.

'Cancer,' I say. 'He's got an enormous lump of cancer in his head that's getting bigger every day. They don't want to give him food in case it makes the lump grow bigger. And he's got a lump the size of a tennis ball in his lungs. Maybe he won't be able to breathe soon.'

'My grandmother lay in a bed for five years before she died. She couldn't move or speak. She could only blink. They asked her what she wanted and if she blinked, they'd give it to her,' Tansy says.

'Oh, no,' says Fraser. 'She must have had a stroke. Cancer in the head won't take so long.'

'My grandmother was run over by a bus. She was deaf and half blind and she didn't see or hear the bus coming,' Pammie says. She waits for us to say something. 'It was ever so sad.'

'My grandfather was killed by a sniper's bullet on the last day of the First World War,' says Fraser.

'What's a sniper?'

'Somebody who hides in trees and tall buildings and has good aim. He can kill people from a great distance,' Hugh tells us. His brown eyes are sad with his own unpleasant truth. He never talks about his father being killed on the beaches at Dunkirk, about the sniper- Messerschmidt who shot his father.

I feel so much better. My friends speak about death as if it is something that happens in every family.

Matron Davies holds me back when the others pack away their sewing in her cupboard. She pretends to look at the cross-stitches I'm sewing on a needle case. I had to pull out a whole row because they were crooked. Matron Davies bends close. I can smell the Rennies pills she sucks for indigestion on her breath.

'You take setbacks well, Karin,' she says. 'I believe you have some difficulty at home now. I'm glad to see you can focus even though your heart must be troubled.' She bends and scratches in one of her drawers. She hands me a tiny card with an angel painted on the front with words: 'And I shall send angels to guard over thee'.

Her puffy, stretched-skin lips are close to my eyes, they tremble a little before she says, 'There's a prayer for the afflicted on this card. Say it every day and you will receive strength of spirit for the dark days ahead.'

Mrs Stevenson holds a book on the Vikings in her hands. She reads aloud how

Viking warriors put their dead leaders on a bed of driftwood in their dragon boats. Covered them with their bear furs, their shields and a sword nearby. 'According to Norse legend,' she says, 'the portals of Valhalla would open to warriors who died sword in hand. Then they set the funeral boat alight with blazing torches and arrows as it drifted to sea on the evening tide. It must have been a glorious sight,' she sighs, 'to see the funeral pyre going up in flames as it drifted towards the setting sun. A flaming boat steering for the burning, dying sun.' She turns her craggy man's face with its lion's mane hair to me and smiles, 'More dramatic. More theatrical than putting a coffin in the ground.'

She reads a Norse legend of Odin impaling himself upside down on Ygdrasill, the World Tree, for nine days and nine nights in his search for wisdom. A magic rune came to him as he hung. He gave this to the world as a gift.

For nine days and nights
I hung on a windswept tree,
Wounded by my own spear, of myself to myself.
With neither food nor drink,
I saw into the depths of being
And from there took up the Runes
Then fell, fainting.
Well-being and wisdom were my prize.

'I'm not religious, Karin,' she says. 'I'm like Peter Pan – I believe that death is an awfully big adventure.'

The four matchbox houses and the tennis court of Dorowa look like toys below as the Dodge creaks to the top of the hill. I haven't been home for two weeks. Ernest bounces the Dodge down the hill, past the Dredger and up to our matchbox house. He stops the motor, takes my suitcase out of the back of the Dodge and drops it onto the gravel. He drives back down the road, the tyres crunching and whipping up a small dust storm.

The bougainvillea eyebrows bristle above the windows. I can smell mangos and oranges, sweet roses and verbena. The compound's dead still and hot. The trees throw pools of deep green around themselves. I love this baking hot stillness.

I hear voices and sounds of snicker-snorts in the dining-room. I carry my suitcase with both hands and go into the house.

'Irene, Irene,' Helen's arm hugs Mom's shoulders. She speaks in a loud whisper, 'Jack's not suffering, he's in a coma. He feels nothing ...'

Mom snickers her tears. Her eyes are red and swollen. She dabs at them with her hankie.

'Aye, Helen's right,' Daisy covers Mom's free hand with her own soft, pudgy one. 'I'll make some tea,' Daisy hauls herself off the chair. She turns and sees me.

'Come in, Karin, come and have tea with us. Happen ye've been awa' a while? Just as weel. Yer father's come tae the end o' the road.'

Not my father, my badgirl voice says.

Does she mean Jack's going to die now?

'Tell Ali not to cook supper,' Mom's voice is thick and the words choke in her throat. 'I'm not hungry.'

'I'll tell him to make sandwiches fer the bairn.'

I poke my head round the bedroom door. The curtains are closed. The room is dark but I can see Death's shape bent over Jack's body. Jack's curled himself up tight so his knees are bent almost to his chest. He's facing the wall. I can't hear his breathing.

Daisy and Helen talk to Mom at the door, 'We'll be back later, Irene, send Ali if anything happens in the meantime.'

Mom waits until they've left the compound, then she takes my hand and whirls me out of the house through the back door. 'I've got to get out of here, I feel like a prisoner. I haven't been out of this compound since Jack left the hospital.'

'But what if something happens?'

'Nothing will happen for an hour and if it does then ... it does. Jack doesn't know whether I'm here or not.'

Mom pulls me across the compound, past the huts, down into the banana grove then up the other side, up the hill dotted with dried grass, termite hills and rocks. Only then does she let go of my hand. She stops, closes her eyes and takes deep breaths. And sighs and sighs.

Mom walks fast. I have to run to keep up with her. She throws herself on the flat rock far up the hill, scaring the lizard into running from its spot.

I feel cold in the hot sun. Mom shivers as well. It's as if Death has followed us up the hill. Mom talks about the deaths of Charlie, her brother, then her father. She talks about the divorce – another kind of death. The sun streaks red across the sky when we leave the rock and walk back. It's awfully quiet as if the whole of Dorowa is holding its breath, waiting. No drums, no dredger, no voices or fires in the compound.

Mom's hand is shaking me. 'Karin, Karin, wake up.'

I open my eyes. Mom's a blue blur behind the net. She lifts it and pulls me from my bed. My feet are cold on the red cement floor. It's early morning, the sky's the inside of a mother-of-pearl shell. I shiver in its chilly newness.

Mom's saying, 'Come with me, come.'

I look at her with sleepy eyes. He face is white as bleached cotton, her mouth sags and her eyes look at me without seeing, they're looking inside her head.

'Come with me,' she takes my hand and pulls me into her bedroom, to Jack's bedside, up close. She looks down at his body, curved in a question mark. She lifts the bottom of his pyjamas to show his back. 'Touch him,' she says. She pulls my finger to his skin and pokes it. It looks and feels like the putty they use to put glass panes in windows. His skin is clammy-cold.

I pull my hand away. 'No,' I whisper. 'I don't want ... is he ...?'

'He's dead. He died in the night.'

I shake, not from fear. I'm free of Jack. I don't know what to say. A dummy made out of putty fills the pyjamas on the bed. Jack has gone.

Mom is trying to make something of this moment but it doesn't feel real to me. At last she lets go of my hand and moves to the wardrobe. 'We should get dressed,' she says, 'I must send Ali with a note to tell Rob and Helen.' She rattles her hangers, pulls a dress from one.

Mom's so slow, slow as a zombie. In the end she stays in her blue candlewick dressing gown, she falls into a chair, like a rag doll, her eyes stitched into sorrow on her bleached cotton face.

Mom's folded in Helen and Daisy's arms, her body shakes with sobs. Daisy rubs her back. 'There, there, Irene, sob awa', let it a' oot.'

Helen pats her hand. 'He didna suffer in the end. The morphine took care o' that.'

Mom squashes down her tears, she dries her eyes with her hankie. She looks into Daisy's eyes then Helen's, 'I loved Jack, you know, in spite of everything. I want you to know ...'

'O'course ye did.'

'Och, Irene, ye dinna ha'e to tell us, we ken.'

Those five words – *I loved Jack, you know.* When they leave Mom's mouth, the words turn into five iron fingers on an iron hand then close into a fist squeezing my heart. I try to breathe and think, but the pain grips my chest. Who would have thought words could hurt so much? Mom has never said she loves me.

I hear their whispers coming from the bedroom. 'We should straighten him oot afore he get's stiff ... Helen, how are we goin' tae make him more presentable? '

'We should wash an' shave him, comb Brylcreem intae his hair.'

Pause.

'Where's his teeth?'

'Irene, do ye want tae ha'e a bath an' get dressed afore the funeral people get here?'

'Rob's gone to sort oot the death certificate in Jos.'

The geyser gurgles out hot brown water and I know Mom's stepping into the dragon bath.

Daisy calls, 'Wha suit do ye want us tae dress Jack in ... the navy blue or the dark grey pin-striped?'

'Wha' aboot a tie? A white shirt I suppose.'

'Ha'e ye got any coins, Daisy?'

'Somewhere in my bag, here's twa pound coins ...'

'Weel done, heavy eno' tae keep his eyes shut until rigor mortis sets in.'

'I thocht it was so the livin' couldna see their own deaths staring at them from the eyes o' the deceased ... I must say, Helen, it's kinda creepy to see Jack's eyes starin' at us when he's gone.'

'Nivver mind, Daisy, we must bind his jaw as weel ...'

Dick and Rob and Andy come in and out. Daisy and Helen make tea and cut sandwiches.

They go in and out of the bedroom to stare at the putty-dummy. Ali, Obafemi and Emoka shuffle in and stand at the foot of the bed and stare at Jack. Jack, grey and quiet, coins on his eyes. White muslin tied under his chin.

I sit on the edge of my unmade bed. I don't even want to read. Shoes patter towards me. Helen crouches down, her eyes look at me, really look at me, she strokes my arm. 'Puir wee bairn. Ye must be so confused. I'll get ye dressed an' brush yer hair. Come, let's straighten yer bed, roll up the nets. Have ye eaten today? No? Let's get ye some food ...'

Helen takes me under her wing, her little brown wren body wraps me in her care, her bright bird eyes keep me tied to her. We walk together across the bush to her house, hand in hand, and she plays me her record of the Luton Girls' Choir singing '*We are in love with you, my heart and I*'.

She talks to me in her sweet bird voice, tells me about herself at my age growing up on a farm in Scotland, makes me Oros, cuts me a slice of cake. She doesn't leave me alone for a second, even when I fall asleep on her chair while she's reading to me. Helen shows me how, even on the worst days, life goes on.

Reverend Roberts' voice sounds like a lonely fog horn wailing over a misty sea. 'In-the-midst-of-life-we-are-in-death.'

We watch as the funeral people lower Jack's coffin on ropes into a big hole. Reverend Roberts wears his black gown and his back-to-front collar. Rays of the sun bounce off his granny glasses and dazzle us, his sweaty face is wet. He opens his Minnie Mouse mouth and the fog horn sounds. 'I am the Resurrection and the Life, saith the Lawd. He-e that believeth in Me-e, even though he-e be-e dead, ye-et shall he li-ve ...'

The fog horn fades. Reverend Roberts lifts his granny glasses and waits. '... and whosoever liveth and believeth in Me-e shall never die-e.' At the end of a sentence, Reverend Robert's voice sounds as if it's diving off a cliff.

I count the tombstones standing in the cemetery of the Anglican Church in Bukuru. Twenty-four. Nothing moves in the still heat, no leaf, no blade of grass.

We're prisoners of the burning orange eye of the sun. Its flashlight glare makes it hard for me to keep my eyes open.

People are dressed like black crows standing round the open hole. Mom's wearing the black felt hat with the dotted veil she wore when she married Jack. It's strange because dummy Jack in his coffin is wearing the pin-striped suit he wore when he married Mom.

Andy and Rob stand on either side of Mom, each holding an elbow in case she faints. Mom's white and shaky. A red rose trembles in her black-gloved hand.

Rob's speaking about Jack now, '... a diligent Scots engineer toiling on foreign soil ... Jack was a late starter ... Jack was struck down in his prime ... he will be missed.'

Not by me, badgirl says.

Oh, no, Brenda MacDonald has stepped up to Reverend Roberts's side and sings as Mom throws her red rose onto Jack's coffin.

'O my Luve's like a red, red rose
That's newly sprung in June
O my Luve's like a melodie
That's sweetly played in tune.

As fair thou art, my bonnie lad,
So deep in luve am I
And I will luve thee still, my dear,
Till a' the seas gang dry.'

Everybody throws single flowers onto Jack's coffin as Brenda MacDonald's voice runs like a sad stream over the grave. Helen's face crumples, her eyes leak tears. Daisy's tears run in little rivers of brown mascara down her cheeks.

Sobby voices, teary-breathy voices, join Brenda's.

'And fare thee well, my only Luve,
And fare thee well, a while,
And I will come again, my Luve,
Tho' it were ten thousand mile.'

Mom's sobbing, moaning into her hankie. Her five-word iron fist is closing round my heart again and it's breaking, breaking. *I loved Jack, you know.*

Don't you dare blub, says badgirl.

Long silence after the song. Everybody stares down at Jack's coffin for so long I think the sad song has cast a spell on them.

Harummph. Reverend Roberts clears his throat then says a blessing, 'The Lawd make his face to shine on thee ...'

Rob and Andy lead Mom away as the grave diggers shovel soil into the hole. I hear the thuds fall on the wood.

A piper plays the bagpipes after they fill the grave, circling round and round. He's dressed in kilt, sporran, cap and stockings. His cheeks bulge as he blows into the mouthpiece. Drums beat in the distance, the sound matches the thin wailing from the pipes. Drums beat out the news of Jask's burial, his final resting place.

Jack-in-the-box is never going to jump out of his box again, says badgirl.

'You musn't speak ill of the dead,' Matron Davies once told us. But why? They can't hear, they won't know. People say bad things about Hitler and the dead Nazis all the time. Will Jack come back to haunt me if I tell Mom things she won't want to hear? I can see the flesh and skin shrivel off Jack's bones. I know nails and hair keep growing after you're dead. His nicotine-stained nails will grow into claws. His Brylcreemed hair will hang over his eyeless sockets. Will his skeleton come back to haunt me? 'Ye wee bugger, haud yer tongue,' his false teeth will clatter.

I can never tell Mom about the things Jack did. If she wouldn't believe me then, she never will now. She's turning him into some kind of saint. He's Saint Jack, patron saint of Scotland and of women desperate for new husbands.

'Jack rescued me,' she cries. 'He rescued me from poverty and loneliness.'

Daisy and Helen come every day just as they did when Jack was dying. They pick through Jack's belongings like magpie birds. His cuff links, his photographs, his certificate from Glasgow University. His father's pipe, a gold cigarette lighter, his watch and his spare set of false teeth. His shirts, shorts, jackets, his kilt made out of the Carmichael tartan, trousers, sporran. Mom decides to give his record player and Harry Lauder records to Andy, his books and magazines to Rob.

'Look at this, Helen,' Daisy lifts up a photograph of a young Jack. 'Does he no look like Rudolph Valentino?'

'Och, aye,' says Helen. 'Who wud a' thought Jack was sae bonnie?'

Mom sniffs.

'Have ye ever wondered why the minister only says "Dearly Beloved, we are gathered together" fer weddings an' no fer funerals? Ey, Helen? Ye'd think he would call his congregation "Dearly Beloved" fer funerals as weel. "Dearly beloved, we are gathered together to honour the departed" ...'

'Daisy – no' now,' Helen lifts one eyebrow as Mom's lips quiver and her eyes flood.

I watch Emoka's shaky arms lift spades of dead leaves onto the fire he's made in a shallow grave at the back of the compound. When he's emptied the wheelbarrow, he trundles off to the heaps of dead leaves and twigs he's swept. I watch his bent back as he disappears round the side of the house. The flames shoot spitfires into the air, twigs crackle like little gunshots. The hot air waves into the smoke. The licky-leapy flames hold my eyes, make me dreamy. I want to make my own fire; I want to burn the image of Jack first into cinders then into ash. I want to give him a Viking funeral. Not because he's brave or because he had a sword in his hand when he died. I want to burn Jack out of my memory.

I wander to the edge of the banana grove, looking down into the ditch. Then I see it. The old juju shrine Amos made has fallen over; the banana leaf fronds are yellow, brown and dry. The carved figure is on its back, still caked with dried chicken blood and feathers. It lies on the wooden poles used to build the shrine, the stomach sticking up, the bosoms like sacks of sand on the chest. I go closer, sliding down the loose gravel. The eyes are holes, the nose a rough beak and the thick lips curl up in a smile.

I run back to the house, into the bathroom. I scratch in the pockets of Mom's hat box. The false teeth wrapped in a hankie. Jack's pith helmet, Mom's fox cape. Its coming to me quickly now. I find Mom's make-up box on her dressing table. I smear lipstick on my lips, down my cheeks, on my forehead, then blue eye shadow and black mascara. I hang the red-brown fox cape round my shoulders. This can be the bear skin Vikings wear. I hear Daisy's and Helen's voices in the sitting-room, talking to Mom, 'In all the years we knew him ... nivver had a lady-friend ... knocked over wi' a feather ... came back from long leave ... married ...'

I run to the back of the compound, Jack's false teeth in one hand, his pith helmet in the other. I slide down into the ditch, go close to the fertility shrine. I open Jack's hankie, put it onto the fat stomach. I do this without touching the false teeth. They smile at the waving green banana leaves above. I cover the carved wooden face with the pith helmet. I find dry leaves and twigs, banana fronds, push them under the pole keeping the shrine together.

I run up to Emoka's fire, sweep more leaves, twigs up into my arms and slide back, pushing them under the shrine. I run up and down a few times. I hear the creak of Emoka's wheelbarrow; hear the sizzle of the flames as he throws more dried stuff on to the fire. He's huffing and puffing. I climb up the ditch a little way and see Emoka bend down into the doorway of his hut.

I creep back up and wait, I hear mutters coming from Emoka's hut, sighs, then snores. He hasn't emptied the wheelbarrow. I take the handles and push it down the slope of the ditch; the wheelbarrow runs away from me and falls on its side near the shrine. I push heaps of leaves on the pile.

My chest heaves up and down with all the running and sliding and pushing. The fox cape is hot. My hair sticks in wet strands to my face.

Here's the difficult bit, badgirl says, *don't chicken out now.*

I bend over the fire looking for something bigger than burning leaves and twigs. Here's a glowing stick Emoka used to start the fire. I hold the end and pull it out. The heap of burning twigs falls and settles a little. I slide down into the ditch. My legs and dress are dirty with soil and leaves. Mom's going to have a conniption fit. I stick the glowing branch into the heap I've built. I wait. Nothing. I blow and blow on the glowing bit until I'm dizzy. Then a little spark, a little flicker. I watch as the sparks catch hold and leap into small flames. It's working.

The flames begin to dance. They dance up to the juju Jack body and lick the dried chicken blood. There's a little roar as the flames take hold of the dead banana fronds and the dry wood poles of the shrine.

I need one more thing. I climb back into the compound and find it. An empty paint tin Ali and Obafemi sit on round their night fires. Two garden trowels. I go back into the ditch. I find a flat rock for the tin to sit on, then, with a garden trowel in each hand, I drum. It makes a tinny sound not a deep boom, but never mind. In my mind I see the drumming push Jack's funeral pyre from the ditch into a fast river flowing to the sea. I begin to chant. Words come to me.

> This dragon boat will sail from me
> Surfer of waves out at sea
> This funeral boat will carry Jack
> Past the portals of Valhalla
> I've set it on fire
> I've set it on fire ...

The Vikings believed the world was flat. I'm sending Jack's burning boat to the edge of a flat sea. I chant and drum. Siward Silk-Hair stands beside me, his long hair waving in the heat of the flames. He raises Brain-Biter to the sky, waving at the unseen Gods of Asgard. 'A-aoi,' he cries.

Hot tears fall from my eyes burning with smoke. The shrine boat is at the edge of the world where the sea turns in on itself. The burning boat and juju body begin to topple over. A little ball of flame. It leaves the edge of the sea and falls into black space. It drifts down, down, falling apart into cinders and ash ... 'A-aoi,' I cry ...

'KARIN.'

I stop drumming and look behind me. Mom and Helen and Daisy stand at the edge of the compound. Their jaws drop with shock. Mom's face is red, her voice shakes, 'WHAT DO YOU THINK YOU ARE DOING?' Her eyes are out on stalks.

I begin to sob. 'I'm burning Jack ...'

"WHAT?'

'I'M BURNING JACK.'

'How dare you take Jack's belongings? How dare you make a fire? You'll set the whole compound alight.'

Daisy calls to Ali and Obafemi to bring buckets of water. They come running, water slopping out of the buckets. Helen slides into the ditch, takes the garden trowels from my hands.

'Och, Karin, whatever is the matter? Come awa', pet, come, lovey, let me clean ye up.'

The fire swishes when Ali and Obafemi pour water on it. They run back to the tap to fill the buckets again.

'What does she mean she's burning Jack?' Mom looks wild.

'Irene, dinna fash yersel'. It looks as though she turned that old juju shrine into an effigy o' Jack ...'

'GOD.'

'She's been awfu' quiet, Helen, if ye think aboot it. Dinna ferget she's also been affected by Jack's dying in the hoose an' the funeral ...'

'Mebbe it's her way o' tryin' tae put it outta her mind ...'

'What? Burning Jack's belongings on top of a fertility shrine? I don't know my own daughter.'

'Mebbe ye don't, Irene.'

'I'm going to give you the hiding of your life, Karin,' Mom's face screws up into her berserker face.

I howl. My howl sounds scarier and lonelier than it's ever sounded. Mom's eyebrows look as if they are going to fly off her face.

'Ye'll do no sich thing, Irene.' Helen kneels next to me and puts her arm round my shaking shoulders. 'Look at the bairn – she's a nervous wreck. Come awa', lassie, we're goin' tae have a hot bath and a wee chat ...'

Daisy calls after us, 'Helen, I'm goin' tae fetch some brandy fer Irene ...'

Helen kneels at the edge of the dragon bath and soaps the dirt off my body, she washes my hair. She pours Mom's lavender bath oil into the water. She murmurs in her soft voice, 'Wha's botherin' ye, lovey? I've nivver seen a bairn take on so ... ye musn't worry ... someday soon this will a' seem like a bad dream ... Wha' did ye rub on yer face? Was it yer mither's make-up?'

I nod. 'I was a pretend Viking.'

'Och, I see, a pretend Viking. Why did ye want tae be a Viking?'

'Because they burn their dead. Sometimes.'

Obafemi's arms are soapy and shiny up to his elbows. The skin on his fingers is always wrinkled from all the washing he does. He bends over the tin bath on the walkway. He doesn't hum his nye-nhe-nhey song. He lifts bloodshot worried eyes every time Mom finds more washing for him to do. Curtains, sheets, towels. It takes forever. He has to wash the white stuff in filter water. Mom's fussy about that. When the washing is crackle-dry, Obafemi sets up the ironing board and irons. I hear sighs coming from his lips like puffs of steam.

The trunk is open on the dining-room floor. Piles of ironing line the dining-room table.

Mom's folding her dresses between sheets of tissue paper. She talks half to herself, half to me as I watch. 'I made this Coco Chanel suit,' she says, 'from a *Vogue* pattern. Coco Chanel was taught her exquisite needlework by the nuns. She always said she would die for neatness and excellence.'

Mom's forcing herself to pack our belongings. But often she collapses on her bed or a chair in the lounge and moans aloud. She sighs, cries, 'Jack, Jack, why did you leave me? I can't be on my own. I'm lonely.'

Everything is packed. It's time to go.

Mom has folded herself into a black suit. She's wearing the black felt hat with the dotted veil even though the sun is glaring hot. She's thinner. She's like a cardboard cutout of herself before Jack died. Dick and Daisy, Helen and Andy join us in the front of the compound. Emoka, Obafemi and Ali load the trunks and suitcases into the boot of the Buick. They bow their heads and put their hands palm to palm.

'Sai an jima – sai an jima,' their voices sigh.

Rob waits at the driver's door.

The moment thins out into a stretch of awkward goodbyes and hugs. Eyes slide away from each other. Mom is so still and silent. 'Bless ye, Irene.' 'Safe journey.' 'Write us when ye're settled.'

I put Frida into Andy's arms. Her slit green eyes follow me, the tip of her tongue shows as she croaks an almost silent meow.

Mom steps into the passenger seat of the Buick, ducking her head under the door. She sits and places her feet together on the mat, folds her hands on her lap. I kneel on the back seat. I take a last look at the house, the gauze-shuttered windows, the gazebo almost hidden by wild clumps of purple bougainvillea, the dark shade of mango trees, the figures of the people who have been my family. The dust from the car wheels blurs them. But they're waving and I wave from the back window of the car. We turn the corner at the bottom of the road and they're gone.

We pass the praying mantis dredger, the avenue of trees leading to Helen and Rob's house, we climb the hill, then descend. Dorowa vanishes. My eyes soak in the watery heat waves on the corrugated dry road, the rows of cactus, the Hausa women swaying under heavy baskets, the traders on donkeys, the hump-backed Fulani cows and their little herders. I think of the dreaminess of a sun-baked compound, the way the air tingles when the rain's coming, the freshness of the rainwashed garden. I close my eyes and remember the karr-karr of the hangkaka, the slithering, croaking, clicking insect noises and the drums. They're drumming now, drumming us into a new life.

I turn to the front, sit on the seat and face the long road coming towards me.

I watch my mother still.

I search her face now, so lined and wrinkled from age and old woes, as she looks up at me, leaning heavily on my arm. Folds line the skin from the corners of her mouth to her chin, her eyebrows have faded into nothing. She appears to be constantly surprised. Her eyes, once so brilliant and blue, are tame now. I feel her frail body jump, then tremble as a guard slams the metal door of the green Fidelity van parked next to us. She halts her faltering walk, leans on her stick and frowns down at her thumb. She lifts it, then shifting her weight onto me, hangs her stick on her arm and strokes the thumb where the nail grows in a hard ridge from the cuticle into a splintered V at the tip. She frowns and rubs as she tries to remember the old injury.

Her hands, knobbly with arthritis, liver-spotted, networked with wrinkles, shake as I arrange her into the passenger seat of my car.

'I don't know what I would do without you, dear,' she says. Dear is a new and lonely term of endearment in her vocabulary.

We have lived in this seaside town since our return from Nigeria. My mother has not heeded any more siren calls to her heart, she has evolved instead into a life of respectable widowhood. She's joined the world of women, widows like herself or divorcees. As in everything, she has been fastidious and painstaking in creating the structure of this life, censoring out the bad memories from the good. My father drifted away into the fog of time, becoming the ghost who chased women and drank. Jack has been raised into a monument to uxoriousness, standing on a plinth like the statue to spring at the entrance to our beach.

She tells me which of her friends have daughters with marital or boyfriend problems.

'Poor Chloe, Mary, Ingrid, Hester, has su-uch trouble with her daughter.' She turns her head slowly to look at me, 'She's getting divorced, you know.' Or, more darkly, 'Ingrid's daughter had an abortion.'

The words 'divorced' along with 'abortion' are now uttered in a hushed tone, not spat out in disgust in her old way. She speaks with quiet scorn of 'separated' or worse, 'they only live together, they've never married'.

I feel her approval wash over me like a warm wave. It has come at a cost. She's very proud of the fact that I am her unmarried schoolteacher daughter.

Why would I marry and have children? I have always had a child to care for.

I draw up outside her cottage where the garden gate always opens silently on well-oiled hinges. Where the crazy paving is always lined with flowers, anemones, freesias, pansies, petunias, in bloom. Where the eugenias are clipped into immaculate balls.

She peers at me with eyes the colour of faded denim, childlike and wistful in her old age. Her puckered lips quiver, 'Don't come in, dear. I want to rest.'

I help her out of the car, her dusty pink coat swirling round her legs in the gusty south-easter. All her clothes are in grandmotherly shades of rose-pink, lavender and blue, although she has no grandchildren.

I know she will make her way to her bedroom as soon as the front door is closed. She will hang up her coat, close the curtains half way, then switch on her bedside lamp even though the summer sun blazes hot outside. She will take out her treasure-trove; a box of mementoes of her life with Jack. She will arrange a nest of pillows and cushions on the bed and sink into it, lying in a circle of light.

The photographs come out first; the wedding photograph where she smiles with tremulous joy at the camera. Photographs of Jack in his youth with his smooth Rudolph Valentino face and slick hair like a publicity still.

Photographs of them arm-in-arm, in the Scottish countryside, at the Yelwa Club at the Christmas dinners, the New Years Eves, the Robbie Burns Birthday Nights. One of Jack in pristine white with pith helmet casting a shadow across the top half of his face in front of the dredger at Dorowa.

She'll finger his gold cuff-links, the cigarette lighter, the pipe. A dried twig of heather. She'll hold it close to her nose and sniff it, although it smells of nothing but the musty inside of a cardboard box.

She'll remember all the endless days of indolent pleasure. Her glory days, as she likes to say, bathed in the glow of perpetual sunshine. So she'll pass the afternoon, dreaming and sighing. She will untie the ribbon binding Jack's letters and re-read the crabbed writing on thin blue paper. She'll weep a little and doze.

I know she'll do this because I have often surprised her in these daily rituals. When I first came across her fingering Jack's mementoes, I felt a surge of guilty relief that I had burned his false teeth on the effigy I'd built in long-ago Dorowa.

I help her through her gate where she stands leaning on the post. I climb back into my car and wave. The sun turns her hair into a white halo, her skin into parchment; my heart stirs for my aged child and her increasing frailty.

Blanched by the harsh glare of the sun, she looks like the negative of an old photograph. She looks like a ghost, I think, with a pang.

Will this be the last time I see her?

My mother came to me in a dream shortly before she died. The dream was like an old black and white movie, haunting and full of unresolved yearning. I unlocked the door to my house, stepped inside and found her waiting for me. Her face was pale and blurred as if she was already shifting into an altered state. *I've come to say goodbye*, she said, without words. *It's time for me to go, Jack's waiting. Walk with me to the road*, she said.

We left the house together, gliding slowly through the garden to the road which became a mist-shrouded, tree-lined avenue. We stood together in the road for the last time. My mother waited for something, someone.

A man appeared out of the mist in the distance. His hands pushed deep into the pockets of his overcoat, the brim of his felt hat tilted over his beak nose.

'Jack. Jack – I'm coming,' my mother cried.

I reached out for her as she left my side, but she moved swiftly away from me. All the words I wanted to say, all the unsaid things, rushed into my throat, then died there in a lump of sorrow. I watched her gliding into the mist towards the waiting figure; the image of her retreating back became etched on my memory.

The two figures met, linked arms, then they vanished.

Glossary

(eet) met lang tande – to toy with one's food

foeitog! – dear me!

wat 'n oulike kind – what a cute kid

kyk na haar mooi gesiggie – look at her pretty little face

jou ouma is so lelik soos die nag, nie waar nie? – your grandmother is as ugly as the night, not so?

maak nie saak nie, hulle is almal dieselfde – it doesn't matter, they are all the same

Engelse – the English

koeksister – def. a deep-fried doughnut soaked in syrup

ag, Moeder, hou nou op – oh, Mother, stop

bly tog stil – please be quiet

ek sal nooit vergeet nie. Nooit. – I shall never forget. Never.

verskoon my asseblief – excuse me please

Acknowledgements

I would like to thank my first readers – Nella Freund, Colleen Oxtoby, Shaida Ali, Máire Fisher and Colleen Higgs – for their encouraging reaction to the first draft of *The Cry of the Hangkaka*.

I acknowledge my debt to Anne Schuster and her creative writing workshops, in particular, the 'Writing a Book' workshop where I discovered that writing a book is not for sissies but, more importantly, I learnt the craft of writing under Anne's gifted tutelage.

Grateful thanks to my daughter, Judy Woodborne, for her beautiful artwork on the cover.

Thanks to Angela Rackham who shared her memories of growing up in Jos at the same time as I did; and to Clare Gibbon and Steve (sorry, Steve, I can't remember your surname) who reminisced about Jos from a different decade.

Finally, I acknowledge my greater debt to Colleen Higgs who was not only one of my first readers but who went on to become my publisher; she was the midwife who encouraged me to give one last push to propel this baby into the light of day.

For more information on Modjaji Books or any of our publications
go to www.modjajibooks.co.za

Printed in the United States
By Bookmasters